A SPARK OF NATURE

A CINDERELLA RETELLING

HEART OF THE QUEENDOM
BOOK 2

SUSANNAH WELCH

Cover Concept and Design by MoorBooks Design
Editing by Nia Quinn

eISBN: 978-1-958568-11-8
Paperback ISBN: 978-1-958568-12-5
Hardback ISBN: 978-1-958568-13-2

www.susannahwelch.com

ALSO BY SUSANNAH WELCH

Heart of the Queendom

A Spark of Storms

A Spark of Nature

A Spark of Seas (Coming Soon)

City of Virtue and Vice

Dance with the Wind

Dance with the Night

Dance with the Dawn

Fight with the Wind

Fight with the Dark

Fight with the Heart

*For the women
who are stronger than they know*

THE QUEENDOM OF
ISANDARIYAH
(AND THE SURROUNDING KINGDOMS)

ISANDARIYAH
TSANYIN
La Veridda
Lake Amyrante
NAERMORE
VERKESHE
Merewyn Bay
Dharijian Sea
ISANDINE
YLIRA
Mt Qira
Mt Qara
YLARA
Uhlirah Desert
ZARIDIA
N
E
S
W

PART I

1

———

PROLOGUE

Elliya prepared the tea for her stepmother as quietly as a mouse. Her stepmother hated the kettle whistling, so Elliya pulled it off the fire before it made a sound. She gently placed the cups and saucers on the serving tray without clinking the fine porcelain and nestled the little spoon into the sugar so it wouldn't rattle against the bowl as she carried the tray.

As she slowly poured the hot water into the teapot, her stepmother slammed open the kitchen door, and Elliya flinched, sloshing boiling water onto her hand. She bit her lip, careful not to cry out.

Her stepmother hissed, "What's taking so long? Are you so worthless you've forgotten how to make tea?"

Elliya didn't answer—silence was a safer alternative than any excuse. She wiped up the spilled water and lifted the tray. "I'm sorry, Stepmother. The tea is ready now."

Her stepmother smoothed a hand across her neatly styled black hair. "Good. Because our guest wants to meet you."

"Me? Why would anyone want to meet me?"

Her stepmother's voice dropped to a dangerous whisper.

"What have I told you about asking stupid questions, girl?" Her fingers flexed, and Elliya held perfectly still, controlling the shudder that threatened to rattle the dishes. Her stepmother glanced at the tray and appeared to calculate the results of an altercation. She huffed out a breath and pointed a finger into the parlor. "Just get out there. Now."

Elliya followed the order, her footsteps silent and quick, with gratitude toward the mystery guest who'd unknowingly stilled her stepmother's hand.

She entered the parlor and found the woman lounging in the sunshine, one arm casually stretched along the back of the sofa while she absently twisted a lock of her pink hair. Her pale blue cape was flung open, revealing the woman's tight navy pants and vest, with golden bangles on her wrists and bare biceps.

Her deep bronze complexion hinted she might be a native citizen of Isandariyah, unlike Elliya, who had inherited more traits from her Verkeshian mother than her Isandariyan father. Her stepmother taunted that Elliya's blond hair and sickly skin proved she was an outsider. But if blond hair proclaimed Elliya as foreign, she had no idea what this woman's pink hair said about her origins.

Which was the same thing Elliya had wondered the last time they met.

Her stepmother's expensive skirts swished as she pranced up to the woman. "Here she is, Miss Geeni. Elliya's not much to look at, especially since she's always filthy and covered in ashes." Her stepmother's high laugh sent a tremor down Elliya's spine, and she used the tea tray to cover the streak of ash on her worn apron.

The pink-haired woman ignored the hateful comment and curled her finger, beckoning Elliya forward. "Come closer, dear. I don't bite."

Elliya lowered the tea tray onto the side table and stood

before her without saying a word. The woman's jade green eyes watched her closely, and Elliya studied her in return. She knew how to read her stepmother's wishes with a glance, but she couldn't tell if this woman wanted her to admit they had met before or not. Since her stepmother didn't approve of her speaking with anyone outside their household, it was probably safer to remain silent.

The woman's rosy lips curved with the smile of a shared secret. "I see she knows when to hold her tongue. A wonderful skill to have." Her stepmother's lips pinched, but she didn't contradict the woman's compliment.

Elliya had met the pink-haired woman two days ago on her way home from the market when her bag of fruit had spilled on the road, bruising the ripe mangoes. She had been angry at herself for not checking the seams of the bag, and as she gathered the fallen mangoes into her apron, she had cried silent tears, dreading her stepmother's reaction. Geeni had come to her aid, though Elliya hadn't known her name until now. All she had known was that a kind pink-haired woman helped her pick up the mangoes, then wiped away Elliya's tears with a gentle smile.

In the parlor, the pink-haired woman slapped her hands on her thighs and stood. "Yes, she will do nicely." She handed Elliya's stepmother a pouch full of coins. "You will receive additional payments each month she remains in my service."

Her stepmother's face lit up as she hefted the coin purse. "She will serve you faithfully, Miss Geeni."

Elliya's head swiveled between the two of them. "Wait ... What's happening?"

Her stepmother grabbed her roughly by the upper arm. "You're going with Miss Geeni, and you will serve her faithfully, just like I said."

Despite her stepmother's sharp nails digging into her skin, she asked a question. "For how long?"

"Indefinitely." Her stepmother's cold brown eyes dared her to ask another question.

A thousand questions raced through her head, but before she could ask, Miss Geeni's hand clamped on to her stepmother's wrist. Elliya looked up to silently warn the pink-haired woman to avoid her stepmother's wrath, but Geeni's jade eyes had turned to glittering steel. "Elliya is my servant now. I gave you enough money to find someone else to abuse."

Her stepmother blinked in surprise, then did something Elliya had never seen before: she bowed her head as if she were the servant. "Of course, Miss Geeni. You're quite generous."

Geeni released her hold, then turned to Elliya. "Gather your things, and we'll be on our way."

"She has no things," said Elliya's stepmother coldly. "Everything in this house belongs to me."

Elliya considered the only items she wished she could take with her, but the books would have to remain in the library until she returned from serving this woman. Geeni raised the hood of her pale blue cape, then led her out to the carriage. Elliya hopped inside, not saying a word as the driver led her further from her home than she had ever been before.

Geeni caught her with a piercing gaze. "You aren't my servant, Elliya. Your stepmother is a terrible woman, and paying her was the easiest way to get you out. In a few days, I will write her a letter informing her you've died. You'll have to change your last name to hide from her. She can't track me, so there will be no way for her to find you."

Elliya just stared at her, unable to respond.

"I don't need additional servants, but I found you a job

as an apprentice to the scholars in the monastery. You'll do a lot of sweeping and cleaning, although compared to your home life, I daresay your new job will feel like a holiday."

Elliya blinked, trying to hold back her tears.

Geeni glanced out the window at Elliya's home disappearing in the distance. "Your stepmother is extremely distasteful. I'm surprised you never tried to run off to the monastery yourself."

Elliya's voice came out as a whisper. "I tried. But she found me before I made it and dragged me back."

"Well, I'm giving you a new identity, and you can start a new life." Geeni patted her hand. "Leaving the only home you've ever known is scary. But believe me, dear, this is for the best."

Elliya swallowed and summoned her words. "I'm not scared. I'm just so ... grateful." She raised a hand to her mouth to cover her trembling lips. The lifetime of fear wrapped tightly around her chest dissipated, and her lungs expanded with a shuddering inhale. She had never breathed so deeply in her life.

Her head spun, and a sob almost burst from her lips before she quickly silenced it. But she couldn't stop the tears that spilled down her cheeks.

Geeni's eyes lit up as she wiped a gentle thumb across Elliya's cheek. "Don't be ashamed of your tears. You've been through a lot. Cry it all out, dear."

Elliya stared at the beautiful woman through blurry eyes. "How can I ever repay you?"

Geeni's smile was kind. "Just be yourself, dear. Do your work and listen, silent as a mouse. The quiet ones always hear the best gossip."

Elliya's face lit up. "I can do that. Thank you, Miss Geeni."

The woman's lips twitched as her grin fell slightly.

Elliya's chest tightened. "I'm sorry, Miss Geeni. Whatever I said, I apologize."

Geeni patted her hand again. "You've done nothing wrong, little mouse. But I do have a favor to ask: never speak the name 'Geeni' in the monastery."

Elliya wanted to ask why, but questions were the fastest way to get in trouble, so she pressed her lips together and nodded.

"Good girl." Her grin had returned. "I knew you were special from the day we met."

Elliya wanted to stay silent, but she couldn't stop a question from bursting forth. "If I can't say your name, how should I address you?"

The question didn't prompt anger. Instead the woman tapped her rosy lips in thought. "How about you just call me Godmother? Whenever you call me that, you can remember this moment when I saved you."

Elliya smiled as more tears flowed down her cheeks. "Yes, Godmother. I will never forget what you've done for me."

Her godmother gave her a warm smile and wiped away her tears.

Every single one.

2

____

Elliya stopped dusting the books and reminded herself to breathe. Even though it had been almost two months since Geeni had rescued her from her stepmother's home, Elliya still caught herself holding her breath at odd times. Her stepmother said she breathed loudly, so Elliya often took shallow breaths to not provoke her wrath. Now that she was studying as an apprentice in the monastery, it was hard to remember the scholars weren't offended by her breathing.

She let the air stream slowly out of her mouth. She was safe. Her stepmother thought she was dead and wouldn't look for her. Once Elliya had proven herself to the scholars, she could take her vows and live out the rest of her life tucked safely inside the monastery.

Safe ... What an unexpected miracle.

The work of an apprentice was strenuous, but nothing compared to her previous life. Her room in the monastery was cool, with plenty of fresh air, unlike her sweltering attic bedroom back home. She ate simple meals she prepared alongside the other apprentices, instead of scavenging scraps from the food she cooked for her stepmother. Instead of rags, she wore a sturdy white dress with a neatly pressed white apron. And if she ended the day covered in ashes and dust? That was no different from home, except that here, no one called her Cinderelliya.

Miss Geeni—her godmother—visited Elliya weekly during her time in the monastery. The pink-haired woman listened to her in a way no one ever had. Elliya had spent so much time in silence that her godmother's attentive presence often brought tears to her eyes. But Geeni always listened to Elliya's stories, lovingly brushing away all her tears.

Elliya longed for some way to pay back the woman's generosity, but what she could offer? Geeni said she just enjoyed hearing the stories about life in the monastery, but Elliya never felt like her stories were enough. She had spent her life watching her stepmother's face to gauge her mood, and she could sense when a story wasn't what her godmother was looking for.

Geeni had liked the stories that involved Prince Jaemin's courtship of Princess Aliyabeth, and their conversations when they visited the monastery. However, she didn't seem surprised to learn the princess disappeared suddenly or that the prince had married the new owner of the theater.

Elliya thought she had finally found a story her godmother would enjoy when she heard about a wild party full of people wearing pink wigs. She thought her godmother would be pleased her pink hair was so trendy, but when Elliya told her about the now legendary party, Geeni's lips tightened while she fidgeted with the gold bangles on her wrists. Elliya apologized profusely, but for what, she didn't know.

Elliya had been listening carefully, but she still didn't have a good story to entertain her godmother with this week. Her dusting became more frantic as she thought of the disappointment on Geeni's face. She had to work harder and listen more so she wouldn't let her godmother down.

She picked up a stack of books from her cart, turning toward their proper aisle, when she ran into a man.

Men weren't forbidden from entering the monastery, but it was rare enough that his appearance shocked her. He bent to gather her fallen books while she blankly stared at the top of his head. His wavy black hair was casually tousled, and his muscular shoulders were visible through his neatly pressed white linen shirt.

He stood, his movements as smooth as a dancer, and offered her the books. "I apologize, Sister."

He was a full head taller than her, with emerald eyes and golden brown skin. Her mouth went dry, but she choked out the words, "I'm not a Sister Scholar yet. Just an apprentice."

His full lips curved into a smirk. "Ah, so you haven't written us off completely yet."

"Who?" she breathed.

"Men." He chuckled. "It's so unfortunate to have a monastery full of lovely women outside my grasp."

She tried to imagine this lovely man "grasping" the older sisters and nearly choked. But the image clarified the type of man he was. And Elliya was much too smart to lose her head over a womanizer.

She cleared her throat and changed the topic. "I apologize for not watching where I was going."

Before she could retrieve the books, he retracted his arms, looking at the book on top of the stack. "*Iet zukta Kalamad* ..." he read. "This is from Verkeshe."

"Yes. It translates to *One Night in Kalamad*."

He held the stack in one hand while he flipped through the pages of the book balanced on top. "I'm studying Verkeshian right now, so this is perfect."

She lowered her head to hide her warming cheeks. "Um

... That's not a proper book to learn Verkeshian. It's a romance novel."

His twinkling eyes shot to her face. "In that case, it's even more perfect than I imagined." He grinned roguishly. "I'm glad to see the Sisters are permitted to enjoy fantasy men."

Elliya tried to imagine which scholar would spend her night reading a Verkeshian romance novel and failed. But she still felt protective toward them. "The Sister Scholars have sworn themselves to pursuing scholarship without restraint. They allow no man to be in authority over them and can read anything they wish."

As soon as the words left her mouth, she was filled with equal amounts of fear and exhilaration. She had never spoken back to anyone like that. Her stepmother had rewarded impudence with swift punishment.

The man's grin turned thoughtful as his emerald eyes studied Elliya. She ducked her head, a remnant of the submissive posture she used around her stepmother, but she watched him, unsure if she should apologize or hold her tongue.

He huffed a quiet laugh. "I appreciate a confident woman. It's one of the many things I respect about the scholars." His eyes sparked with a mischievous glint. "I'm sure you are clever enough to join the sisterhood, but it will be a sad day when you do." He handed her the stack of books but filched the top book with graceful fingers. "I'll keep this for study. The vocabulary will come in handy." He winked.

She released her held breath as he walked away, but no matter how many deep breaths she took, she couldn't still her racing heart.

3

Elliya assisted the other apprentices in cooking the evening meal, then ate alongside them in the long dining hall. Most of the apprentices were close to her age of twenty, but a few older women had come to the monastery, seeking sanctuary later in life. Even though the scholars and apprentices welcomed her into their conversations, Elliya still felt removed. She had spent most of her life in silence, so talking over a meal was foreign to her.

After dinner, Sister Ethelwin found her at the sink. "Good evening, Elliya. I didn't think you were assigned to cleanup duty this evening." The scholar's loose hood rested across her shoulders, revealing the woman's long gray braid and kind face.

Elliya lowered her head, quickly wiping her hands on her apron. "I apologize, Sister Ethelwin. It's difficult to hand someone else my dirty dishes. I'm very sorry."

Ethelwin's lips quirked into a small grin. "Based on your prolific apologies, Elliya, one would expect you to be involved in all manner of mischievous activity, but I haven't caught you in even a single shenanigan. Not even one!"

Elliya bowed lower. "I apologize, Sister Ethelwin. I ..."

She trailed off as she thought through the scholar's words. Was she reprimanding Elliya or not?

Ethelwin sighed and whispered under her breath. "Blessed Twins, now I've got her apologizing for her apologies." She bent to catch Elliya's gaze during her bow. "Once you have satisfied your need to tidy up, I have a new job for you. The queen has requested a small personal shrine in her room. A monk will light it every morning, but I need you to collect the ashes each night."

Elliya raised her head and fidgeted with her apron as she took in the news. "Of course, Sister Ethelwin. I will tend to the queen's shrine as you wish." Though it was difficult, she moved away from the sink, leaving the dishes for someone else. "I will go right now."

After the sun had set, the tropical heat was manageable, and Elliya's footsteps were light as she made the short walk from the monastery to the palace. But before she made it to the palace gates, a carriage pulled up beside her, the door opening from within.

Her godmother's pink hair was tucked inside the loose hood of her cape. The blue silk garment was thrown back against the seat, revealing her bronze arms adorned with gold jewelry. She lounged on the carriage seat with one ankle crossed over the other knee, a curl of smoke rising from the pipe held loosely in her hand.

Elliya hopped onto the adjacent seat and smoothed her messy apron. "What are you doing here, Godmother?"

Geeni raised a pink brow. "I was going to ask you the same thing, dear. I didn't realize they allowed apprentices to wander around Isandine at night."

Was her godmother upset? Elliya had only left the

monastery on Sister Ethelwin's order, but the thought of disappointing her godmother sent a spike of alarm through her.

"I'm sorry, Godmother. I wasn't wandering, I promise. The Sisters assigned me to sweep the ashes from the queen's personal shrine each night."

Geeni's lips curved in a slow smile. "You are a treasure, little mouse. Goddess Qira truly blessed me on the day we met."

Elliya didn't know how to react to such kind words, and she studied the floor to hide her blush.

The pink-haired woman raised her pipe to her rosy lips and puffed thoughtfully for several moments, then looked Elliya up and down. "Since this will be your first time meeting the queen, I need to make sure you are prepared." She sorted through her gold necklaces, then lifted one over her head. "Wear this."

Elliya held the necklace reverently in her palm. The thin chain held a gold charm with an odd symbol that shimmered as if wet. "What is this?"

"It's protection, little mouse." Geeni pointed her pipe in the direction of the palace. "Protection from the queen."

Elliya's fingers instinctively closed around the necklace. "Why do I need protection from the queen?"

Geeni breathed out, releasing a long curl of smoke. "Because the queen has magic."

Elliya smothered her immediate reaction, silently studying the necklace. Her scholarly mind wanted to dismiss the idea of magic, but her tongue refused to speak a contradictory word to her godmother. A thousand questions sprang to life in her mind, however stupid questions had been the quickest way to make her stepmother furious. She didn't want Geeni angry with her, so she held her tongue.

Geeni watched her reaction while she continued

smoking her pipe. "I'm surprised you aren't assaulting me with questions about that revelation."

Elliya hunched her shoulders. "I'm sorry, Godmother. I—"

Geeni waved her hand dismissively. "Questions about magic are expected, so I'll tell you what you are too afraid to ask. The queen has magic, and she isn't the only one. You haven't heard about it, because the queen and her advisor, Drazen, collect everyone they find with magic and keep them as her pets, like the animals in her menagerie."

Elliya's eyes widened as she listened, but she waited patiently while Geeni took another puff of her pipe before continuing. "The magic is called a Spark, and each person's Spark is different, granting them unique abilities. The queen's ability is to steal the Spark of others, keeping it for herself. No one knows for sure how many Sparks she has stolen, so I don't know exactly what she could do to you. That's why you need protection."

Elliya studied the gold necklace on her palm and whispered, "And she can't hurt me with magic if I wear this?"

Geeni avoided her eyes as she rested her pipe in a marble bowl, then she answered smoothly, "It will keep you beneath her notice. With that necklace, you can be in the same room as her or Drazen, and they will barely notice you at all. You'll just be a quiet little mouse sweeping ashes."

Elliya traced the shimmering symbol with her finger. "How does it work? Does it have a Spark of its own? Who made it?"

Geeni smiled, but it didn't reach her eyes. "You ask a lot of questions, don't you, dear?"

Elliya shrank at the irritation in Geeni's voice. "I'm sorry, Godmother. My stepmother punished me for asking so many questions. Please forgive me, Godmother. I'm so sorry." Elliya bit her lip to keep the embarrassing babble of apologies from streaming out of her mouth.

Geeni gently cupped Elliya's chin and lifted her head until she was forced to look the woman in her jade eyes. "I'm only upset because I want you to trust me. Don't worry about how the necklace works. Just keep it hidden beneath your clothes and trust it will keep you safe. Trust *I* will keep you safe. Don't you trust me, little mouse?"

Elliya's eyes filled with tears, and she whispered, "You rescued me, Godmother. Of course I trust you."

Geeni's attention flitted to the tears hanging from Elliya's eyelashes, and her lips bent in a small smile. "You're such a dear little treasure."

Elliya blinked, and the tears fell, but Geeni softly swept them away before the tears slid down her cheeks.

As Geeni fiddled with a bangle on her right wrist, Elliya took the moment to collect herself. She lowered the necklace over her head, then tucked it beneath her dress. "Thank you, Godmother. I will treasure this necklace as the gift it is."

Geeni picked up her pipe again and blew out a slow curl of smoke before she answered. "I grew up in a home much like yours, Elliya." Her jade eyes stared into the distance. "An only child, living with a violent woman ... I know exactly what you always wished for: safety ... peace ... falling asleep with no fear of what the next day would bring ..." Her eyes refocused on Elliya. "It's how I knew you needed rescue. Because of the pain I suffered, I have a gift for knowing exactly what people need. And in return, I always find myself blessed."

Elliya's throat constricted painfully as she considered the violent childhood of the confident woman before her. "I'm glad you survived, Godmother. And I'm so grateful for everything you've done for me."

"I know you are, dear." Geeni smiled kindly. "Just keep quietly doing your job and enjoying the safety of the monastery. You have nothing to worry about anymore. I won't let anyone hurt you ever again."

Tears pricked at Elliya's eyes, but she held them back. "Thank you, Godmother."

Geeni studied her eyes for several moments, then her lips twitched. "Well, I guess that's all for today. Take care, little mouse." She opened the carriage door, and Elliya scurried out.

4

———

Elliya knocked on the queen's door and trembled as she waited. In one hand, she held a decorative dustpan with a stiff brush, while her other hand flitted across the front of her white dress, feeling the comforting gold charm hiding beneath. Geeni said the charm would protect her, and Elliya needed to trust her.

No sound came from within, and she bit her lip. Should she knock again? She glanced at the guard on her right, and the woman gave a slight jerk of her head, signaling Elliya to enter, before returning to her stoic position.

Elliya wiped her sweaty palm against her apron, then quietly opened the door.

The empty sitting room was lit with a few candle sconces burning low. The thick rug muffled her footsteps, though she stepped as quietly as always, moving past the cluster of sofas and approaching the open door to the left. The room beyond was dark, with only a flickering light shining from within. Elliya took a deep breath and peeked inside.

The queen kneeled in a puddle of satin skirts before the dying embers of a flame.

The queen's shrine was a small brazier with a wide bowl of black volcanic rock resting on a pedestal with delicate bronze legs. Most people didn't have the luxury of a personal shrine and instead traveled to the public shrines to drop their written prayers into the continually burning flames. Inside the queen's small shrine, embers still clung to chunks of hardwood, and charred paper bits lay scattered along the edges—the remains of written prayers the queen had burned as offerings to the Blessed Twins.

Elliya had never seen the queen before—she made few public appearances, and her sons handled most of the work of administering the queendom. But Elliya recognized her as a queen instantly.

Though she sat on the floor, the queen's back was ramrod straight, her head slightly tilted as she stared at the remains of the holy fire. Her chestnut hair was woven into an intricate braid that shone red in the flickering light. Elliya couldn't tell the color of the woman's eyes, but they stared unblinking at the shrine, the flame burning in their depths.

Elliya hovered in the doorway, waiting for a signal to approach, but the queen never moved. Perhaps she should ask permission to leave and return later? Familiar anxiety raced through her blood, freezing the questions on her tongue. Shame curdled in her gut because she couldn't figure out the answer on her own.

Though Elliya's head remained bowed, she studied the queen's face, hoping to find the answer that would keep her safe. She brushed a hand across her hidden charm. What kind of magic did this woman possess? Was she strong? Could she move things without touching them? Could she read Elliya's thoughts? And if she possessed so many Sparks, ensuring her place as the most powerful person in the queendom, why did she appear so sad?

Elliya tried to push down the string of questions—she

would never risk asking them out loud. Even if the queen looked sad, that didn't mean Elliya was safe. She had often found her stepmother staring wistfully at one of Elliya's father's handkerchiefs, but the woman could turn from sadness to fury with just a single look at Elliya.

So she chose the safest option. She sat on her heels and waited.

What did a queen pray for? Were her prayers similar to those of the people who visited the shrine? Did the Goddesses listen to her above everyone else? Queens of Isandariyah were descended from the First Queen, Twice Blessed, in an unbroken line of matrilineal succession. Did that make this queen more blessed than everyone else?

Elliya ground her teeth, frustrated that she couldn't stop the questions from bubbling up in her mind. If she were smarter, she would know the answers and wouldn't have to burden others with her constant questions. She forced her mind to be still and watched the flame as it burned up the last of its fuel.

When the last ember died, the queen closed her eyes and breathed out a long sigh. Then she stood, absently smoothing her skirts, without glancing in Elliya's direction. She silently retreated to her inner bedroom and closed the door behind her with a soft click.

Elliya held her position for several breaths, watching the queen's door. When it remained closed, Elliya scooped the ashes from the shrine and departed the queen's quarters without ever saying a word.

As she left the palace, a guard told her the path through the menagerie was the quickest way to reach the gate. Lanterns lit the curving path through the queen's animal collection, but it was so late that the animals had all snuggled up inside their dens, and the only hint of life was the soft coo of birds. The presence of the slumbering animals soothed her, and she stepped lightly to not disturb them.

Animals were much less complicated than people. Horses didn't care if she asked too many questions. Mice just wanted a little snack, then they'd sit with her in comfortable silence. And birds sang the same joyful songs each morning, no matter how bad the day was.

She skidded to a halt as a kitten darted across the path.

Elliya crouched to peek into the bushes lining the brick walkway. The kitten cowered, its tiny body in a tight, shivering ball.

"Aww. Poor baby. You can't make yourself disappear by hiding. Believe me, I've tried." She reached out a slow hand. "I promise I won't hurt you."

The kitten sniffed Elliya's fingers tentatively, then, determining her safe, rubbed its face against her open palm.

Elliya slowly scooped up the kitten and walked beneath a lantern. "What a pretty ginger lady you are! Where do you belong, little one?"

The kitten studied her with slow blinks, then cuddled against her palms and started purring.

"Don't fall asleep on me! I need you to show me where—"

"There you are!"

Elliya hunched at the sound of the masculine voice and pulled the kitten protectively against her chest. "Who's there?"

The shadowy figure stepped into the lantern's light, and Elliya recognized him as the stranger she had met earlier in the monastery's library. And he wasn't talking to her, but to the kitten.

"Why did you run off?" He pointed a scolding finger at the kitten. "I even gave you a treat, you little rascal."

The kitten was still snuggled in Elliya's hands, and didn't appear afraid of him, just mildly disinterested.

The man huffed at the kitten, then his eyes finally rose to Elliya's face. "Hello again, Sister." He gave a proper bow. "I apologize for my rudeness. This kitten escaped from me while I was examining her, trying to determine which tomcat is her father."

Her mouth opened to remind him she wasn't a scholar yet, but a piece of knowledge floated to her lips instead. "Her father is a ginger cat. Ginger fur is a recessive trait, so for a female cat to have orange fur, her father must be ginger and the mother either ginger or calico."

He tilted his head, studying her in a new way. "I thought I had met all the Sisters involved in this type of scholarship. How do you know this?"

Her gut clenched as she considered the source of this knowledge: a stack of books, lost to her forever inside her stepmother's home.

She whispered, "I read it in a book."

The man took a step closer, and the kitten began purring louder. His emerald eyes roved across her hair and face. "Was the book from Verkeshe?"

He was too polite to ask her if *she* came from Verkeshe, though her blond hair suggested it was a possibility. And though the books were in fact from Verkeshe, she couldn't bring herself to speak about their author. So instead, she asked a question of her own. "Why are you trying to determine the kitten's father?"

An embarrassed flush colored his face. "Just a little scientific experiment I was conducting. I guess now I know it was the ginger tomcat who fathered this litter."

Elliya tried to keep her eyes from widening as she imagined this man conducting experiments. He seemed more likely to spend his time styling his perfectly tousled hair or picking out clothes to highlight his chiseled form.

She focused on more scholarly thoughts to still her wandering eyes. "Even though the ginger tomcat sired this kitten, the rest of the litter could have different fathers."

"A single litter can have multiple fathers? How is that possible?"

The answer came quickly to her. "A female cat can be in heat for several days, and anytime she encounters a male cat, they can ..." Elliya's words slowed as she realized the suddenly awkward conversation she had found herself in.

The stranger's eyes widened in understanding. "So one litter can have different fathers, and there's no way to know who inherited what from whom ..." He groaned. "That blazing calico can't help me study inherited traits if she fools around with every tomcat inside the palace walls. Now all I've got is a basket of mismatched kittens of ill repute."

Elliya held the kitten closer to her chest as she looked the man directly in the eye. "The kittens aren't of ill repute, because there is no shame in siblings having multiple fathers. Consider the princes—they all have different fathers, and there's nothing disreputable about them."

The stranger's mouth fell open.

Elliya stopped breathing. She never made contradictory statements to anyone. Apologize, duck your head, and agree: that had been her strategy to survive, but this was the second time she had contradicted this man.

He shut his open mouth, and his lips curved. "I appreciate your conclusion, Sister. I retract my rude comments about the kittens' parentage."

His smooth grin distracted her into giving another small contradiction. "It's just Elliya. I'm not a scholar yet."

He hummed deep in his chest. "Well then, good night,

Elliya." His eyes drifted to the kitten in her hands. "And good night to you, little kitten ... What was the name the stable girl gave you ... Lacey?"

Luci.

The strange thought popped into Elliya's head, and she whispered, "Luci?"

His eyes lit up. "Yes, that's it! Luci." He smiled warmly at the kitten. "Good night to you, too, Luci."

The man bowed to her in farewell. She had so many questions for him, and she opened her mouth, but he answered her first question before she could ask.

"Hawthorne." His lips twitched as if he knew a joke. "And the answer to your next question is *Yes.*" He winked at her before he strode into the shadows.

She whispered, "*Prince* Hawthorne?"

The kitten purred in affirmation.

5

Elliya woke up with a slight pressure on her chest, and when she opened her eyes, she found the culprit: a kitten staring at her with pale blue eyes.

I'm hungry.

Streaks of dawn filtered through the window slats of her simple monastery bedroom, and Elliya's blurry eyes focused on the kitten as she struggled to understand.

Elliya drew in a deep breath and did something that felt quite silly. She asked the kitten, "Did you say something?"

I'm hungry.

The answer came to her in the same way she had known the cat's name. Not as speech, but as an idea planted directly in her mind. The cat understood her, and Elliya "heard" the response.

Elliya chewed her bottom lip as the kitten calmly licked her paw. She had always had an affinity with animals—they seemed to find her presence comforting. Back in her attic room, birds would gather outside her window, singing her awake, and mice curled up to watch her do chores. But she had never heard them *speak*.

She knew of afflictions where people heard voices—was that what was happening to her? She didn't feel sick. Would she know if she were?

"What should I do?" she asked the kitten. "If they find out I'm sick, they'll kick me out of the monastery." A shudder ran through her as she imagined returning home to her stepmother.

I'm hungry.

Elliya sighed as she got out of bed, nestling the kitten on the pillow to wait. "Okay, I'll get you something to eat, but then I have to figure out what to do with you."

She had been so distracted by the prince the night before, she had failed to ask him where the kitten belonged. When she had found her way out of the menagerie and to the palace gates, she'd thought the guards would accuse her of smuggling the queen's property, but when she tried to hand the kitten over to them, they'd just laughed and ushered her outside the palace walls. She didn't want to upset the scholars, so she had hidden the kitten inside her apron pocket until she made it to her room. But now it appeared she had accidentally become the kitten's guardian.

I'm hungry.

"I'm hurrying!" Elliya pulled on her white dress, tied her apron around her waist, then offered her hand to the kitten. "You can wait in here or hide in my apron."

The kitten walked regally to Elliya's outstretched hand and stepped onto her palm.

Elliya tucked the tiny cat into her pocket, then grinned. Good thing apprentice aprons had deep pockets.

~

Elliya finished washing her breakfast dishes and tucked the kitten inside her apron pocket for the dozenth time that morning. Luci kept bounding away to chase a butterfly or sniff a feather or taste a fallen scrap of food. As Elliya exited the kitchen, she pinched one more bite of sausage and slipped it into her apron. Luci's rough tongue washed Elliya's finger clean, then the kitten jumped out of her pocket and ran into the courtyard.

Elliya darted after her, but pulled to a stop—Sister Ethelwin waited for her. She forced her attention away from the kitten scampering in the grassy courtyard and opened her mouth to apologize, but she wasn't sure what for yet. Sorry for washing her dishes when she wasn't scheduled, sorry for secretly keeping a kitten in the monastery, sorry for possibly going crazy ...

Before she found the right words, the gray-haired scholar spoke. "Good morning, Elliya. Instead of dusting the library today, you are assigned to assist two scholars with a project."

Her silent apologies were quickly replaced with unvoiced questions: What kind of project? Which scholars? Why her?

A young scholar burst into the dining room. She skidded to a stop at the sight of Ethelwin and smoothed out her white robes, adopting a serene expression that belied her previous sprinting.

"Good morning, Sister Ethelwin. I am not late." The young scholar tucked a loose curl underneath her disheveled hood.

Ethelwin raised an eyebrow. "You are right on time, Sister Kensley." Her lips curled in a wry smile. "And it's perfect timing for you to take Elliya with you."

Kensley bowed primly. "Of course, Sister." She watched the older scholar walk away, then pulled a biscuit out of the sleeve of her lightweight robes, and took a big bite. "Nice to meet you, Elliya," she said with a full mouth. "I'm Kensley. Let's go!"

Elliya followed her along the covered walkway surrounding the courtyard, peeking around each column to keep an eye on the kitten. The scholar opened a door to their left and ushered Elliya inside.

Morning sunlight filtered through the tall windows, striking chalkboards filled with equations and sketches. In the middle of the room, a red-haired scholar sat at a tall table with books piled in stacks, her face tilted down as she read.

When Kensley pulled Elliya to the tall worktable, the red-haired scholar raised her head and looked Elliya up and down. "We have no need for a maid."

Kensley rolled her eyes. "She's not here to clean, and you know it, Lliadain. Sister Ethelwin said she will join us on this project at Prince Hawthorne's request."

Elliya's eyes widened. She had been recruited for this position by the prince?

Kensley patted a stool to summon Elliya. "No reason we can't chat while we wait for the prince to arrive."

Elliya eased onto the stool, scanning both scholars as she tried to understand what she was doing here. "I'm not very good at chatting—"

Lliadain looked back down at her book and mumbled, "Kensley talks incessantly, so you needn't do much."

Kensley ignored the other scholar, leaning across the table toward Elliya. "How old are you? No, let me guess ..." She squinted and studied Elliya's face. "You're twenty years old."

Elliya nodded. "Yes, that's right."

"I just turned twenty-two," said Kensley. "I've only been a Sister Scholar for a few months, but Lliadain has been here for years." She lowered her voice to a conspiratorial whisper. "She's basically an old woman." Kensley mouthed the words *twenty-nine*.

Lliadain shot her a glare, then returned to her book. Kensley gave a wicked grin, and Elliya bit her lip to keep from giggling.

"Prince Hawthorne is twenty-seven, but since he's the second-born son of Queen Illorienne, everyone knows how old he is." She laughed. "But don't tell him I said that. He doesn't need any encouragement about his popularity, especially with women."

Elliya wasn't sure what to say about the prince, so she adopted her most diplomatic voice and said carefully, "Prince Hawthorne is quite ... charming."

Lliadain snorted but continued reading.

Kensley threw her head back and laughed. "That's an understatement. Prince Hawthorne is a beautiful man, and he knows it." The curly-haired scholar lowered her voice. "But there's something about the prince that not everyone knows ... Would you like to hear a secret about the 'too-charming' prince?"

Elliya's mouth dropped open. "A secret?"

Kensley leaned across the table and whispered, "Prince Hawthorne ... is a nerd."

Elliya stared at her.

Kensley laughed brightly. "He's read quite extensively in his lifetime, though I doubt he admits it to many people. I don't think it fits well with his playboy image." She sighed. "It's a shame he was born a man. He would have made an excellent scholar if he were a woman."

Lliadain raised her head. "If Prince Hawthorne were a woman, he'd be queen."

An uncomfortable silence fell over them, followed by a cleared throat from across the room.

"Yes, unfortunately for the queendom, I'm not a woman." Hawthorne stood in the open doorway, and despite Lliadain's flippant remark, he grinned. "But all the women I know are very grateful I'm a man."

Elliya opened her mouth to offer an apology, but for what, she wasn't sure.

The prince interrupted her by placing a book in her hands. "But that's why we're here—to find a solution to the queendom's lack of an heir."

She looked down at the book, and her cheeks warmed. "Animal husbandry? The queen gave birth to seven sons, so I assume she understands the process."

Kensley barely smothered her grin. "We are trying to prove bloodlines, other than relying on the traditional method of matrilineal succession."

Elliya tried to will away the warmth in her cheeks. "So there's no hope she can still give birth to a daughter?"

The prince's voice was matter-of-fact, as if the discussion of his mother's breeding were commonplace. "The queen is forty-seven. A pregnancy at her age is unlikely and also dangerous. Besides, the queen is ... busy." His eyes flicked away, like the topic had finally become uncomfortable.

Elliya frowned. What was keeping the queen so busy she couldn't worry about an heir? Considering she'd given birth to all seven sons in less than eleven years, at one point, she had been fairly diligent about the process.

Lliadain huffed out a breath. "The whole idea is sacrilegious. The blood of the First Queen, Twice Blessed, has been passed down from mother to daughter in an unbroken line. The thought of a king on the throne gives me the chills."

Prince Hawthorne's smile froze on his face. "No one is suggesting a king."

Elliya cringed at his chilly tone, but still asked, "If a king isn't an option, then why are you studying bloodlines?"

Prince Hawthorne's voice settled into his usual confident tone. "Beyond the theological reasons, there is a practical reason for matrilineal succession—it's the only way to know the bloodline is pure. Any child born of a queen has her blood, whereas the same cannot be said with certainty for a king's child. So while my brothers and I are clearly born of the First Queen's bloodline, we could not guarantee the same of our children."

Elliya nodded as his logic clicked into place. "You want to have a daughter and prove her bloodline so she can inherit."

He laughed. "My daughter? No, I don't plan on settling down. Actually, Jaemin is the oldest, so I thought it should be his daughter. Although that was before anyone knew his choice of bride ..."

She lifted the animal husbandry book. "So you are studying this, not to produce certain traits in future generations, but to work backward, to see if certain traits can prove ancestry."

His eyes locked on hers. "Exactly. I knew you would understand."

The intensity of his emerald eyes startled her, but she couldn't look away.

He moved closer. "When we met, you mentioned dominant and recessive traits, which is a topic I've been studying for the last year. I've been researching the work of a Verkeshian scholar ahead of her time. All her work is over twenty years old, so I planned to travel to Verkeshe to look for her, but Drazen said the queen doesn't want me to leave." His shoulders heaved in a sigh. "It's a shame because this scientist must have made progress over the last twenty years. By now, she must have discovered something that holds the answers we need."

Elliya's breathing grew more shallow the longer he spoke. A question hovered on the tip of her tongue, but she couldn't make her lips move. She pulled in a slow breath and was pleased her voice didn't tremble. "What's the scholar's name?"

"Yulia Zaleska."

Elliya's throat closed with the sudden grief of hearing her mother's name spoken by the prince. Her mother had been a gifted scholar, but Elliya hadn't expected to find anyone else who had read her work.

Even though she had no memory of her mother, the writing in her mother's books gave Elliya a crystal clear image of the woman, even clearer than the memory of her father, who had died when she was five. Yulia Zaleska was truly brilliant, with a library full of research, despite her death at the age of twenty. She was the one who belonged at the monastery, not Elliya.

Everything Elliya knew about her mother was thanks to the textbooks in the small library inside what was now her stepmother's home. Elliya's stepmother liked to keep the library door locked, only granting permission to enter when Elliya had completed all her chores perfectly. And since perfection was nearly impossible in her stepmother's eyes, anytime Elliya made it inside the library, she picked a new book to memorize in case it was the last time she was allowed to enter.

Leaving her mother's books behind had been the hardest thing to sacrifice when Geeni rescued her, especially her mother's journal hidden in her bedroom. The journal was a mixture of scientific observations, doodles, and scattered personal recollections. It was how Elliya knew that when her mother fled Verkeshe, she'd left behind the name

Zaleska, taking a new name on her arrival to Isandariyah. In those pages, she saw her mother's story unfold, with each choice leading to her untimely death.

Lliadain groaned. "Prince Hawthorne, why do you keep wasting time on dead ends? Studying inherited traits will not lead to the conclusive evidence we need."

Prince Hawthorne leaned against the table. "It's the best plan we have so far. The only plan. We have to find an answer. If we can't, hidden forces will tear the queendom apart."

Elliya's head tilted at his mysterious words. "What hidden forces?"

Lliadain's sharp focus shifted, choosing Elliya as her next target. "We are dealing with sensitive matters of the queendom's future, and yet we suddenly have a stranger listening in. Remind me how you came to be in the middle of this very critical research, Elliya ... Perhaps *you* are one of those hidden forces."

Elliya's mouth went dry. She wanted to explain that her mother was the scholar Prince Hawthorne was seeking, but she couldn't reveal that without admitting she wasn't who she said she was. She was only in the monastery because of the fake identity Geeni had given her. Admitting she was the daughter of Yulia Zaleska would not only sound like a lie, she would also risk being discovered by her stepmother.

Her stepmother would drag her home and never allow her to leave again.

Prince Hawthorne stepped to Elliya's side, pulling the scholars' focus his way. "Elliya and I had a conversation about inherited traits thanks to a wayward kitten I was chasing through the menagerie. There are no hidden forces at work here. Just my good fortune to find someone with a scientific background."

The prince's smile was charming, but there was a hint of

challenge in his words. Lliadain opened her mouth, probably to question Elliya's scientific background, but Kensley leaped in smoothly. "Perhaps we should give Elliya a chance to speak for herself." She turned her golden brown eyes on Elliya.

Instead of explanations, a question rose to Elliya's lips. "What happens if the queen dies before an heir can be proven?"

The question splashed like cold water over the prince and scholars. The prince's head sagged, and Lliadain's eyes dropped as she made an unconvincing show of reading the book in front of her.

Kensley recovered first and turned a comforting smile on Elliya. "That won't happen. We are dedicated to finding an answer."

Elliya turned to the prince. "And what if we never discover more research by Yulia Zaleska?" Her mother's name tingled on her lips.

The prince straightened his shoulders. "We will continue her research ourselves, or uncover a new method to find the answers we need."

Elliya put on her peaceful smile, willing her heart to be calm. "Can I see the book?"

"Of course! Come with me." The prince led her to the shelves at the back of the room, scanning the titles before he pulled out a book with a worn cover. "Is this the same book you've read?"

Her hands trembled as she opened the book, reading the words both familiar and unfamiliar. "No," she whispered. "I've never read this one."

The prince's eyes lit up. "You've read another of her works? Where is it now?"

She cleared the lump in her throat. "Those books are lost."

"Books?" breathed the prince. "You've read more than one?"

She nodded absently as she rubbed her hand across the front of the worn cover. "Where did you find this one?" Elliya had thought her mother's complete collection of work was on the shelves in her stepmother's house.

"In the queen's library." At her confused look, he continued. "Many generations ago, Queen Idrisana opened our borders to refugees from warring kingdoms. She gifted those refugees with their own portion of land to settle and farm. The only thing she asked in exchange was a book from their home country. Even though the queendom doesn't gift land anymore, some refugees still continue the tradition of offering a book when they arrive." He looked at the book in Elliya's hands with fondness. "Apparently, someone brought this with them from Verkeshe and donated it when they arrived at the port."

The very reason the prince wanted Zaleska's scholarship was exactly what had caused her mother to flee her home country. According to her mother's journal, her knowledge had labeled her a threat to the Kingdom of Verkeshe, which was constantly plagued with disputes over bloodlines. When she arrived at the port of Isandine, she had shed the Zaleska name but had given one of her precious books as an offering of gratitude.

"I found the book in the queen's library," said the prince. "I've had others help me translate, but I'd love for you to look it over to confirm my translations are accurate."

Elliya longed to flip through the pages to see if her mother had scribbled notes in the margins like she had in her other books, but she stilled her hand on the front cover. This book linked Elliya to the life she had abandoned. To admit she was Yulia Zaleska's daughter meant confessing she had entered the monastery through deceit. She couldn't risk anyone discovering the truth of who she really was. She should run as far away from this book as the monastery's walls would allow.

She pulled the book against her chest. "I won't stop reading until I've memorized every word."

6

Elliya spent her morning translating her mother's book with the prince and the scholars. Each word was precious to her—they were the last remnant of her mother's existence. Elliya tried to hide the tears springing to her eyes every time she imagined her mother working on the experiments detailed in the book.

They broke for lunch, and the prince excused himself, saying his brothers needed him at the palace, but he would be back the following day. His lingering glance at Elliya said he would be glad to see her again.

She pretended she didn't notice.

During her free time after lunch, she grabbed Luci, tucked the kitten into her apron pocket, and smuggled her out of the monastery.

As she walked down the palm tree-lined streets, she whispered, "Am I crazy, Luci? Obviously, I'm crazy for talking to a cat and hearing her respond, but am I also crazy to get involved in this work with the prince?"

The kitten peeked out of the apron and started climbing the front of Elliya's dress. Elliya carefully disconnected the kitten's pin-like claws from her dress, then placed the kitten on her shoulder. Luci grabbed hold of Elliya's collar, snuggling underneath her fall of blond hair.

I'm hungry.

Elliya sighed. "Yes, you are always hungry. When we get to the café, I'll get you a little snack."

Bad dog.

Elliya looked around the busy street. "What are you talking about? I don't see any dogs."

Bad dog is scary.

She grinned at the kitten's improving vocabulary. "If we see a dog, I will protect you, okay?" She rubbed a finger under the kitten's soft chin. "You're safe with me."

Elliya crossed the cobblestone street and stepped inside the café. When Luci spotted her godmother, the kitten hissed, then clambered down Elliya's dress into her apron, needle claws scratching all the way.

Elliya stifled a hiss of pain, then put on a warm smile. "Hello, Godmother. It's good to see you!"

Geeni lounged inside her usual private booth, a wide-brimmed hat on the table and her pink hair styled into smooth curls. Today she wore the clothes of a wealthy merchant—a light silk top, cropped at the waist, with flowing pants gathered at the ankles. Her usual profusion of gold necklaces and bangles shimmered in the soft light filtering through the café windows.

"Have you been crying, dear?" Geeni patted the rattan chair next to her, letting Elliya take a seat. "Is someone being mean to you at the monastery?"

"No, definitely not! Everyone is so kind to me." Elliya's lips twitched as she struggled to hold on to her smile. "I was just thinking about my mother today."

"That's understandable. Anytime you want to talk about her, I'm happy to listen. I'm not offended by tears."

Elliya's heart warmed. "Thank you, Godmother. You're so sweet to me."

Geeni held her gaze for several moments before settling back in her chair. "So tell me about your life in the monastery ... Anything exciting happening?"

Elliya had considered many stories she could tell her godmother, but the woman's kindness convinced her to confess what was weighing most on her heart. "Godmother, I'm worried I'm unwell." She lowered her voice to a whisper. "I've been hearing voices ... Well, only one voice, I guess. I heard my kitten speak."

Irritation flashed across her godmother's face, but it was quickly replaced with a cheerful smile. "I doubt you are crazy, dear. The more reasonable explanation is that you have a Spark."

Elliya's mouth dropped open. "A Spark? You think I have magic?"

"Magic has been growing more common in recent years, despite how Drazen and the queen have tried to keep it hidden. You must have the ability to speak to animals."

Elliya still couldn't comprehend the idea. "But I've only heard the kitten speak, and she's only spoken a few words to me. If it's magic, it doesn't seem very strong."

"Your Spark will grow the more you use it. Now that you know you have a Spark, you should spend time developing it. Try listening to some other animals." Geeni laughed lightly. "I'm sure there are more interesting animals to talk to than a kitten!"

A tiny growl rumbled inside her pocket, but the kitten didn't peek out. "People will think I'm crazy if I'm seen talking to animals! How will I convince them it's actually a Spark?"

Geeni's eyes widened. "Do not tell anyone about your Spark! Haven't I already told you? Drazen and the queen kidnap anyone they find with a Spark so the queen can steal their magic. The only reason you have been safe from them is because of the necklace I gave you."

Elliya reached up to touch the gold charm hidden beneath her dress. "So I should just secretly talk to animals?"

Her godmother smiled. "Think of it like a game, dear. Just ask the animals to tell you their secrets. Mice can sneak into the most secure fortress. I'm sure they must know some fabulous gossip."

Elliya twisted her fingers in her lap. "Of course, Godmother." She wasn't sure what mice would make of human secrets, but the idea was both intriguing and a little unsettling.

Geeni leaned forward, resting her arms on the table as she considered Elliya. "I want the very best for you, dear. I know your childhood was awful, but now you have the chance to get what you've always wanted—a fresh start, a new life. No more violence or wild outbursts of anger ... just a perfectly safe life. As long as you can hold your tongue about your true identity and about your Spark, you can live out the rest of your days in safety inside the monastery." She clasped Elliya's hand warmly. "That's what you want, dear, isn't it?"

Elliya imagined her days stretching before her in a neat progression—each day harmonious and safe. "That sounds lovely, Godmother." She sighed as comfort washed over her, and she shoved down the part of her that longed for something more.

PART II

7

———

Elliya's days fell into a routine, more peaceful than she ever imagined. She spent her mornings with the prince and the two scholars, writing out an accurate translation of her mother's notebook. The prince had a rough translation already, but since Elliya was more familiar with her mother's writing, she made connections the other scholars had missed. She didn't know how to pronounce the Verkeshian words, but thanks to her mother's notes written in the margins, Elliya knew what the complex terminology meant.

After assisting with the translation, she spent the afternoons doing the usual chores required of an apprentice: sweeping, dusting, and pulling weeds in the monastery courtyard. Luci followed her around most afternoons, pouncing on bugs and complaining about how hungry she was. Elliya tried to keep the kitten hidden from the scholars, but she wondered if a few of them secretly knew. Luci looked more plump than the amount of food Elliya fed her warranted. If the kitten was leading a double life with a few caretakers, Luci kept that information to herself.

Each evening after dinner, Elliya walked to the palace

and swept the ashes from the queen's personal shrine. She hadn't seen the woman since the first night, and based on the lack of paper scraps in the ashes, she wasn't sure if the queen had dropped any prayers into the shrine again.

She finished each night by walking home through the menagerie. The collection of animals provided the perfect testing ground for her newly discovered Spark. Despite Geeni's suggestion to ask the animals about gossip, Elliya discovered most animals had very little interest in humans. The animals inside the menagerie were mostly tame from their time around people and went about their work as if humans were just another part of the scenery. The only "conversations" she had with animals were about their own interests.

She learned about building a nest from a scarlet sunbird, and from an iguana, the best trees to sleep in at night. A zebra led her to a pool of still water where she listened to the slow, unhurried monologue of a turtle. She found their thoughts fascinating and wanted to share them with someone, but she didn't think a lemur's eating preferences were the kind of gossip Geeni would find interesting.

And on nights like this one, as she lay on her stomach in the grass, peering into a small den while a mother rabbit gave her a tour, Elliya wondered if she actually was going crazy. Geeni had told her she had a Spark, but what if the woman was wrong? What if the animals' voices were just a grand delusion? What if Geeni was just trying to be kind to Elliya by not telling her she was going insane?

Elliya rolled onto her back. The moon had traveled far since she arrived at the menagerie. The scholars hadn't chastised her for how late she came back from the palace, but anxiety flickered within her as she imagined that tonight might be the first night they noticed. She stood, brushing dirt off her dress, and thanked the rabbit for the tour. Even if she was going crazy, it was still best to be polite.

Over the last few nights, she had grown comfortable in the dark menagerie, with the soft chatter of the animals drifting into her mind as she passed each pen or walled enclosure. She hopped over the low wall that contained the rabbits and headed back toward the curved path dotted with lamps.

The animals' voices went silent.

Her slippered feet gliding across the grass felt strangely loud. She froze, straining her ears for any hint of danger, just like the other terrified animals in the menagerie. A hysterical laugh threatened to burst from her throat—was this a new form of her insanity?

A rustle at her back caused her to spin. Elliya stopped breathing, her panic stilling all movement by instinct. She couldn't even blink.

There, in the shadow of a weeping willow, stood a tiger.

The tiger watched her, just as still. But instead of Elliya's cowering posture, the tiger stood with each paw firmly planted on the ground, each muscle of its sleek form holding potential just waiting to be unleashed.

Elliya's mind raced with questions. Why wasn't this tiger inside a pen? Had it escaped? Why hadn't anyone noticed before now? Did tigers eat people? Should she run or stay perfectly still? And why couldn't she hear the tiger's thoughts?

She strained her new abilities, trying to detect something from the tiger. If she detected fear, she would try to scare it away. If she detected mere curiosity, she would lower herself into a submissive posture and hope it wandered off. But if she detected a hungry rage ...

From the other animals nearby, she sensed a fluttering terror. They held their breath just as surely as she did. But she couldn't hear anything from the startling creature. The tiger was a silent void, hovering in the moonlight.

The tiger hadn't yet moved a muscle, but Elliya's forced stillness sent a tremor racing down her legs. She had to break the moment, one way or the other. And since there was no way she would turn her back on this animal, even to run away, she only had one option available. Elliya slowly sank to her knees, bowing her head with her eyes locked on the tiger.

The tiger's eyes flashed in the moonlight as it followed her movement, but it still didn't relax its vigilant posture.

Even though she couldn't hear its thoughts, could she communicate her peaceful intentions? "I'm sorry for disturbing you, proud tiger." Her voice trembled but carried easily through the stillness. "You are obviously the ruler of this menagerie. I apologize if I've stepped too loudly."

The tiger's eyes shone with reflected moonlight. Then the tiger lifted its front paw and placed it silently, stalking toward Elliya.

Her eyes widened as the tiger moved closer. She couldn't outrun a tiger, but as the animal stalked toward her, its dark stripes gleaming in the dim light, she wanted nothing more than to flee. Except she had lost all feeling in her fingers and toes, making it impossible for her to even stand.

She expected the animal to close its last few steps in a pounce, but the tiger stopped just beyond her reach. Then it sat on its haunches and tilted its head, watching her.

Elliya drew a shaky breath, then wet her lips. "You are quite terrifying, Sir Tiger."

The tiger narrowed its eyes.

She cleared her throat. "Lady Tiger?"

The tiger watched her in silence as Elliya's heart pounded in her chest. Then the tiger rose to its—her—feet, flicked her tail, and sauntered away.

Elliya couldn't move until long after the tiger had faded into the darkness. The surrounding animals had started chattering again, sending a wave of relief through her.

She covered her face with her hands as a hysterical laugh finally burst out. "Did that really happen? How am I still alive?"

The animals grew quiet again. Elliya bit her lip, her head swiveling to spot the tiger.

Hawthorne stepped out of the shadows. "Elliya? What are you doing?"

She hurriedly rose to her feet, but her lingering fear weakened her legs, and she stumbled into his waiting arms. She found his nearness startling, but her knees trembled so badly she wasn't sure she could stand on her own yet.

He led her gently back onto the path underneath a lantern. "I heard your voice. Who were you talking to?"

She turned away from the intriguing sight of his golden brown skin shimmering in the flickering light and focused on the shadows beyond. "I saw ..." She cleared her throat, ashamed of how her voice still shook. "I saw a tiger."

He raised an eyebrow. "Oh, really? A tiger." His lips curved in a smirk. "Now, Elliya, there's no need to lie if you are meeting someone out here for a secret midnight tryst. You can be honest with me, of all people. I'm quite a fan of trysts."

His implication sent an uncomfortable thrill through her body, and she stepped out of his arms. "A midnight tryst? I'm training to be a scholar, Prince Hawthorne. I have no desire to engage in trysts." She folded her arms. "And what are you doing out here so late? On your own midnight tryst?"

A wink was his only answer.

She huffed, but her attention was drawn back to the

shadows. "I'm telling the truth. There was a tiger right over there!"

His eyes flicked to the shadows as a hint of a frown tugged at his smirk. "There are no tigers in the menagerie, Elliya. You must have seen something else."

She narrowed her eyes at him. "The tiger stalked so close to me I could have reached out and touched it ... touched her." She ground her teeth. "You don't believe me. You think I'm crazy."

He turned from the shadows and looked her in the face. "I didn't say you were crazy. It's just ... extremely unlikely."

"No matter how unlikely it is, there is a tiger in here. You should ask yourself whether it snuck inside the palace walls or if someone let it in."

"Either option is unsettling. I will let the menagerie guardians know." He breathed out a sigh, his eyes pulled back to the shadows. "I hope they find it quickly, because they will tease me incessantly until they do. Would you like to have company on your way out of here?"

A twinge of pride prickled her neck. "I'm not afraid to walk alone."

He grinned and offered her his arm. "Well, maybe I am. Humor me?"

She reluctantly took his arm as they headed down the path. "Why will the menagerie guardians tease you about seeing a tiger?"

"Because of the children's rhyme." At her confused look, he spoke the verse in a singsong voice. "*Look in the closet, look under the bed. Find the cursed tiger, and you'll end up dead.*"

She tripped a step, but Hawthorne's arm kept her upright. "What an awful rhyme!"

He laughed. "Have you met any kids? They say awful stuff all the time." He grinned. "Parents say the rhyme, too. You must have been an obedient child, otherwise your parents would have threatened a tiger coming to get you if you didn't finish all your vegetables."

An image flashed through her mind—her as a child, seated between her mother and father as they ate a meal. She had dreamed of this imaginary scenario many times over the years as she ate cold scraps all alone, quietly hiding from her stepmother. The parents of her imagination wouldn't threaten her with a tiger attack.

And her stepmother didn't need to threaten her with a tiger when she was so violent herself.

Hawthorne pulled gently against her arm. "Are you okay?"

She didn't want to discuss any part of her family situation. "Oh, I guess I'm still shaken from seeing the tiger. I can see why tigers would scare children. It was terrifying."

"Yes, and considering the way the regent was killed, it's no wonder tigers are the scariest thing children can imagine."

She turned her head, trying to watch him without tripping again. "The way the regent was killed?"

He slowed to a stop and studied her under the lamplight. "I'm sorry, Elliya. I assumed you went to school here in Isandariyah and know all our history, but that's very presumptuous of me." It seemed like he wanted to ask if she was originally from Verkeshe, but was too polite to ask.

"Oh ... I see ..." Even though she didn't want to discuss her family, avoiding the conversation would be suspicious. So she gave him an answer as close to the truth as she was willing to get. "My mother was from Verkeshe, and my father was Isandariyan, but they both died many years ago. My father taught me to read when I was very young, but after that, my education was fairly ... nontraditional."

The only memory she had of her father was her sitting on his lap as a child while he read to her. Beyond that teaching, her only schooling was found in stolen moments spent in her mother's library.

Hawthorne's eyes softened. "I'm sorry to hear that, Elliya. It must have been difficult to lose them at such a young age."

She had revealed more than she had planned, so she tugged his arm to get him to keep walking, letting her avoid his eyes. "Yes, well, it means my knowledge of Isandariyan history is limited to what I read in a book."

He allowed himself to be pulled forward. "You aren't likely to find the story in a book, since it's usually only whispered about. The regent was the queen's father, and most historians find it impolite to publish books about her while she is still alive."

She looked at him again, intrigued by the story. "The regent ... your grandfather. He became regent when his wife died." The queen's mother had died in childbirth. That part of the story had always stuck with her.

"He was smart enough to always rule as regent, never calling himself King, although he acted as one in all but name. He almost plunged us into multiple wars, constantly looking for conquest. It was a very dark time in the queendom."

She kept her voice low. "What happened to him?"

"The queen, my mother, was scheduled for her official coronation on her seventeenth birthday, but the day before the ceremony, the regent announced his engagement." His lips twisted. "To her."

Elliya gasped. "He wanted to marry his own daughter?"

Hawthorne's eyes grew dark. "He was determined to hold on to his power, no matter the cost."

Elliya pictured the last time she saw the queen kneeling before her personal shrine. She tried to imagine the woman as a seventeen-year-old girl with a father who'd just announced he'd marry her to hold on to his power. "What happened?"

Hawthorne's eyes glittered darkly. "The morning of the ceremony, a tiger killed him."

She whispered, "A tiger?"

He shrugged. "That's what they say based on the bite marks on his neck, but no one ever found the animal, so who knows?"

"Are you suggesting the tiger I saw tonight ..."

"It can't be the same tiger. The regent was killed thirty years ago, and tigers don't live that long." He grinned and dropped his voice. "Although the nursery rhyme does say *cursed tiger*, so who knows how long *they* live?" He waggled his eyebrows menacingly.

She swatted his arm. "That's not funny! A tiger killed your grandfather, and yet you aren't concerned I saw one!"

He gave her a solemn look. "I believe you, Elliya. I'm just not afraid of it. The tiger that killed my grandfather is called two different names. When it's used to scare children, it's called the *cursed tiger*. But all the people who were alive back then call it by a different name."

His emerald eyes sparkled in the bright lamplight. "*Blessed Tiger*." Hawthorne stared sightlessly ahead. "Even violent tigers can be blessings, if their target is right."

Elliya silently considered the fate of the last man in Isandariyah to consider naming himself king.

8

———

When Elliya arrived to assist with translating her mother's book the next morning, Prince Hawthorne wasn't there. Elliya began copying her translation in neat lines into a clean notebook, while Kensley chatted about the latest feud brewing between scholars. Lliadain ignored them both, as usual. Elliya found it odd the prince hadn't arrived yet. He was usually very punctual.

Perhaps he'd stayed out too late because he actually did have a midnight tryst in the menagerie.

She tried to push away the image of the prince engaged in whatever activities were involved in a tryst. She had no interest in that sort of thing. Sure, she had agreed to take his arm so he could lead her out of the menagerie, but that was only because she'd been shaken from seeing the tiger. It was natural to take his arm in that circumstance.

And if her mind kept reflecting on how warm his arm had been, with firm muscles beneath his fresh linen shirt ... Well, she took pride in her scientific mind. It was normal for her to notice such things.

Like when he threw his head back and laughed at some-

54

thing she said, and she breathed in the scent of citrus and warm spice ... Purely a scientific observation.

She rubbed her palm across her face and forced her attention back down to her mother's book.

"You seem distracted today." Kensley bit into a carrot while she examined Elliya's face.

Elliya's cheeks warmed. "Um ... I didn't sleep well." Which was the truth. Before falling asleep, her mind had kept replaying the moment Hawthorne had left her at the palace's gate. She'd released his arm, but before he'd let go, his hand had trailed down her arm and clasped her own hand as he said good night.

Lliadain snorted but didn't look up from her book. "A common malady of girls who spend too much time with Prince Hawthorne."

Elliya's mouth fell open, and she had no idea how to respond.

Kensley covered her giggle behind her hand. "Don't feel bad about it, Elliya. He's turned flirting into an art form. You aren't to blame if his tricks work on you."

Her back stiffened. "He has pulled no *tricks* on me, and even if he had, I'm smart enough not to fall for them."

Lliadain lifted her head with a single red eyebrow raised. "Those penetrating emerald eyes ... A touch that lingers just a little too long ... A slow smirk designed for you to watch his lips ... That man has practiced a long time to gain his skill to charm unsuspecting young women." Lliadain looked Elliya up and down. "I just didn't think you'd be quite so ... unsuspecting."

Kensley pointed her carrot at Lliadain. "It's not her fault. It's obvious she doesn't have much experience with men. And to have the first guy who notices you be Prince Hawthorne, well, that's like being thrown into the deep end of the lake."

Warmth flooded Elliya's neck and flowed across her cheeks. "It's not like that ..."

Prince Hawthorne chose that moment to arrive, sweeping into the room with a stack of books in his arms and a grin on his lips.

"Elliya! I've got something for you." His dark plum vest was tailored perfectly across his broad shoulders and narrow waist, but he had hastily rolled his linen shirt up on his forearms. His wild curls looked as if he had tumbled out of bed and come right to find her.

She hid her face in her notebook to hide her glowing cheeks. "Good morning, Prince Hawthorne. Lliadain and Kensley are also happy to see you."

He ignored her attempt to draw the scholars into the conversation, instead pulling up a seat next to her, scooting it closer than was strictly necessary. "I talked to the menagerie guardians this morning, and they said there have been many tiger sightings recently."

Lliadain snorted. "Superstitious nonsense. Tigers don't live this close to the city. They live deeper in the jungle, surrounding the Twins." She jerked her head eastward, toward the two volcanoes named after the Twin Goddesses.

Hawthorne ignored Lliadain, his attention still on Elliya. "The guardians haven't seen it themselves, but they believe you really might have seen a tiger in the menagerie last night."

Kensley's eyes widened. "You were in the menagerie last night with the prince?"

Hawthorne turned to Kensley with a wicked grin. "Scholars have given up having fun, but Elliya is still just an apprentice. I told her last night there is no shame in enjoying midnight trysts while she has the chance."

Lliadain rolled her eyes, and Kensley gave Elliya a look that was half-playful, half-pity.

Elliya's head spun around to the prince. "There was no midnight tryst!"

"Speak for yourself," he said with a wink. He didn't wait for her to close her open mouth before he slid a book in front of her. "These are the menagerie guardians' log books. They've tracked the recent tiger sightings."

Lliadain gave him an arch look. "What does this have to do with our current project? I'm only here to further research into heredity. If you want someone to help you track down monsters from children's rhymes, you'll need to find someone else."

He focused his smooth grin on Lliadain. "We are still studying heredity, dear scholar. However, we've finished the translation of this book and still haven't found a definitive answer. My brothers all look different, thanks to our different fathers, and there are no inherited traits common among all of us. There's nothing to prove we are descended from the First Queen, other than the queen giving birth to us, so there will be no proof for our daughters either. We need to find more writing by this author to continue." He turned back to Elliya. "The books you read by Yulia Zaleska ... Are you sure we can't get them? If you know where they are, I'm sure I could persuade the owner to sell them to me." His lips curved into a smirk. "I can be very persuasive."

She cleared her throat to hide her uneasiness. "No, the books ... They're lost."

He sighed. "I have another plan in mind, but while I sort it out, I need something interesting to study." His emerald eyes focused directly on Elliya. "Unless you can imagine something else more diverting to pass the time?"

She had never seen eyes so green. Like sunlight glinting off a raindrop as it trickled down an orchid leaf ...

Lliadain snapped her book closed. "Thank you, Prince Hawthorne, for proving once again why scholarship at the monastery is limited to women. Your presence is not conducive to scientific inquiry. Perhaps it's best if you leave until you have further research to share."

Hurt flickered behind his green eyes, but he kept a calm smile on his lips. "If that's what you wish, Sister. I apologize for hindering your research." He stood smoothly, sparing one more look at Elliya. "If you'll permit me to make one last suggestion—you probably shouldn't take the path through the menagerie at night until the tiger is located. I'd hate to see you injured by a tiger, either real or cursed."

The blush had faded from her cheeks, but the way he spoke like it might be the last time they saw one another sent dread crawling through the pit of her stomach. "Thank you for your concern, Prince Hawthorne." And because she hated the hurt expression still lingering behind his eyes, she added, "Might I suggest you find another location for your midnight trysts as well?"

His lips curved into a genuine smile. "I will keep that in mind." He bowed with a flourish and strode out the door.

9

———————

After Hawthorne left, Elliya's morning with the scholars passed slowly. She finished writing out one of the last chapters before heading to lunch, then spent her afternoon doing her usual chores, accompanied by Luci. The kitten's vocabulary had expanded, but it was mainly just food words, along with a few words that didn't have exact translations into Isandariyan. Elliya assumed they were cat curse words.

At dinner she considered eating with Kensley, but the scholar was sitting with a group of scholars Elliya didn't know, so instead, she ate alone again. When she walked to the palace to sweep the queen's personal shrine, the guards waved her through the gate with barely a second glance, and she realized she hadn't spoken a word since Prince Hawthorne left.

She had spent most of her life before the monastery in silence. Her stepmother didn't want to hear anything Elliya had to say other than an occasional affirmation that she was following orders. Elliya would occasionally sing quietly to herself, but only when her stepmother had left the house. Sometimes days passed in silence. She had found a new home in the monastery, but would she ever learn how to speak freely?

The guards at the door barely glanced at her as she carried her dustpan inside the queen's quarters. The sitting room was just as silent and pristine as always. So silent that the voice seemed unreasonably loud.

You won't find anything.

Elliya froze. Her eyes darted around the room, looking for the source, but she didn't see him until she crouched to peek under the sofa.

A chubby mouse was scrubbing his face with his paws. *She actually finished her meal today and only left me a few crumbs on her plate.* He sighed dramatically. *If she starts eating her meals again, I'll probably starve.*

The chubby mouse looked unlikely to starve, but Elliya was too polite to tell him so. Instead, she pulled a bread crumb from her pocket, one she had saved to feed the birds later. The round little mouse was so cute, the birds would just have to share.

The mouse's eyes lit up as he took the crumb from her fingers and began methodically chewing around the edges. She brushed off her skirt as she stood and stepped into the queen's inner chamber.

The queen kneeled before her shrine.

Elliya froze again. She wasn't sure if the queen spent her time in another part of the palace or if she was always behind the closed bedroom door, because Elliya had only seen her once. But now the queen kneeled in front of her shrine as she had that first day, watching the last scrap of a prayer burn away.

Elliya didn't want to look like she was impatient with the queen, so she dropped to her knees, resting her dustpan in her lap. Then she waited, watching the queen, while trying to look like she *wasn't* watching.

As the last flame melted away, the queen closed her eyes in one final prayer, took a deep breath, then stood in a smooth swish of silk. She turned toward her bedroom door, then paused as her eyes landed on Elliya.

It wasn't until this moment that Elliya remembered the queen possessed magic. Geeni said she had numerous Sparks, but she hadn't told Elliya what any of them were. As thoughts of all the magical ways the queen could kill her raced through her head, she longed to reach for the gold necklace hidden beneath her dress. Geeni said it would protect her, and Elliya had to hold on to that promise.

The queen took a slow step toward her, and Elliya's pulse pounded hard in her chest. She wanted to look up at the queen to gauge her reaction, but she was too terrified to watch the woman stalk closer.

A squeak in the sitting room was followed by scurrying feet as the chubby mouse shot beneath Elliya's dress, which pooled around her as she kneeled, the fabric slightly muffling his terrified squeaks.

"Hush now, little one. Shh ..." Elliya crooned a comforting sound, and the mouse quieted immediately.

The queen paused, tilting her head as she stared at Elliya.

"I'm sorry for disturbing your prayers, Your Majesty. I'm sorry ..." Elliya's apology faded away—should she also apologize for the mouse? She wasn't the one who'd scared the mouse, but it was usually safer to apologize than not to.

Before she could open her mouth to apologize for the squeaky mouse, the queen spun in a rustle of skirts, entered her bedroom, and closed the door behind her.

Elliya shot to her feet, causing the mouse to scamper behind a hanging tapestry. She swept out the ashes, then hurried back through the sitting room and out the door.

The guards barely twitched as she flung open the door

and dashed down the hall. She brushed the ashes from her hands onto her apron, and as she raised her head, she found Prince Hawthorne before her.

"Elliya! It's a pleasure to see you. What are you doing here?"

She told herself her heart was still racing from her interaction with the queen, and not from his grin. "I just finished sweeping the ashes from the queen's personal shrine like I do every night."

A shadow passed over his eyes, and Elliya couldn't tell if it was from sadness or suspicion. "You just came from the queen's quarters? What did she say to you?"

Elliya had done nothing to make him suspicious, but a part of her felt guilty just the same. "She said nothing to me. This is only the second time I've ever seen her."

He looked toward the queen's quarters, as if he could see her through the walls, a small frown tugging his lips downward. Then he shook his head, facing Elliya again with his usual grin. "Well, it's wonderful you are here. I'm on my way to start a fight, and I could use someone in my corner." He reached out his hand. "Come with me. You're just what I need."

She obediently gave him her hand without asking any more questions.

He led her past the queen's door, heading deeper into the palace than Elliya had been. The guards raised their eyebrows but didn't make any move to stop them.

The prince opened a door and tugged her inside. Instead of the bright fabric that hung throughout the palace, faded tapestries and ancient scrolls framed in glass lined the walls. Dark wooden artifacts lined the ceiling-high shelves, and though Elliya wanted to study them to determine their origin, her eyes were drawn to the man seated behind the wide desk.

He leaned over a book on his desk, his long gray braids contrasting with his black robes. She found his age hard to guess. His dark brown skin had faint lines around his eyes and forehead, but his long beard made him look positively ancient.

The man glanced briefly at the prince, before his attention landed squarely on her. His dark brown eyes roved over her soot-stained hands before focusing on her face. She took a step back under the weight of his penetrating stare.

The prince pulled her closer to his side. "Elliya has read a Verkeshian textbook from the same author as the one I found." He looked down at her with a comforting smile. "Tell him what you've read."

Elliya stared at the prince, who was still clutching her hand. She couldn't answer because her dry mouth was sealed shut.

The prince looked at her expectantly. "About inherited traits ... recessive and dominant ... tracking lineage ..." He spoke as if his words would shake the knowledge loose from her mind, but her tongue couldn't form the words.

The gray-haired man leaned back in his chair, steepling his fingers near his chest. "There's no need to convince me of your theories. Tell them to the Sister Scholars."

The prince's smile stiffened. "The scholars have grown tired of a man studying with them, Drazen."

Elliya examined the man closer. Drazen—the queen's advisor. Geeni had told her this man had magic, like the queen. She clutched her apron to keep her hand from wandering up to the hidden locket under her dress.

Drazen's skin was a darker brown than most of the people in Isandariyah, meaning he might have come from Zaridia, which would explain the foreign artifacts filling his study. He answered in a calm baritone voice. "The Sister Scholars are our best hope for discovering the answer we need. Work with them, not against them, and they could provide you with inspiration."

Prince Hawthorne groaned. "I don't need inspiration, Drazen. I need a scientific answer. And for that, I must travel to Verkeshe."

The prince stared at Drazen, and Elliya's mind raced in the silence. Verkeshe? Why would he—

Drazen's mouth hardened into a tight line. "The queen wants all of you here."

"So you say, but she rarely speaks to us at all." The prince cleared his throat, turning his frown into a smooth smile. "I need to find Yulia Zaleska. She made these discoveries over twenty years ago, and will have continued her research. I just have to go to Verkeshe and find her."

Elliya's lungs constricted tightly. The prince planned to travel to Verkeshe to find her mother? She wanted to tell him that would be a waste of his time, but couldn't form the words.

Drazen leaned forward, resting his forearms on the desk. "The relationship between Isandariyah and Verkeshe is strained right now. You can't waltz in there and demand they hand over one of their scholars."

"I'll sneak in and find her."

Drazen gave him a flat look. "The Verkeshian people won't reveal their secrets to someone who is clearly not from their country, Prince. How will you track down this scholar on your own?"

"I'm taking *her* with me." He punctuated the word by tugging Elliya closer.

Elliya looked down, surprised he still clasped her hand. Her lips parted, but she couldn't ask a question before Drazen chuckled.

"You think one of the scholars' apprentices will take your side over theirs?"

Hawthorne said confidently, "Of course, because she's a scientist."

Elliya gaped at him. A scientist? How could he say that with a straight face? She would have laughed if she weren't so confused.

The prince straightened his shoulders. "We will return with the Verkeshian scholar and solve everything."

Drazen frowned, but before he could speak, the prince spun on his heel and dragged Elliya out of the study.

She followed him several steps before digging her heels in. Someone of his size could pull her off her feet, but he released her hand at her gentle tug of resistance. She put her hands on her hips, very aware of how cold her hand felt now that he let her go.

She huffed, "You told him I would go with you to Verkeshe without even asking me!"

He bit his bottom lip as if he enjoyed being scolded by her. "I apologize. That was inconsiderate of me. But tell me truly ..." He flashed his bright smile. "Doesn't a secret mission to Verkeshe to find a missing scholar sound fascinating? I promise I'll be a delightful traveling companion."

Besides not knowing he was chasing a dead woman, he was so arrogant he believed Elliya would jump at the chance to go with him. His cocky grin stirred an angry snake that coiled in her gut. "It does *not* sound fascinating! It sounds ridiculous!"

He took a step closer and whispered in a husky voice, "Come now, Elliya ... Most women would fight to go on a secret adventure with me."

She swatted away the butterfly fluttering in her stomach and focused on the snake in her gut. "A secret adventure with you—your tailor, your stylist, and the troop of women required to stroke your ego." The words spilled out in a confident flow, but when they ended, she was left with a cold dread. She had barely spoken all day at the monastery, and now she was in a verbal sparring match with a prince. What had gotten into her?

Her eyes shot to his face, searching for an indication of his reaction. Would he only verbally rage at her? Or would he resort to violence like her stepmother?

His body was as still as hers and close enough that his wide frame filled her vision. His brows pulled together, but not in anger. The expression reminded her of the times he read an interesting passage in her mother's book. Brows scrunched as he uncovered a mystery, and eyes devouring something wondrous.

That was how he looked at Elliya now.

The butterflies burst to life, fluttering against her rib cage and soothing the angry snake. He wasn't angry at her outburst, but his expression alarmed her in a different way.

His lips parted, and he spoke in a sultry drawl. "You are truly stunning when you're angry." His eyes roved over her face. "Your cheeks flush in the most becoming way."

He lifted a hand as if he might stroke her cheek, but she flinched away. He blinked at her sudden movement, his eyes studying her again as he evaluated a new mystery.

She pressed her lips together, then said calmly, "I'm not angry." She took a deep breath, willing away the last traces of anger and burying the other unwanted feelings. "I don't let myself get angry."

He raised an eyebrow. "Perhaps you don't share your anger with others, but you have no problem revealing it to me." He tipped his head in a small bow, drawing his face closer to hers. "I'm honored."

His nearness stilled the air in her lungs. Each breath felt too loud, but it was nothing compared to the heartbeat pounding in her chest.

His expression shifted from wonder to smug delight. He

knew the effect he had on her. Knew the effect he had on all women.

The angry snake twitched its tail, startling some butterflies.

He tipped his head closer. "So, have I convinced you to come with me to Verkeshe?"

She wanted to offer a denial, but her mouth was so dry she couldn't speak. She wet her lips.

His eyes shot to her mouth, a cocky grin spreading across his own lips.

The snake in her gut flared back to life. The desire for confrontation was so foreign to her she tried to shove it down alongside all her suppressed wants, but his smug grin stirred up more feelings than she could contain.

She pasted on the most peaceful smile she could manage. "You shouldn't rely on your pretty face to make your arguments, Prince. It's a lazy form of debate."

He chuckled and took a step backward. "I look forward to proving my debate expertise to you, Elliya." He bowed gracefully. "And thanks for noticing my pretty face."

He winked, then strode away, leaving her to settle the snakes and butterflies at war in her stomach.

10

———

The next morning, the scholars had moved on to something else. Yulia Zaleska's book and Elliya's translated notebook sat in a neat stack at the edge of the desk, while Kensley and Lliadain hunched over a row of vials.

"It's blood," said Kensley at Elliya's unasked question. "We're studying the differences and similarities between the blood of family members."

Elliya picked up one of the glass vials and looked at the blood inside. "What does this have to do with what we just translated?"

Lliadain took the vial out of Elliya's hand and replaced it in its slot. "It doesn't. Now that the prince isn't limiting our research with his twenty-year-old foreign textbooks, we can move on to more current experiments."

Kensley gave Elliya a comforting look. "I think we can use the knowledge from Zaleska's work as we study these blood samples up close." She collected a sample from one vial and dropped it into a fresh vial. "If we can determine similarities and differences in blood, maybe we can use it to prove the queen's bloodline."

Her words shook loose an idea from another of her mother's textbooks. "You're studying the similarity in blood types between family members."

Lliadain's head snapped up. "How do you know about blood types?"

Elliya was saved from devising a way to sidestep the question by the arrival of the prince.

"Good morning, ladies! Have you missed me?"

Lliadain glared at him. "You've barely been gone a full day, Prince."

He swept up to their table with his usual swagger. "I regret to inform you I will be unable to join you for the foreseeable future. I hate to deprive you of my presence, but I must, in the name of science."

Lliadain rolled her eyes and dropped her head back to the vials.

Kensley smiled fondly. "Where are you headed, Prince Hawthorne?"

His face split in a wide grin. "Thank you for being so kind as to ask, Scholar Kensley. I'm headed to Verkeshe to find Yulia Zaleska."

Lliadain's lips pinched with disdain. "With all due respect, Prince, that's an idiotic plan."

Elliya's eyes widened as she turned to see the prince's reaction to the scholar's impertinence.

The prince only chuckled. "I always appreciate your due respect, Sister Lliadain. However, I'm afraid I must still bid you farewell. I'm leaving for Verkeshe tomorrow."

"Tomorrow?" gasped Elliya. "You can't do that!"

He grinned. "I've already told you that you are more than welcome to join me, Elliya." He slid closer to her side of the table, resting his muscular forearm on top of a stack of books. "I know you said I shouldn't use my pretty face to persuade you, so how about this for a compelling argument?" He dropped his voice to a sultry whisper. "An adventure to a foreign land … Discovering a brilliant scholar …" He drew close enough that his breath stirred her hair. "Exploring the frontiers of knowledge until everything is revealed …" His last word hung in the air as a barely exhaled breath.

Lliadain slapped her palm on the table, breaking the spell. "Prince Hawthorne—"

Elliya cleared her throat. "With all due respect, Scholar, I can answer for myself." Elliya avoided the scholar's glare and studied the prince with a neutral expression.

The prince leaned against the desk, head tilted back as if to get a better perspective on the show.

Elliya calmly folded her hands at her waist. "Thank you for the very … descriptive invitation, but I'm happy here in the monastery where I belong. I can explore the frontiers of knowledge on my own with no …" She pointedly looked him up and down. "… distractions."

His lips curved in a small smirk. "What a shame. I would have made sure the adventure was worthwhile." He bowed to her, then to the scholars. "I'll return with Yulia Zaleska. I hope you take her more seriously than you take me." He bowed to them, then headed for the door.

"Don't go!" The words burst from her mouth before she could draw them back.

He spun in the doorway, giving her a final smirk. "Come find me in the menagerie tonight if you change your mind. Or if you want to give me a kiss goodbye."

The thought of kissing the prince drowned out any clever comebacks. She could only gape as he walked out the door.

"That idiot is going to get himself killed," grumbled Lliadain.

The image of the prince in the menagerie shocked her awake. "You think the tiger will kill him tonight?"

Lliadain rolled her eyes while studying the vials.

Kensley patted Elliya's hand. "Not the tiger, dear. Verkeshe." She frowned at the closed door. "It truly isn't a wise decision. No matter how desperate he is."

Elliya drew in a deep breath, her mind fully functioning now that the prince had left. "You think he will die in Verkeshe?"

Kensley sighed. "Verkeshe and Isandariyah have a strained relationship. King Ruzgar always has his eyes on his next conquest, and his sons are even worse. An Isandariyan prince 'kidnapping' a Verkeshian scholar would be the perfect excuse to go to war."

Lliadain looked up with a fire behind her eyes. "Hopefully Prince Hawthorne makes an inappropriate comment to someone's daughter and gets himself killed before revealing he's an Isandariyan prince."

Elliya gasped. "How could you say such a thing?"

Lliadain shrugged. "Better than starting a war." She concentrated on the vials.

Elliya just stared at the woman, unsure what to do with the scholar's dark thoughts.

Kensley sighed. "I hope someone talks him out of it. I don't wish for his death, but the queendom can't handle an invasion by Verkeshe. Not with the inheritance still undecided."

Elliya gazed at her mother's textbook at the end of the table. "But that's exactly why he feels like he needs to go, isn't it? He sees the question of inheritance as a ticking clock. No one will persuade him to stay if he thinks a scholar in Verkeshe holds the answer."

Kensley forced a smile. "Maybe he will find her and everything will work out." She used a dropper to combine two blood samples and studied the result with a determination that belied her hopeful words.

Elliya moved to the end of the table, completely forgotten by the scholars. She flipped open her mother's textbook, the comforting pattern of Verkeshian words blending in her mind. An idea formed of how to stop the prince from leaving, but it terrified her. A tremor passed down her spine as the plan took shape.

Was it worth it? She barely knew the prince. Maybe she should just let him go to Verkeshe, even though he chased a ghost. If he got himself killed or started a war, neither of those things would be her fault. Prince Hawthorne should know better than to make rash decisions.

Except she could see why he was making the decision. There was no heir. If the queen named him or one of his brothers as heir, the queendom would be no more. And depending on the truthfulness of the children's nursery tale, declaring oneself king was a quick way to get mauled by a tiger.

No, Isandariyah would not and could not have a king. There had to be an answer.

She rested her hand on her mother's textbook, hoping to receive her blessing. She wasn't sure if her mother would approve of her decision, but she only saw one path before her. To convince the prince to stay in Isandariyah, she would do something that shook her to the core.

Elliya had to go home.

11

Elliya knew her stepmother's schedule better than she knew the scars on her own back. Some of those scars had been caused by Elliya miscalculating the exact moment the tea would finish brewing or her ability to answer the door before the postman knocked. Even at the monastery, Elliya still woke up at exactly the same time each morning. Perhaps one day she could convince herself that staying in bed five minutes longer wouldn't result in harm.

Standing outside the home filled with a lifetime of disturbing memories made that hard to believe.

Elliya retrieved the hidden key from the bushes and cracked open the back door. A quick glance told her the kitchen was empty, so she tiptoed inside. Not that she'd expected her stepmother to be working in the kitchen. But her stepmother had probably hired someone to take over the housework now that her only servant was gone, and Elliya had thought they might be inside.

Judging by the dirty dishes in the sink and the clean cook pot, her stepmother couldn't afford to pay the new maid to stay the entire day and do all the work Elliya had done for free. The woman would have to learn to live with less than perfection, which brought Elliya a small amount of glee, but it also sent a new ripple of fear through her. If her stepmother found her standing in the kitchen now ...

Elliya's fingers went numb from clutching her skirt so tightly. She shook out her hands, then tiptoed to the door out of the kitchen into the parlor. She usually took the staircase directly to her attic bedroom, but for this quest, she needed to venture through the parlor and up the wide staircase to the library.

She tiptoed up the stairs, repeating her stepmother's schedule under her breath. Today, she would be at the tea shop with friends and wouldn't be home until right before dinner. She had at least one hour until the woman arrived home.

Elliya cracked open the door to the office, still terrified despite knowing her stepmother wasn't here. Everything in the office looked just as she'd left it, though slightly dustier.

Her stepmother would be furious about the dust.

She breathed through her anxiety and headed to the bookshelves along the wall. Even though the disorderliness disturbed her, Elliya had mixed her mother's books in with the others, hoping her stepmother wouldn't notice the name of her husband's previous wife. Either her father hadn't mentioned his first wife's scholarship to his new wife or the woman had simply disregarded it. Elliya was grateful for the oversight. She knew with a certainty that if her stepmother knew how important her mother's books were to Elliya, she would have destroyed them long ago.

As it was, her stepmother used the small library to punish or reward Elliya. Since the rewards were few, Elliya had memorized as much of her mother's writing as she could. One day she'd felt particularly bold and had stolen her mother's last journal and hidden it under a floorboard up in the attic. Even if her stepmother discovered the truth about the books in the library, Elliya would have one journal the woman would never find.

Retrieving the journal was her next stop, but first she needed one of her mother's textbooks. She skimmed over the titles, careful not to disrupt the thin layer of dust and give away her presence. If only she could take the entire collection with her! But that would tip off her stepmother, who would call the authorities, believing she had been robbed. Elliya couldn't risk the threat that they might track the books back to her.

She found the textbook about blood types and pulled it gently off the shelf, scooting the books on either side closer to one another to hide the gap. Surely this book would be enough to convince the prince to stay. Even though the book itself didn't provide the answer he needed, maybe along with the scholars' other research, they could discover an answer together. She clutched the book to her chest as she imagined working in the lab with the prince, heads bent together over the book, fingers brushing as they both moved to turn the page ...

The front door opened.

Elliya stopped breathing, mentally repeating her stepmother's schedule. Today was the day her stepmother went to the tea shop with friends. She wouldn't be home until right before dinner, when Elliya would quietly place a lovely meal before her ... Except Elliya wasn't cooking dinner right now.

A metal pan slammed onto the counter.

Her stepmother was cooking her own dinner.

The woman would be furious.

Elliya clutched the book before her like a shield, even though she knew if her stepmother found her, a book wouldn't protect her. The woman would pick up anything nearby to use as a weapon. Elliya scanned the library, her eyes falling on her father's cane by the door, and a sick dread washed over her—that would be the first thing her stepmother reached for.

Elliya had to get out. Now.

She canceled her plan to retrieve her mother's journal from the attic. She had already abandoned the journal once before, so she made herself let it go again. But she held tight to the textbook as she planned her escape route.

Elliya only knew a few ways to sneak out of the house. She had used them all to run away, but every time she'd escaped, her stepmother had found her and dragged her back, literally. The only thing protecting Elliya was that her stepmother believed her dead. So if Elliya could use one of those escape routes without being detected, she would still be safe.

Walking out the front door was a definite no. Besides the fact the kitchen was just on the other side of the parlor, the front door had a noisy deadbolt. It would take too long to silently unlock it while unnervingly keeping her back to the kitchen door.

The library window was also not an option. Once she had climbed down the trellis and run away to hide in a neighbor's shed. Her stepmother had hauled her all the way home, then forced her to rip the roses off the trellis without gloves, before her stepmother took a hammer to it. Elliya rubbed a scar on her palm. That day she had just been grateful her stepmother hadn't taken the hammer to her.

Other than the back door through the kitchen, she couldn't think of another way out. Panic set in as her stepmother slammed the pots and pans. Elliya imagined her using them as a weapon against her, and she backed closer to the window, her breath coming in gasps.

Hello, friend.

A bird landed on the open windowsill. He fluffed his bright blue feathers, then perched comfortably. *I thought you had left. I missed hearing your quiet songs.*

Though the panic was closing her throat, she whispered, "I left, but now I'm trapped here again." She clutched the book tighter. "I have to get out of here."

The bird tilted his head. *You can't fly?*

"Not without breaking an ankle, or worse. Then I couldn't run, and she would find me."

The bird tilted his head the other way. *Take the squirrels' path.* He hopped to the edge of the sill and looked down.

Elliya crept closer and risked a glance down. A tree had grown close enough to the house that a branch hovered just beyond the top portion of the trellis that her stepmother couldn't reach. Elliya was surprised she hadn't noticed it before.

Except over the last few years she hadn't even attempted to run away. She had stopped believing escape was possible.

You should go. The bad one is coming.

Elliya didn't think. She shoved the textbook into her apron pocket, clambered over the sill onto the trellis edge, then flung herself onto the branch, as close to the trunk as she could manage. The rough bark scraped her hands, but she clung to the branch until she got her feet underneath her.

The library door opened.

She froze, expecting her stepmother's face to appear at the window any moment. She glanced down, but the ground was still too far for her to jump, and her stepmother would definitely hear her land.

The bird had flitted into the branches when she scrambled out the window, but it landed once again on the windowsill and "spoke" in a gentle voice.

Fly away, silent songbird. We can escape easier than you.

Two squirrels zipped across the branch before balancing neatly on the windowsill. Then they followed the bird through the window.

Squealing erupted from inside.

Elliya didn't waste time—she just started climbing down. Crashing echoed from the room, and she feared her stepmother would hurt the animals. As she slid the last few feet to the ground, she spared a look up to the window in time to see the bird flutter out.

Fly! he commanded before he headed back in.

She obeyed the bird and ran.

12

———

Elliya's stomach rumbled loudly in the quiet menagerie. She had skipped dinner so she could finish the last of her chores before heading to the palace. Not that she could have eaten anything with her stomach still a churning mess. The wild sprint away from her stepmother's house, followed by the long walk back to the monastery, had not been enough to calm her terror.

By the time she walked to the palace, exhaustion had set in. Even though her days were always filled with manual labor, she never had to run for her life or shimmy down trees. When she found the queen's quarters empty, she sighed, relieved that at least one part of her day was easy.

After sweeping the ashes from the shrine, she took the dark path through the menagerie and wondered again if she was insane. Not just because of the animals' voices chattering away in the back of her mind. No, her current fear of insanity was that she had actually risked everything to go back to her stepmother's home. Her mother's textbook was a comforting weight in her pocket, but she still wasn't sure if it was worth the risk.

From the darkness came a voice as smooth as warm honey. "You're here."

She stopped walking directly beneath a lantern and waited for Hawthorne to approach. No way was she following him into the shadows.

He stepped into the light, and she realized why he had hidden so well. In addition to black pants and boots, he wore a black sleeveless tunic that showed off his muscular arms.

She gave him a quick look up and down. "Is this your uniform for all your midnight trysts?"

His eyes lit up. "Oh, is that what this is?"

"What? No, of course not." She hoped her blush wasn't visible in the dim lantern light.

He chuckled softly. "Well then, why are you here? If you didn't come to kiss me goodbye, does that mean you are coming with me to Verkeshe?"

"I'm not here to kiss you or to follow you to Verkeshe. I'm here to convince you to stay."

He raised his brows, intrigued. "You won't change my mind, but I'll enjoy letting you try."

"That's not how—" She cleared her throat and started over. "I have something for you."

"Oh, I bet you—"

She cut off his slow drawl by pulling the textbook out of her apron and shoving it against his stomach.

"What is this?" He opened the book and angled the pages so the lantern light fell on the words.

"Another textbook by Yulia Zaleska with theories about blood types. I hope you find it interesting enough to stay."

His long fingers skimmed gently across the page, and his face lit up in innocent wonder so unlike his usual flirty grin. He turned the pages carefully, his fingers tracing the hand-written notes in the margins.

He spoke in a reverent whisper. "I thought you said the books you'd read were lost."

"Um ... I found one." She bit her lip to keep from saying more.

His eyes were still skimming the words. "You think this holds the answer we need?"

Because of the notes in her mother's final journal, she knew the book wouldn't solve the queendom's inheritance problem. But revealing that wouldn't convince him to stay. "I think it might help continue the scholars' other research. When we show them this book—"

His head shot up. "You haven't shown them yet?"

His complete focus disoriented her. "Um ... no, not yet."

He lowered the book, stepping closer. "You came to me first."

She swallowed, highly aware his closeness let him read everything on her face. "I had to find you before you left."

He inched slightly closer with the book pressed between them. "Why didn't you just let me go to Verkeshe? While I was gone, you and the scholars could have studied this with no ... distractions."

She borrowed Lliadain's haughty arrogance to rescue her from his closeness. "I didn't want you to accidentally start a war!"

A slow grin spread across his lips. "And is that the only reason you didn't want me to go?"

"Well, you *are* a prince. It would be a shame if you ran off and got yourself killed."

His grin continued to grow. "And?"

She clung tightly to her faked confidence. "And even though you aren't a scholar, you're still quite helpful in the library. You can reach the top shelves." Her voice came out shakier than she wanted, but she thought she could play this game all night.

He lowered his head and whispered, "And?"

The soft word fluttered against her skin, and she realized she was outmatched. She drew in a deep breath to calm herself, but he was so close she breathed in his scent of citrus and warm spice. She had severely miscalculated her ability to remain detached. He had won, and even though he could read the truth plainly on her face, she surrendered by speaking it out loud.

"And ..." Her voice fell to a whisper. "I would miss you."

She expected his smug grin to widen with proof of his victory, but his eyes softened into the same wonder he'd had for the treasured book. He seemed almost surprised by his own reaction. "I ... I would miss you, too, Elliya."

His quiet admission startled her. It was nothing like his proud swagger and cocky self-confidence. He seemed almost vulnerable. As if he really would miss her.

She looked up at him, her indrawn breath filling her senses with his nearness. His impossibly long lashes blinked slowly, his emerald eyes locked on her face. Her mouth was so dry, she desperately wanted to wet her lips, but if his eyes shifted focus to her mouth, she might pass out. She was so caught up in the sight of him, she almost missed it.

The animals had gone silent.

"The tiger!" She pried her eyes away from Hawthorne to scan the shadows for the animal's approach.

His eyes widened as her words finally sank in. "The tiger? Where?" He grabbed her by the waist, pulling her behind him.

She momentarily forgot about the tiger at how suddenly he had moved to protect her. True, he had no idea where the tiger actually was, and he had no visible weapons other than the large textbook in his hand. Nevertheless, his first instinct was to protect her.

She was glad he couldn't see her face, because rapture

would have been written plain. She closed her eyes and savored the feeling of his strong back against her chest, his bare arm snaking behind him at her waist, his eyes searching the shadows for the tiger.

Oh, yes. The tiger.

"Where did you see it?" he asked.

"I didn't see it. I heard it. Um ... I guess I actually heard all the other animals get quiet when the tiger approached."

He kept his hand on her waist, but faced her. "You must have excellent hearing. I haven't heard any animal sounds since I entered the menagerie."

He was right. The animals were almost silent at night, except for their quiet chatter as they settled into their dens. She couldn't exactly tell him she had heard a mother meerkat go silent as she tucked her baby into bed.

She chose a little misdirection. "I guess you were distracted." The animals were still silent, so she turned in a slow circle, looking for the tiger. "She's here somewhere. I just don't see her."

He pulled her closer, scanning in the opposite direction. "She? How do you know the tiger is female? How close did you get to this thing?"

She had only inferred the tiger was female based on the animal's reaction, because her Spark was noticeably not involved.

"She just seemed like a girl." She pitched her voice slightly louder. "Lady Tiger, we're sorry to bother you. We'll just be on our way now." She took Hawthorne's arm and hauled him down the path toward some chattering animals in the distance.

He allowed himself to be led away. "Lady Tiger? So, you talk to her?"

She laughed awkwardly. "Um ... I guess so. But it's not like she talks back."

He gave her a strange look, then scanned the shadows inside the pens they passed. "Are you sure the tiger is nearby? I didn't hear—" He stopped walking and looked at her. "Did you lie about hearing the tiger to distract me? Were you scared I might—"

"No!" She cut him off before he could finish the question with the words *kiss you*. Of all the feelings she'd had in that moment, she wouldn't admit that *scared* wasn't one of them.

"The other animals went silent, just like they did the other night. The tiger was close. I just didn't see her."

He hummed noncommittally in response.

She searched the shadows but couldn't see anything, though the soft chatter of animals had returned. "I guess she's gone now."

He offered her his arm, and they headed toward the menagerie exit. They walked for several minutes in silence before he murmured, "Just so you know, there's never a need to lie to escape a situation you don't want to be in with me. I enjoy flirting, but I'd never pressure you into anything."

His candid words surprised her. "Thank you for saying that."

The moment between them felt fragile, and she wasn't sure what to say. She thought he might speak first, possibly crack a joke, but he just chewed on his lip in silence.

They approached the lit exit of the menagerie with the gate to exit the palace grounds just beyond it. He studied her with serious eyes. "Are you sure you're okay walking back to the monastery in the dark?"

She smiled at his concern. "I'm fine. It's not a long walk." She looked over his shoulder into the menagerie. "You won't walk back to the palace through the menagerie, will you? The tiger is still in there somewhere."

The corners of his mouth curved in a small smile. "I'll take the long way back."

She glanced at her mother's book held loosely at his side. She couldn't let him leave without asking him the question he still hadn't answered. "Will you stay?"

His smile faded until all that remained was a focused calm. "I'll stay while we translate this book to see if it holds an answer. But if not, I'm going to Verkeshe."

His serious tone left no room for argument. If this book didn't hold an immediate answer, he would leave anyway.

He lifted the book and traced a gentle finger across the cover. "I'm reluctant to hand this over to the scholars. They'll want to read it first. You know, before I get my 'man hands' all over it."

She had to choose between looking at his grin or the way his man hands stroked the cover.

She chose the grin.

He ducked his head, as if to prepare for an embarrassing question. "Elliya, I know you're a scholar apprentice, but I have to ask ... would you read this to me before you give it to the scholars?"

The question was so vulnerable that she replied before thinking. "Yes," she breathed.

He lifted his eyes, pinning her in place. "Tomorrow morning. Unless you're needed to assist them?"

She frowned. "Now that I've finished translating the other book, they have little for me to do. I assume they'll send me back to the library to sort books."

A smile lit his face. "Great. Then tomorrow morning you can meet me at the palace instead. If anyone asks, just say you're sorting books in the queen's library."

"That's where I should meet you? In the queen's library?"

He grinned. "Yes, but you'll have to wait for me to let you in. It's very ... private."

The way he said the last word sent a shiver down her spine, but not in a bad way.

Hawthorne appeared to reconsider his choice of word. "Of course, what I said earlier still applies. I do nothing without a woman's consent."

"Yes, of course." She suddenly wondered how many women he'd taken to this "private" library.

His lips twitched in a suppressed grin. "I prefer my women willing." He waggled his eyebrows. "Oh so willing."

She rolled her eyes. "Good night, Hawthorne."

His chuckle faded as they each walked different ways.

13

———

Elliya found the queen's library the next morning thanks to a helpful maid. When she told the woman she was there to meet Prince Hawthorne, the maid gave her a knowing look.

"Enjoy yourself, dear." She patted Elliya on the back and winked before walking away.

This "private" library was a busy place.

Hawthorne strode around the corner, his cocky swagger only slightly offset by his cheerful grin. He held her mother's book loosely at his side, but she got the feeling he had to restrain himself from clutching the book against his chest like a delighted schoolgirl.

"I'm so excited to show you the library." His eyes sparkled as he pulled a key out of his pocket.

She gave him a flat look. "Judging by the number of maids who winked as they walked by, you've been excited to show a lot of women this library."

He grinned. "True, but I think you'll enjoy it in a way they did not." He swung the door open and let her step inside.

Her hand floated unconsciously to her mouth to cover

87

her gasp. The library was unlike anything she had ever imagined.

Even though she could only see the rows of books on either side, she got a sense of the enormity of the room when she looked up. Morning light streamed through the glass roof, the curved ceiling stretching so far that she couldn't see it past the tall shelves at her sides.

Hawthorne closed the door behind them. "I knew you'd love it." He offered her his arm. "Care to join me on a stroll to the center?"

She lowered her hand from her open mouth and took his arm. "What a strange layout! Why does the door lead into this small enclosure instead of opening into the whole room?"

"Because it's a labyrinth." He led her to the bookcase before them, then turned right, which revealed another set of shelves curving around the edge of the domed ceiling. "There are books around every corner, but only one path leads to the center."

She let him lead her down the correct pathway, amazed at the sheer number of books. "How old is this library?"

"My seventh-great-grandmother had it built for her husband, who was a noted scholar. That was before the Sister Scholars built the monastery, so there were many male scholars back then."

She looked at him, though he kept his eyes focused on navigating the maze. "I think it's unfortunate they limit the monastery to women scholars."

His lips twitched with a suppressed grin. "But just think how distracting that would be. You'd never get any work done."

She gave a small huff. "There are still plenty of distractions among women scholars."

His eyes took on a faraway look. "Unfortunately, becoming a scholar isn't a possibility for me."

"But you're a prince. Surely you could get the rules changed."

His lips hardened into a line. "I can't challenge the ban on male scholars. I need to prove the First Queen's bloodline to crown the next queen, not seek more power for myself." He chuckled darkly. "It doesn't end well for men who reach for power that doesn't belong to them."

She whispered, *"Find the cursed tiger, and you'll end up dead."*

He nodded slowly. "But if I can discover a way to prove the First Queen's bloodline, and Jaemin can provide a daughter, then maybe the queendom will have a chance to reexamine its policy on male scholars." He led her around one more corner, and the enclosing bookcases fell away to reveal the center of the library.

Circular bookcases surrounded the center, with the way they entered the only exit leading back into the labyrinth. Curved leather couches lined the perimeter, and directly in the middle, crescent tables circled a massive stone candelabra.

Her fingers trailed across book bindings as she walked the perimeter of the library within a library. She breathed out, "It's so beautiful! No wonder you bring all the girls here!"

He threw his head back and laughed. "Yes, but they choose to show their appreciation by holding me, not the books."

She slid a book back onto the shelf and raised an imperious brow. "Perhaps you should only invite women who believe libraries are for reading."

He gave her a shocked look. "And limit my choices? I hardly think that's wise. But today I invited an apprentice scholar. I'm just not sure that will lead to the results I wanted."

She crossed her arms. "Considering you asked me here to read to you, I think I can safely say you will get what you wanted."

"I want many things, Elliya, but today I will settle for reading." He sat on a curved sofa and patted the seat next to him. "Come read to me."

She stalked over and plucked the book out of his hands. "I'm not snuggling on the sofa with you, Prince. This is a scholarly endeavor. We sit at the table."

He grinned. "As you wish, Scholar."

She set the book on the smooth table and scooted onto the circular bench. When the prince climbed over the bench and sat at her side, she realized why he'd given up the sofa so easily. The curved bench positioned him close at her side.

He rested his chin on his palm and looked at her expectantly. "Read to me."

She wondered if she had made the right decision, bringing the book to him before the scholars. But she sighed and began to read.

She read several chapters about her mother's study of blood types. His face lit with wonder at the information, and she could almost hear him thinking through the experiments to help prove her mother's theories. However, the more she read, the more his attention seemed to shift from the words to her.

"Are you paying attention?" she snapped.

He answered smoothly, without missing a beat. "Of course. Her theory is that there are three key components of blood, and a child inherits one component from each parent, creating a unique type from the combined two."

Elliya was impressed with his very tidy summation.

Apparently, he *had* been paying attention. "Yes, that's right. I'll continue."

She read each paragraph in Verkeshian, then translated the words into Isandariyan so he could hear both. She had just finished reading the original when she looked up and caught him staring at her lips.

When she stopped reading, his eyes met hers. "Your Verkeshian accent differs from any I've heard."

She had imagined him thinking about something else, but his statement was embarrassing in a different way. She lowered her eyes back onto the page. "Um ... I've never really heard Verkeshian spoken. I only know how to read it. You shouldn't trust me for proper pronunciation."

"You've never heard it spoken? Then how did you learn to read and translate it so well?" His eyes searched her face as if trying to uncover a wonderful mystery.

Her cheeks warmed. "I read a lot of books like this with notes in the margins and notebooks with Verkeshian and Isandariyan translations. I just figured it out, I guess."

His eyes widened. "That's amazing. I can't believe you taught yourself Verkeshian."

She brushed a hand across the words, needlessly smoothing the page to avoid his eyes. "Besides not knowing the proper pronunciations, I doubt I could carry on a full conversation with anyone from Verkeshe. My Verkeshian vocabulary is limited to mostly scientific terms."

A wicked grin played across his lips. "So that Verkeshian romance novel I picked up at the monastery library the first day we met ... Did you understand all that vocabulary?"

She wanted to tell him she hadn't read it, but it was hard to lie when his emerald eyes never left her face. Her voice came out as a rough whisper. "I had to make a lot of assumptions based on the context."

The corner of his mouth tugged upward. "Perhaps we

should read that book together next. For purely educational purposes, of course."

She had no response to that. He suddenly felt closer than before, though he hadn't moved. His knee pressed against hers, even through the thick fabric of her work dress. A fold of her skirt rested on top of his thigh, which felt strangely intimate.

He leaned closer, his arm propped on the table at their side. "You are a fascinating woman, Elliya."

His low whisper sent a tingle racing across her skin. Her rational mind realized what was happening, how close he was and how she had leaned forward by instinct. She calculated the inevitability of his kiss, like the conclusion of a well-planned experiment—the natural result of a chemical reaction. The magnetism of his lips pulled her forward until his eyes were the only thing she could see.

Her eyes drew closed, his breath warm against her skin. How could he still breathe in a moment like this? Elliya's lungs had stopped functioning in the midst of overwhelming stimuli—the rising temperature of the room, the brush of her hair against her neck, the warmth of his closeness. Every sense attuned to the moment his lips would finally touch hers.

"Elliya, may I kiss you?" His whisper was barely more than a breath against her lips.

She choked out her answer, her whisper even softer than his own. "No."

Though her eyes were closed, she felt him process the word.

Slowly.

She opened her eyes the same moment he did. They hadn't moved apart, so she could see the confusion clearly on his face. His eyes dropped to her lips still parted from her whispered answer, then moved back to her eyes.

"No," he repeated. "Um ..." He leaned back slowly, his brow furrowing. He appeared unsure what to do next.

She raised a nervous hand to her lips, which still tingled from the warmth of his breath. "I guess women rarely tell you no."

He ran his fingers through his hair as if searching for something to do with his hands. "I ... um ... I usually pay close attention and only ask women I think will say yes. I guess I misread the signs." He looked her in the eyes, then bowed his head. "I'm sorry, Elliya. I should have realized you weren't interested sooner."

Seeing such a self-confident man so vulnerable and unsure forced the truth from her lips. "You didn't misread the signs, Prince." She swallowed the lump in her throat and continued with her confession. "My lips are more enthusiastic than my vows will permit."

He looked up, confusion still on his face.

She scooted a little further away, pulling her skirt off his leg. The slight separation helped clear her mind enough to explain. "I'm in training to be a scholar, and though I haven't taken those vows yet, I am focused on that future. I can't stray from it."

"Oh." He nodded, biting his lip. "Yes, of course. I understand."

The vulnerability on his face tugged at her heart. "Before I came to the monastery, I didn't think I'd live much longer."

She hadn't realized it until she risked going home. It had been years since she last tried running away, and on her long walk back to the monastery, she'd realized it was because she'd thought she might die soon. She hadn't imagined taking her own life, but there had been days when her stepmother had injured her so badly, Elliya had wondered if one day the woman would go too far and kill her.

Hawthorne watched her with concern. She doubted he had been prepared for such a revelation.

She sighed, and continued, "When the Sisters accepted me as an apprentice scholar, they granted me a second chance at life. I can't waste this opportunity." Not even for the most beautiful man she'd ever met.

He nodded gravely. "Thank you for sharing that. You didn't have to ... but thank you." His eyes were warm with understanding, and though his knee no longer touched hers, his closeness still pressed against her.

She cleared her throat. "Perhaps it's best if we continue our study at the monastery and not in the *private* library?" She grinned playfully to ease the tension.

His expression remained serious as his eyes caught hers. "I will respect your wishes, Elliya. Just know if you ever change your mind, the private library is always open for you."

14

Elliya and the prince made their way back through the labyrinth library in silence. She wasn't sure what she could say to make the situation any less awkward. She couldn't shake the embarrassment of how much his nearness affected her.

As they rounded the last corner of the maze, a knock sounded on the door.

"Hawthorne? Are you in there?"

The prince's eyes widened. "It's Jaemin," he whispered.

A different voice. "If you're in there, I assume you aren't alone." Then several low chuckles.

Hawthorne sighed. "And Finn. Why couldn't they have waited a few more minutes to find me?" He turned to Elliya with a resigned look. "My brothers think I only come to the library to woo women."

She could see why they assumed that, but was kind enough not to say it. "And you would like me to tell them we were here working on research and skip that whole ... last bit." Her cheeks were still so warm that she hoped their almost-kiss wasn't visible on her face.

He rubbed a hand through his hair. "Actually, the opposite. If they knew how often I come here to read, they'd never let me live it down. They don't know—"

Elliya grinned. "That you're a nerd?"

He huffed out a breath. "That I'm researching a scientific solution to our dilemma."

She giggled. "Don't worry, Prince. Your secret is safe with me."

He opened his mouth to protest, but a key rattled in the lock, and the door opened.

Three men stood outside the door. One wore a Queen's Guard uniform, another was dressed as a monk, and the youngest was dressed as if he had been riding all day.

Hawthorne pasted on a smirk. "Hello, brothers. Does the phrase 'private library' have no meaning to you?"

The one in the Queen's Guard uniform gave him an imperious look. He appeared to be the oldest, so Elliya guessed him to be the firstborn prince, Jaemin. "You get plenty of private time in the library, Hawthorne. It's time for sparring practice."

Hawthorne crossed his arms. "You mean it's time for the three of you to pummel me?"

The youngest one grinned. Elliya recognized Finn's red hair and honey-gold eyes from the posters that recently celebrated his eighteenth birthday. "You'd improve faster if you weren't always so worried about protecting your face."

Hawthorne gave a scandalized gasp as he touched his cheeks. "And risk damaging the Goddesses' finest creation?"

The monk gave him a flat look. He wore the traditional red pants of a monk with a sleeveless red tunic as well. "There are more worthwhile activities than using your pretty face to seduce women." He studied Elliya's white apprentice scholar uniform. "Especially women dedicated to the Goddesses."

Elliya's cheeks reddened, but she couldn't decide if she

was more embarrassed about the monk's assumption or angry that he felt entitled to judge her.

Hawthorne smoothly stepped in, putting a comforting hand behind her back, but not actually touching her. "This is Elliya, and she has violated no vows you need to concern yourself with, Edric. She merely needed help to find a book the scholars requested."

Elliya was surprised he'd defended her, especially since he wanted to protect his playboy image.

Edric raised an eyebrow. "I'm sure everyone told her you were the best one to ask, considering how much you use the 'private library.'"

Finn's lips twitched. "And you knew where to locate this book? I'm surprised, considering how much time you spend in the library in the dark."

Hawthorne's lips clenched, and Elliya couldn't tell if he wanted to defend her or protect his reputation. She decided to rescue him.

She lifted her mother's book out of his hand. "Thank you for locating the book, Prince Hawthorne. I will take this with me back to the monastery." She hoped the look she gave him communicated how much she wanted him to meet her there later to read some more. And then, because she felt a little defiant toward the other princes, she added, "Thank you for the lovely tour of the queen's library. It was ... a pleasure."

His lips curved at the private joke. "It truly was." His eyes sparkled with a longing he didn't hide. "And remember what I said, Elliya. You're always welcome in this library."

She didn't trust her voice not to tremble, so instead she bowed to all the princes and strolled away. Once she turned the corner at the end of the hall, she lifted her skirts, dashed to the servants' corridor, and ducked inside to catch her breath. But no matter how many deep breaths she took, her cheeks felt permanently reddened with a blush.

The princes would pass her hiding spot, so she hovered by the door, peeking out to wait for them. She had used up all her boldness in that conversation, and now she had nothing left. She would probably need to be silent for the rest of the day to recover.

The princes talked as they drew nearer. They spoke with the relaxed tone of brothers who cared for one another. What must it be like to live with a family who actually loved each other? She let the wistful thought drift away as they approached.

"Has this Elliya revealed any of the monastery's secrets? Did she let anything slip about Sparks?" asked Jaemin.

Her head snapped around so quickly she nearly slammed it into the wall. This was the first mention she'd heard of Sparks besides what Geeni had told her. Elliya had still wondered if the idea was a fanciful notion Geeni had made up to explain Elliya's crazy idea she could speak to animals.

"That's not why Elliya was here today," said Hawthorne. "I have other goals besides just discovering what the scholars are doing with Sparks."

Edric, the monk, spoke with disdain. "There are more important goals than seducing women, brother."

Hawthorne's voice remained playful. "Just because you've sworn off women doesn't mean the rest of us must."

Finn's voice faded as they passed the door. "But can't you do both, Hawthorne? Seduce women *and* figure out what secrets the Sisters are keeping from us?"

Elliya also wanted to know Hawthorne's answer to that question.

She cracked open the door, waited for them to turn a corner, then tiptoed as she followed them inside a large training room. The viewing area was empty, so she picked up a hand towel from a neat stack and wiped it along the frame of the window that looked onto the sparring area. If someone came in, she could just pretend to be cleaning.

Hawthorne stood at the edge of a mat with his arms crossed. "Is this honestly necessary? You know I'm a better lover than fighter."

Edric scowled. "You need to be able to protect yourself. There are people out there who would harm you if they could."

Jaemin gave Hawthorne a stern look. "And we have to be prepared to fight people with unknown Sparks. We have no idea what Sparks our enemies now possess."

Finn nodded in agreement. "We don't even know how many people with Sparks the scholars are hiding, and the scholars are supposedly on our side."

Hiding inside the monastery? Were people with Sparks being held against their will? Geeni had alluded to that, saying the queen and Drazen captured people with Sparks, but Elliya hadn't noticed anything unusual at the monastery. Elliya needed to take everything her godmother said more seriously.

Jaemin stepped onto the mat across from Hawthorne. "An apprentice scholar as a 'friend' is perfect. She might be more amenable to sharing secrets than a full Sister who has already taken her vows. For once, I think your womanizing might pay off."

Hawthorne's usual smirk hardened into a stiff line. "I'm not tricking Elliya into confessing any of the scholars' secrets."

Finn gave him a compassionate look. "Okay, but just promise, if your pillow talk produces anything useful, you'll tell us, okay?"

Hawthorne's mouth dropped open. Elliya wondered if

he was now picturing pillow talk like she was. She closed her own open mouth.

Jaemin didn't give him time to reply. "Stop procrastinating. It's time for practice."

Hawthorne's shoulders sagged. "Fine, but please, avoid the face when you pummel me, okay?"

Finn grinned. "I'll go easy on you today, big guy."

Hawthorne sighed, then pulled his shirt off over his head.

Her hand holding the towel dropped lifelessly to her side, all pretense of cleaning gone. She had felt his bicep when she had taken his arm in the menagerie, and his golden brown chest looked just as firm. He spun in a slow circle, stretching his neck from side to side, and rolling his shoulders. The muscles in his back flexed as he stretched his arms overhead. Even though Hawthorne protested the sparring match, he wouldn't lose from lack of muscles.

Finn's laugh startled her, and she jerked back—her ogling had almost caused her to slip into view.

"Come on, brother," said Finn. "No more procrastinating."

Elliya had been so focused on Hawthorne's bare chest she had missed Finn removing his shirt as well. Though he wasn't as broad as Hawthorne, his muscles were more defined. Did that mean he was stronger than his older brother? Finn raised a hand and beckoned Hawthorne in challenge.

Hawthorne sighed, then ran toward Finn. The youngest prince slipped out of his grasp, stepping to the side, then grabbed Hawthorne's arm and twisted it behind his back.

Hawthorne shifted and used his bigger size to pull loose from his brother. Though he escaped from the hold, he frowned. "Are you patronizing me? Why don't you just take me down and win?"

Finn smiled. "I'm not letting you off the hook that easy, brother. You need to practice."

Hawthorne huffed, then ran at him again. They grappled, and Elliya wasn't exactly sure who was winning, though by Hawthorne's expression, the younger prince might be purposefully downplaying his skills. Even though she didn't understand the intricacies of their match, she found their dance around the mat fascinating. Finn's fair skin and Hawthorne's golden brown, their muscles flexing and hair tousled. Hawthorne's hands were powerful enough to push Finn away, yet she had seen his fingers brush so delicately across a page while he read ...

"You're barely trying, Hawthorne," snapped Edric.

Elliya had forgotten about the other two princes standing on the edge of the mat, watching with arms crossed.

Finn had pulled his older brother into another hold, and Hawthorne grumbled, "I'd appreciate no comments from the crowd."

Edric muttered to Jaemin. "We've gone too easy on him. He has no discipline for anything except chasing women."

Hawthorne was quite disciplined with reading scientific textbooks and learning Verkeshian, so either his brothers thought little about his studies or they didn't know.

Hawthorne appeared to rally at the monk's rebuke and redoubled his attempt to pull his younger brother down to the mat.

Jaemin raised an eyebrow. "I'll gladly support his womanizing if he uses that skill to figure out what the Sister Scholars are hiding."

Hawthorne's lips twisted, and he stumbled before seizing the younger prince to steady himself. Elliya pulled her eyes away from Hawthorne and locked on Jaemin. She wanted him to say more about the scholars, but all the brothers appeared to know exactly what he meant.

Edric had watched Hawthorne's stumble and turned to Jaemin with a furrowed brow. "He's so easily distracted even by the thought of women ... You shouldn't encourage him."

Jaemin shrugged. "We have to use the skills the Goddesses gifted us with." He tapped his finger against his lips. "Hawthorne should invite that girl to the ball."

Elliya's mouth fell open, and she missed how Finn over-powered his older brother, only seeing Hawthorne flip into the air, then suddenly land on his back on the mat.

A huff of air exploded out of his lungs as he hit, and he sucked in a single breath before casually asking, "The ball?"

Finn barely seemed out of breath as he offered his brother a hand to help him rise. "Yes, Jaemin is throwing a ball for his wife."

Jaemin sighed, as if the idea pained him. "Apparently, she didn't get enough dancing at our wedding. She says I still owe her, since we never danced at our first ball."

Hawthorne rubbed the sweat off his brow with his arm. "Isn't Alanna the one to blame for that? Her Spark caused a windstorm to blow through the ballroom."

Jaemin gave him a meaningful look. "It was her Spark, but she didn't cause the windstorm."

All four princes suddenly grew solemn.

Elliya's mind raced. So, Prince Jaemin's wife, Alanna, had a Spark. But someone else had caused a windstorm at the last ball ... Was it the queen?

Her thoughts were interrupted by the other two princes stripping off their shirts and taking their place on the mat.

Hawthorne flopped onto a bench and grabbed a towel. "I'm not the only one distracted by women, Jaemin."

Jaemin's stern lips curved into a grin. "I'm not distracted by women, brother. Just a single woman."

Hawthorne crossed his arms over his glistening chest and opened his mouth, but Elliya missed his answer because the door opened.

In the doorway stood a cute maid who appeared just as surprised as Elliya. "Oh, sorry ... I didn't realize someone was already in here."

Elliya's mouth moved as she tried to offer a reasonable explanation.

The maid glanced at the towel held loosely in Elliya's hand and grinned. "That's the excuse I was planning to use, too. The spectator room is just so ... dirty." The maid was not looking at the room at all. Instead, her eyes roved between the four shirtless princes. She bit her bottom lip as she stared. "I'll stay and help you clean up."

Elliya glanced around the small space. It might be the cleanest room in the palace.

The maid drew closer to the window than Elliya had dared, and she worried the princes would turn their way. She handed the maid the towel and backed toward the door. "I should go."

The maid didn't spare her a glance. "Mmm-hmm ..."

The sound was either an acknowledgement of Elliya's departure or just a low hum of appreciation. Either way, Elliya slipped out the door and closed it quietly behind her.

She needed to return to the monastery. Although, thanks to the handsome princes, she realized the monastery might not be as safe as she'd thought.

15

Elliya hid when Prince Hawthorne arrived at the monastery the next morning. She peeked around a column in the courtyard as he swaggered into their usual research room with Lliadain and Kensley, but she couldn't bring herself to walk in as if nothing had happened.

After listening to the princes' conversation, she had returned to the monastery for her afternoon chores. But instead of sweeping her usual locations, she'd wandered into rooms she had never entered before. No one gave her more than a cursory glance before returning to their work and allowing her to sweep. She was allowed into any room she wanted, but she still found nothing suspicious. What did the princes think was happening?

She sank against the column at her back as she remembered the princes' conversation. She had believed Prince Hawthorne spent so much time at the monastery because he was interested in knowledge, but maybe that had all been an excuse to get inside and look around. Even though he protested Jaemin's ideas about using Elliya to gain information on the monastery, maybe that had been his secret goal the entire time. Maybe all his attention for Elliya had been an act. Maybe he had been patiently waiting for secrets to pour out of her mouth.

Maybe that was why his attention so often dropped to her lips ...

Her hand drifted to her mouth as she remembered how close they had come to kissing. She recalled his warm breath against her cheek and the slow blink of his long lashes ... She breathed in the warm citrus scent of him, almost as if he was right beside her ...

"Elliya?"

She ripped her hand away from her lips and smoothed out her apron as Prince Hawthorne stepped around the column.

"Good morning, Prince." She tried to infuse her voice with all the fake calmness she could muster.

"I need you to rescue me." He grinned, and Elliya willed her heart to stop beating so fast. "Lliadain is bullying me by asking why I haven't left for Verkeshe yet. Please show her the book you discovered, so I have a good excuse."

Elliya had almost forgotten about her mother's book. If she didn't bring them the book to study, the prince would leave for Verkeshe on his mission to find a ghost. She had to face them and continue their work if she wanted the prince to stay.

Although, she could just hand her mother's book to Hawthorne and the scholars, leaving them to study it while she quietly swept the monastery floors. That would keep her beneath the notice of both the prince and the scholars. It might not be completely safe, but it would be safer.

She pulled her mother's book out of her apron pocket and imagined handing it to the prince, letting him read it with the scholars without her.

"Let's go." She clutched the book to her chest. "I'll save you."

His lip darted up into a grin, and he lifted a hand, urging her to lead the way.

~

When Elliya showed the scholars the book, they had mixed reactions.

Lliadain studied her with narrowed eyes. "What is this?"

Elliya avoided her gaze. "It's another book by Yulia Zaleska. The one I read before I got here."

Kensley flipped through the book, devouring the pages with her eyes. "I thought you said it was lost."

"Um ... I found it?" She couldn't keep the last word from rising in a question.

Hawthorne folded his arms proudly. "See? I told you she found it."

Lliadain stared at her with a flat expression. "Yes. Isn't she clever." It wasn't a question, but an accusation.

Elliya moved closer to her mother's book, which brought her closer to Kensley as well. The young scholar raised her head. "This book is more recent than the one we already have. Maybe it contains something that will help us further our research."

Hawthorne joined them at the table, scooting so close to Elliya their shoulders touched, though he didn't appear to notice. "Zaleska discusses how a child's blood is a combination of each parent's type. There are similarities between family members, though the parents' blood often combines in different ways. I think this might give us the answer we are looking for."

Lliadain's glare slid away from Elliya and transformed into a curious expression as she studied the book. "Does she say how to test the blood type? Perhaps we can gather samples from your brothers and the queen and see what we can discover."

Elliya's fear lessened without Lliadain's harsh stare, and she felt confident enough to contribute to the conversation. "It would be better if you had a larger sample size. Do you have any other family members in Isandine?"

Lliadain's head shot up, and her glare returned. Elliya thought she had asked a reasonable question, but Kensley looked embarrassed on Elliya's behalf.

The prince frowned as he considered her question. "The queen's cousin is in Isandine, but I doubt Ginevere wants to help us with this project."

Kensley jumped in and quickly changed the direction of the conversation. "We should begin with other subjects so we can test them over multiple generations. Maybe mice?"

Lliadain turned to the prince. "It will take several weeks to read through Zaleska's notes and put this experiment together. Are you canceling your fool's mission to Verkeshe to see this through?"

Hawthorne's face was resolute. "Postponing, not canceling. But yes, I will see this through." His eyes hesitantly moved in Elliya's direction. "Besides, there is a ball coming up."

Elliya ducked her head into her mother's book as her cheeks warmed. Not because she thought the prince would actually invite her to the ball, but because her mind wandered back to the conversation where he discussed the ball with his brothers. The conversation where Hawthorne had his shirt off ... where he was glistening with sweat ...

Lliadain huffed. "Just what the queendom needs right now. A frivolous ball."

Kensley rolled her eyes. "Don't be so stiff, Lliadain. A ball is romantic."

Lliadain raised a brow. "And will you be taking someone to the ball, Sister?"

Kensley sniffed. "Of course not, Sister. I'm devoted only to the Goddesses. But I don't begrudge others their chance for true love."

Lliadain's lips twisted, but she didn't respond.

Hawthorne leaned across the table to gain their attention. "So, have we decided? We'll work on this experiment ..." He looked at Elliya. "... together?"

Lliadain huffed, "Fine."

And Kensley smiled. "Of course!"

Elliya was slower to answer, as her mind was still filled with questions about the scholars' secrets and Hawthorne's true motives for spending time at the monastery. How could she work by his side if she didn't trust him? They'd need to spend days reading her mother's words and doing experiments, making new discoveries and learning how to work with each other.

Her answer frightened her, but she forced herself to look him in the eye and tell the truth. "I look forward to it."

16

Organizing the experiments with the prince was so pleasant that Elliya almost forgot about her weekly meeting with Geeni. She had spent the last three days with the prince, finding mice for their experiment, most of them convinced to join by Elliya's whispers that they only had to donate a little blood in exchange for regular feedings. Once she mentioned the food to the chubby mouse from the queen's chamber, they had found a crowd of mice nestled right inside the monastery's front gate.

She couldn't stop the smile that spread across her face as she went to meet her godmother. Even though she still questioned the prince's intentions with the monastery, he was a skilled researcher with a keen mind. Working with him each day on scientific projects was a delight. Eventually they'd come to the end of her mother's research, and he would leave, but until then, she wanted to savor every moment.

She slid into the seat across the table from Geeni. "Good afternoon, Godmother. It's so nice to see you!"

Geeni signaled to the waitress and asked for two mint

teas. "You're cheerful today. I trust the scholars are treating you well?"

Elliya shoved down her unanswered questions about the monastery and answered more generally. "I have plenty to eat, and the work isn't difficult. I'm truly blessed that you rescued me, Godmother."

Geeni gave her a fond smile. "You're so sweet, Elliya. Nice girls are always such valuable associates."

Elliya lowered her gaze, focusing on the mint tea as the waitress poured it into her glass. "I don't know how valuable I am, Godmother."

"Nonsense." Geeni waved a dismissive hand. "Just drinking tea with you is valuable to me. Your stories are so intriguing!" She scooped a heaping spoonful of sugar into her cup and stirred it delicately. "Tell me about life in the monastery. Didn't you tell me you're cleaning the queen's chambers now? How exciting!"

Elliya shrugged. "I wouldn't say it's exciting. I've only seen the queen twice."

"Really?" Geeni leaned forward as if intrigued. "What's she like?"

Elliya sipped her tea as she considered. "She's beautiful and regal. I've never heard her speak, so I don't know much about her. Except ... except she looks sad."

Geeni's eyes glittered. "Sad?"

Elliya shook her head. "I guess it's silly for me to think that. She's a queen, after all. I'm probably just imagining things."

Geeni's golden bangles clinked as she rested her arm against the back of the padded bench. "I'm sure queens have a lot on their minds. Especially queens with too many sons."

Elliya frowned. "That's true. I'm sure that's a heavy burden to bear. Hopefully, our work in the monastery can help with that."

Geeni's eyebrow arched. "Really? Are you assisting the scholars with something that could solve that conundrum? I thought they only let you sweep."

"I guess I am helping, though I'm still not sure why they allow me to work on the blood type experiments. I'm sure there are much more skilled scholars who could assist."

Her godmother's eyes lit up. "Experimenting with blood types ... Aren't you clever? I bet you'll solve the queen's dilemma in no time."

Elliya sighed. "No, I don't think so. I know the result of the research we are doing. It won't lead us to a definitive answer."

"Really? How do you know for sure?" She took a casual sip of tea, though her eyes remained locked on Elliya.

Before she fled Verkeshe, her mother had recorded the last discovery she made in the journal hidden in Elliya's old room. Yulia Zaleska had tested the blood of two brothers, and using their blood types, determined one brother *might* belong to his mother's husband, but the other surely did not. The thought of how the information might be used had scared Yulia enough that she fled Verkeshe on her own, despite being a young woman.

Even though Elliya trusted her godmother, she couldn't bring herself to reveal her mother's secrets. Elliya avoided her eyes and said, "Just a hunch."

Geeni hummed noncommittally as she took another sip of tea.

Elliya bit her lip, upset with herself for bringing the conversation to a halt. She sat up straight as she remembered the only other news Geeni might find interesting. "There's going to be a ball."

"Oh! How lovely! Do you get to attend?"

Elliya nervously twisted her hands in her lap. "Why would I attend? I don't even know how to dance."

Geeni laughed lightly. "Not to dance, obviously! I meant, do you get to help clean up?"

"Oh, to clean ..." Elliya's cheeks reddened with shame. "I think the palace has enough people for that."

Geeni leaned forward and patted her hand fondly. "Well, if they ask you to assist, do it! The beautiful dresses, the music and dancing ... If you have the chance to watch something so thrilling, you should take it."

Elliya's heart warmed at her godmother's thoughtfulness. "Thank you, Godmother. You are kind to say so."

"Yes, I am." Geeni's lip curved in a little smirk. "I hope you go to the ball and have a wonderful time."

Elliya walked inside the courtyard and found a small patch of gardenias with weeds that needed to be pulled. The sunshine and familiar work usually helped her organize her thoughts, but before she had pulled more than a dozen weeds, a kitten bounded through the gardenias and pounced on her hand.

"Luci! Where have you been?"

I'm hungry. The ginger kitten sat and began licking her paw with a haughty glare at Elliya.

She whispered to the kitten, "I know you've been getting food from other scholars. Your tummy is so round!" She poked a finger at the kitten's midsection.

Luci swiped a paw at her. *Rude.*

Elliya bit back a grin. "I apologize. I just meant that you appear quite healthy."

The kitten looked mollified as she tipped onto her side and allowed Elliya to rub her round ginger belly.

"Your coat is so shiny!" she cooed at the tiny kitten. "Has someone been spoiling you with fish?"

The kitten languidly stretched her paws above her head. *Lliadain gives me fish.*

Elliya's eyes widened. "Sister Lliadain gave you fish?"

Someone gasped behind her, and Elliya spun.

Lliadain stood above her. "How did you know that?"

"I ..." Elliya didn't know what to tell the scholar, but admitting the cat talked to her was not high on her list.

"No one saw me feed her." Lliadain glanced between the kitten and Elliya, and thoughts raced behind her eyes. "The kitten told you."

Elliya laughed awkwardly. "What? That's silly."

Her eyes locked on Elliya cowering at her feet. "You can talk to animals. That's your Spark."

Terror washed over Elliya at the familiar feeling of kneeling below someone with power over her. She couldn't find any words, whether to deny it or beg for mercy.

Lliadain grabbed Elliya by the arm and yanked her to her feet. "Come with me."

Elliya allowed herself to be pulled along by the scholar, too terrified to resist.

Lliadain opened the door to one of the study rooms and jerked Elliya inside. Her gaze shot around the room, and though it was empty, she whispered, "Whatever you do, don't tell anyone you have a Spark. Especially not a scholar."

Elliya tried to find enough breath to answer. "Why?" Her voice came out as a rough whisper. "But you're a scholar ..."

Lliadain's eyes still scanned the empty room. "You haven't said anything to Kensley, have you? Has she seen you do anything suspicious?"

"Suspicious?" Too many questions popped into Elliya's mind. "What's going on here? Do scholars really capture people with Sparks?"

Lliadain continued searching the room, though Elliya wondered if it was just so she didn't need to make eye contact. The scholar bit her lip but then answered, "If they discover you have a Spark, they will control you, and you will never be free again."

"Control me? How?"

Lliadain roughly grabbed both of Elliya's arms, and her eyes finally locked on Elliya's. "Listen to me closely. There are many people who would try to control you if they know about your Spark. Possessing magic is a secret that is best taken to your grave. Do you understand me?"

Elliya had stopped breathing. Lliadain had asked her a question that demanded a response, but the woman's firm hands clasped around Elliya's arms had sent panic through her system. Her stepmother was the last person who had laid hands on her, and all those memories rushed back. She couldn't find the air to make a sound.

Lliadain's eyes shifted as if she finally recognized Elliya's terror. She released her grip and took a small step back, her head tilted as she studied Elliya's face.

Elliya pulled in a ragged breath, and her shoulders sagged with exhaustion. She still had so many questions for the scholar but had no energy to ask.

Lliadain smoothed back the hair that had come loose from her tight bun. "You are caught in the middle of something bigger than you understand. Seek out the other scholars for friendship or kindness, but I'm the only one who can be trusted with knowledge of your Spark. Stay below everyone's notice, and you might make it out of here alive." She gave Elliya a stiff bow, then strode away.

17

Elliya had returned to pulling weeds, though it did nothing to soothe her thoughts. She had fantasized about the monastery her whole life. On dark nights, she had imagined the monastery as a sanctuary, a place of learning and peace. When Geeni rescued her and deposited her at the monastery, she'd thought her life had finally changed. Finally, she would be safe. But the monastery was no safe haven.

She was still in danger.

The memory of Lliadain's harsh grip burned her arms, even though the scholar had left no bruises. Elliya had imagined one day confessing her Spark to the scholars, but after Lliadain's warning, she didn't want to tell a soul. Why had this strange magic suddenly happened to her? She just wanted to live quietly, below the notice of anyone who might want to harm her. Why did she need to have a Spark that brought her to the scholars' attention?

Even though she didn't want to confess her own Spark, Elliya still had so many questions for the scholars. What secrets were they hiding about Sparks? Were they holding people prisoner just because they had magic? And who did they think they were to hide this information?

The questions raged in her mind, but the thought of actually voicing them out loud terrified her. The monastery was supposed to be safe. By becoming a Sister Scholar, she'd thought she would gain a home, an occupation, and safety for the rest of her life. But nowhere was safe for her.

Sister Ethelwin beckoned to Elliya, and she brushed the dirt off her hands and ran over. The older scholar had a kind presence, but Elliya couldn't control her instinct to panic anytime the woman summoned her. Ethelwin didn't slow her walk through the courtyard, merely assuming Elliya would follow her.

Elliya followed the gray-haired scholar to a bench underneath a mango tree where two women sat. Based on their similarities, Elliya thought they might be related ... Maybe mother and daughter? But that didn't make sense, because the older woman wore white scholar's robes.

Ethelwin leaned down to speak to the older of the two women. "Did you enjoy watching the birds, Sunah?" Ethelwin spoke as if the black-haired woman were her elder, even though Ethelwin was a few decades older. She offered her hand. "Let me take you back to your room now."

The woman looked up at her with confusion in her eyes, as if she didn't recognize Ethelwin. The gray-haired scholar brushed Sunah's shoulder, and a contented smile spread across her lips.

Ethelwin helped her stand, then gently supported her under the arm. "Elliya, please help Alanna find her way out of the monastery."

Elliya looked at the younger of the two women—Alanna—then at the doorway out. She could point to the exit from here. Why did Elliya need to escort her?

She had not dared ask the question, but Ethelwin must

have sensed it. "Even though the exit is close, Alanna often gets 'lost' in the monastery and ends up wandering in odd locations. Please help her find the most direct way out."

The young woman smirked. "How kind of you, Sister Ethelwin."

The scholar gave her a motherly look. "You are always welcome here, Alanna. As long as you remember to behave."

Alanna smiled innocently. "I have many skills, but being well-behaved is not one of them."

Ethelwin pursed her lips and led the older woman away.

Alanna's eyes trailed after the woman who looked like her mother, then she shook her head, turning a sparkling smile on Elliya. "So, you're my minder today? Elliya ..." She examined Elliya's apprentice uniform, and her eyes lit up. "Wait ... Are you Hawthorne's girl?"

Elliya choked, then covered her mouth with her hand. "I'm an apprentice scholar. I'm not anyone's girl."

Alanna's lips curved into a grin. "If anyone could steal a girl directly from the Goddesses' hands, it would be Hawthorne."

Elliya's mouth fell open, and she whispered, "That's sacrilegious."

Alanna made a dismissive gesture. "Nonsense. Qira the Trickster would bless him for his thievery." Her copper eyes studied Elliya's face. "Though if he's planning to steal you from the Goddesses, he's certainly taking his time. He speaks about you much differently than he does other women."

Elliya's eyes widened. "He speaks about me?"

Alanna gave a bright, twinkling laugh. "Oh yes. His brothers tease him incessantly about you."

The idea of Hawthorne not only thinking about her when they were apart, but talking about her, made her stomach turn warm and gooey. She remembered how the princes had teased him during their sparring session, and the words "pillow talk" came back to her mind.

She cleared her throat. "Um ... Sister Ethelwin said I should escort you out." She lifted her hand to show the way.

Alanna stood smoothly and fluffed out her full skirt. The warm amber fabric shone brightly against her golden brown skin, and a gold ring with a fat emerald glittered on her finger.

Elliya finally made the connection. "Alanna ... You're Prince Jaemin's wife."

"Yes, I'm guilty of that and many other surprising things." She winked and walked toward the arches leading out of the courtyard.

Elliya scrambled to catch her. "What are you doing here?" Ethelwin had said Alanna wandered around the monastery ... Was she trying to discover the scholars' secrets like the princes were?

Alanna's face grew serious. "I was visiting my mother."

Elliya recalled how similar Alanna looked to the older scholar. "Your mother is a scholar? How?"

Alanna gave her a wry smile. "My mother wasn't as well-behaved as she should have been, either."

The admission startled Elliya, but she didn't respond.

Alanna stepped through an arch into the cloister. "My mother fled La Veridda after my father died in the war. She was a brilliant scholar, but wouldn't have been permitted to join the monastery with a child, so she kept me hidden." Her eyes clouded, as if the memory pained her. "The scholars are kind enough to allow me to visit, even though my mother is ill and doesn't remember me."

Elliya recalled how the older woman had left with Ethelwin without a backward glance to her daughter. Elliya had never known her own mother, but what must it be like to watch your mother slip away? She felt an immediate kinship with the young woman and offered her what comfort she could. "She seemed comfortable in your presence. Even if she can't consciously remember, you are part of her, formed of her essence. She must sense that about you."

A tear shone at the edge of Alanna's eye, but she blinked it back. "Thank you for saying that. You're very sweet." She breathed out a soft sigh. "I can see why you have Hawthorne so off-kilter, and why the girls in the palace have been sighing nonstop."

Her logic didn't make sense to Elliya. "The palace girls are sighing?"

Alanna gave her a significant look. "Because he's telling them no."

"Oh." Elliya laughed awkwardly. "Well, he doesn't have to. He should ... do whatever he wants."

Alanna stopped at the monastery exit and met Elliya's eyes. "I know what he wants. And if it doesn't work out, I'll be quite sad, for both your sakes." She tipped her head in a bow. "I will offer a prayer at Qira's shrine in your honor for the way you've stolen Hawthorne's heart." She winked as she walked out the front gate.

18

Elliya had arrived early to the lab, as she did each morning. She found it easier to draw blood from the mice without Hawthorne or the other scholars watching her. The mice were quite chatty as they patiently waited to get their blood drawn and receive their snack as a reward. She had taught them the least painful way to draw blood, so now the mice walked right into her palm. The behavior was so unusual she worried the scholars would realize her Spark, so she drew the blood before the others arrived.

The mice were fascinating creatures. Geeni had jokingly said mice probably heard a lot of gossip, and that was actually true. However, their gossip revolved around topics that interested mice—like which humans were sloppy eaters and dropped food on the floor.

The chubby mouse from the queen's chamber had mentioned the queen rarely finished her meals, and Elliya assumed that was why he had grown so round. As she handed him his small snack, she asked him why he had left a home with better meals than she provided.

You've got something better than an undisturbed platter. He gobbled down the snack, then licked his paws to smooth down his whiskers. *The ladies.*

"Ladies? You mean the female mice?" It took a moment for his meaning to sink in. "Oh ..."

The scholars had chosen mice for the experiments because they could reproduce rapidly. Over the last few weeks, multiple litters had been born, leading to the testing of the parents' and children's blood. The chubby mouse had personally fathered three litters. He was a literal stud.

Elliya held out her palm, and he stepped inside, then she carried him to the cage of his newest lady mouse friend.

As she placed him inside, the female mouse looked him up and down. *Hello, handsome.*

Elliya quickly shut the cage, then gave them their privacy.

She went to the last cage, which was filled with the youngest litter. They were finally big enough she could safely draw their blood. She peeked inside at the wide-eyed creatures. "Don't be frightened, little ones. You're part of a grand experiment, and to honor you for your work, I promise to treat you well. I do need to poke you with something sharp, but if you hold still, I will be so fast, you'll barely feel it. After I'm done, I've got a treat for you." She lowered her hand into the cage. "Who is brave enough to go first?"

One little mouse walked calmly into her palm.

"What a courageous little mouse!" she cooed. She drew his blood efficiently, then set him on the table with his snack between his paws. His brothers and sisters gathered at the cage bars, trying to sniff his treat.

"If you promise to be calm, you can all come out and watch."

She sensed agreement from the teenage mice. She set them on the table, where they sniffed her syringe and the sealed container with treats. They lined up patiently for their turn, then nibbled on their snacks while she tended to each sibling.

She labeled each tiny vial of blood, then turned back to the mice. "Time to go back to your cage. Line up, please."

The mice stepped into a neat line and watched her.

Hawthorne breathed, "You have a Spark."

Elliya froze and stared at the prince, who hovered just inside the door. She perched on her toes, one step away from fleeing, a similar posture to the little mice on the table. Panicked, Elliya and the mice barely breathed, but she recovered her voice enough to whisper a response. "What? No, that's ridiculous."

Hawthorne hadn't moved, but his eyes flitted from her face to the crouching mice, then to the mice in their cages. "They've all been remarkably calm, almost uncannily so, and I couldn't figure out why. But it's because of you. Because you can speak to them."

"Stop saying that!" At her sharp tone, the mice scattered, darting under the table, their panic finally too great.

She crouched beneath the tall exam table and caught a mouse as it tried to hide under her dress. Its little body trembled in her hands, and she made calm cooing sounds, even though her own heart pounded.

Hawthorne squatted across from her under the table. His hands were lightly clasped before him, and Elliya could sense a young mouse fluttering wildly inside. She didn't want to reveal her Spark any more than she already had, but the mouse's terror pained her.

"Hush, little one. Hawthorne won't hurt you. Curl up and rest in his hands."

The fluttering stilled, and Elliya sensed a calmness from the mouse as it curled into a ball and relaxed against Hawthorne's fingers.

The prince looked at his hands with awe, and even though he couldn't see the mouse, Elliya knew he could tell the mouse had settled at her command.

He raised his emerald eyes to her and whispered, "You're magnificent."

His heartfelt exclamation startled her so much that she almost dropped the mouse in her hands. "No, it's nothing special. Nothing unusual at all."

He scooted closer to sit beside her, his hands still gently closed. "You have a Spark, Elliya. Magic." He tilted his head as he studied her. "Isn't that why you're in the monastery? Do the scholars not know?"

"Please don't tell them!" she gasped.

He scanned her face with concern. "You're scared of them."

The mouse hopped out of her shaking hands and curled up on her skirt. "It's nothing, Hawthorne. Please, don't say anything."

Hawthorne let the mouse scamper out of his hand to join its sibling on Elliya's skirt. He took her hand in his. "I won't tell anyone, Elliya. I promise."

Was that a promise he could truly keep? His brothers would love to know she had a Spark and would probably be curious to know why she hadn't told the scholars. That was exactly the evidence they had been encouraging Hawthorne to get from her. Now that he knew information his brothers were desperate to find, would he keep her secret? She looked into his eyes, searching for the answer, and found it.

"You won't tell anyone," she breathed in awe. "You'll keep my secret."

"Yes," he whispered.

His declaration stole her breath. Why would he do that for her? The answer flickered at the edge of her awareness, but she refused to face it.

She withdrew her hand from his. "Let's just pretend none of this happened and get back to work."

"We can't just return to work, Elliya. I need to know why you don't want to tell the scholars." Even though they still hid under the table, he dropped his voice. "Are you in danger?"

She wanted to respond with a short answer and get back to work, but she couldn't. She didn't know if she was in danger, but Lliadain's harsh warning made her think she might be.

His eyes read her expression. "If you're in danger, we have to get you out of here."

"No, I can't—"

"I'll help you escape. They'll never find out about your Spark." He spoke so quickly, she couldn't interrupt. "I'll take you somewhere they can't find you."

"Hawthorne, the monastery—"

His eyes lit up, and he took her hands. "Run away with me, Elliya."

She couldn't breathe. "What?"

He grinned with the excitement of a brilliant plan. "Come with me to Verkeshe. It's the perfect time. We can leave these experiments to the scholars, and you can come with me to search for Zaleska. Just imagine it! A grand adventure, searching for the missing scientist, just you and me."

Her mouth went dry. "That sounds ..." *Romantic* was the word she couldn't bring herself to utter.

He squeezed her hands. "So you'll come with me?"

"No," she whispered. "I can't." She shook off his hands, gathered the sleeping mice off her skirt, and stood.

He scrambled out from under the table. "I know you told me no before, Elliya, but if you are in danger from the scholars—"

"I made a vow, Hawthorne. I can't leave the monastery."

He shook his head. "You're still an apprentice. You haven't sworn your service to the Goddesses yet."

"I made a vow before I ever arrived." The time they had almost kissed, she had only told him the partial truth, and now confessing her actual vow was more difficult than she imagined. Hawthorne's face was so open and warm and ... handsome.

But what was the use of a vow if it was easy to make? She swallowed and confessed, "I didn't vow to serve in the monastery. I vowed to the Goddesses that I would never fall in love."

Hawthorne's eyebrows shot up at her admission. Then he laughed. "The Goddesses won't hold you to an impossible vow."

Her back stiffened at his casual dismissal of her very serious vow. "It's not impossible. Scholars make that vow all the time."

His laugh faded, and his face drew into stern lines. "No, they don't, Elliya. They vow to forsake a future family, husband, and children so they can focus on their work. But they don't make the impossible vow to never fall in love."

She realized the truth of his words, but it didn't change her mind. "Maybe they don't make that vow, but I did. I won't fall in love."

He breathed out in exasperation. "But you can't possibly hope to keep that vow. You can't control love." He moved closer, his voice dropping to a low rumble. "One day you'll be going about your normal life, and then, out of nowhere, an intriguing and frustrating person will appear. You'll think about them when you're apart. You'll read something and can't wait to discuss it with them. Every thought you have will slowly begin to revolve around them until suddenly you realize your lives are impossibly intertwined. And the thought of separation feels like cutting off a part of yourself." He shook his head slowly. "You can't control that. And I don't know why you'd even try."

She sucked in a deep breath, trying to pull herself out of his hypnotizing story. "Because it's dangerous."

He snorted. "Falling in love is *not* dangerous, Elliya."

"It's what killed her, Hawthorne!" she snapped. "Falling in love killed her."

His movement stilled, and he watched her carefully. "Killed who?"

She realized her words sounded like a leap in topic, because he didn't know the *who* she was referring to was Yulia Zaleska. He didn't feel her presence lingering over every experiment, haunting every moment Elliya spent with him. But she gave him the less complicated version instead. "Love killed my mother. She would still be alive if she had never fallen in love."

Hawthorne bit his lip, clearly wrestling with how to respond. He wanted to dispute her point, but the conversation had grown too delicate.

She avoided his searching eyes by refilling the water bottle in the cage. "I have my mother's journal from back then, from when she fell in love. I read how their relationship started ... how much she loved my father and how that love intoxicated her ... Of course, she would marry him and have his child. It was the inevitable conclusion—the boulder crashing down the mountain that couldn't be stopped. She would have lived if she didn't have me, and the only way to prevent that was if she never fell in love."

Arguments flared behind Hawthorne's eyes, but he answered carefully. "Elliya, your logic is ... faulty."

His accusation stung. "My logic is sound. It's simple cause and effect."

"Love is not simple, Elliya. And love is not what killed

your mother. You're a scientist. If you want to make vows to the Goddesses, promise to spend your life studying how to make childbirth safer."

She snapped shut the mouse's cage. "I didn't ask for your assistance in making new vows."

"But you're being ridiculous! Living without love won't bring your mother back. It's just punishing yourself for something that wasn't your fault." His eyes widened in understanding. "That's what this is really about. You don't truly believe love killed your mother—you blame yourself. You vowed to never fall in love to punish yourself."

Her hand clenched the edge of the cool metal table. "No, it's not—"

He stepped closer, placing his warm hand atop hers. "You said you read her journal ... She must have talked about being pregnant, talked about *you*." His voice brushed against her, gentle as a feather. "She loved you even before you were born, didn't she?"

"Yes. She loved me." She blinked back her tears. "Which further proves my point—love killed her."

He took her hand in his, pulling her closer. "Her death was not your fault, Elliya." His soft voice wrapped around her in an embrace. "She loved you and wouldn't want you to punish yourself for her death." He swallowed and spoke slowly, as if unsure of his words. "Please don't cut yourself off from love—your mother's or ... mine."

Time slowed around her. She heard the indrawn breath of the mice as they watched her and Hawthorne, wondering what would happen next. He held her hand between them, near his chest, and she wasn't sure if the thundering pulse was his or her own. But louder than those sounds were the clanging bells in her mind, warning her of danger.

This moment was the boulder perched atop the mountain. It needed no push to tip it over the edge ... All it required was a single word, lashes fluttering closed, lips parted in anticipation ... The slightest yielding would start the boulder's inevitable descent.

A descent into love, happiness, family, risk, pain, death ... She had surrendered the hope and fear of that life long ago, so she braced herself to hold the boulder in place.

She let go of his hand. "I'm sorry, Hawthorne."

He drew in a shaking breath. "Elliya, please—"

"I can't give you what you want. I'm sorry."

His shoulders sagged. "I don't need an apology. Just don't give up on—"

"Apologizing is what I do best." She gave a mirthless laugh. "I was born with an apology on my lips."

He opened his mouth, but she couldn't bear to hear any more of his kindness. "I'm truly sorry, Hawthorne." She fled the lab, away from his eyes, which longed for something she couldn't give.

19

After her painful conversation with the prince, Elliya avoided the lab while he was there. She woke before sunrise and collected the blood samples, then spent her mornings cleaning the far edges of the monastery. She saw him once, lingering outside the lab door, but she stayed hidden until he eventually left.

Seeing him caused a sharp pain deep in her chest. He didn't walk with the same swagger, and the sparkle was missing from his eyes. She longed to run to him, to see his eyes light up as he smiled, but that feeling just proved her decision was the right one. If the sight of him already caused her physical pain, it would only get worse if she allowed those feelings to take root. Better to shut those emotions off now, before the boulder crushed her.

She knew his schedule at the monastery, but she was terrified she would see him each night as she went to clean the queen's shrine. Other than reading in the labyrinth library and sparring with his brothers, she didn't know what he did at the palace. Every time she turned a corner, she worried she'd walk into him. She imagined crashing into his broad chest, looking into his eyes; his warm smile ... his indrawn breath ... his lips parted ...

She shook her head to banish the images and made her way out of the palace into the dark night. The queen hadn't been praying at the remains of the fire, so Elliya had cleaned the shrine quickly and peeked around each corner on her way out of the palace. As she headed to the well-lit path, a familiar voice forced her into the shadows.

"Sorry, Jaemin, you won't change my mind." Hawthorne's voice was resolute, with no hint of his usual playfulness.

Elliya pressed herself against a tall hedge, her breath held.

"It's a foolish mission, Hawthorne," said Jaemin. "The chances of you finding her—"

"I have to do something!" His voice echoed before he dropped back to his usual low rumble. "Zaleska's books prove nothing definitively, so I have to find her and see if she's discovered something new. We have no answer, and time is running out. You've seen the queen. She's ..." He sighed. "I don't know what else to do."

Jaemin didn't answer right away, but then he sighed. "I understand, brother. Go to Verkeshe with my blessing. I pray you can find this scientist and she can give us a solution."

Elliya clutched the leaves of the hedge to protect herself from racing out to stop him. He was back to his foolish idea to run off to Verkeshe already? She'd thought her mother's book had convinced him to stay until they confirmed their experiments matched Zaleska's findings, but the next generation of mice wouldn't be born for several weeks yet.

"Thank you, brother. I'll leave the day after tomorrow."

She slapped her hand over her mouth to cover her gasp.

"Is that because you've decided to come to the ball

tomorrow night?" asked Jaemin. "I thought you might not come, especially with the way you've been moping after that girl—"

"I'll attend the ball and fulfill my duty as prince and brother."

"Good," said Jaemin. "Now, let's discuss how to not get yourself killed in Verkeshe ..." His voice faded as the two of them walked down the well-lit path.

Elliya couldn't bear the thought of them turning around to discover her, so she bolted down the dark menagerie path instead.

She hadn't been through the menagerie since the night she'd been there with the prince. Even though it was the shorter path, she hadn't wanted to risk seeing the tiger. But tonight the tiger seemed less frightening than seeing the prince again.

The animals chattered as they settled into their dens for the night, and their peaceful conversations helped calm her thoughts. The prince was leaving. That was fine with her. She had been avoiding him, anyway. It would be very easy to avoid him if he was in Verkeshe.

Verkeshe. Sure, the kingdom was highly militant and didn't appreciate strangers. Especially good-looking princes asking about one of their women. He'd do everything in his power to find Zaleska, including using his skills to charm answers out of beautiful women. He'd lay delicate kisses on their hands, touch their arms as he whispered private jokes in their ear, pull them into alcoves to ask if they'd ever heard the name Zaleska ...

Her gut churned painfully, and she shook the images out of her head, angry at herself for allowing thoughts of him to cause her physical pain. She needed to forget him and focus on her future as a scholar. Life in the monastery was more than she'd ever dreamed. As long as she kept her Spark a secret and avoided charming princes, her life would be free of pain and risk. She would be safe.

Safe and alone.

She shook her head again and focused on the dark path. The *quiet* dark path. Her footsteps slowed. The animals had grown quieter the deeper she went into the menagerie, and now they were completely silent.

There, at the edge of a shimmering pool of water, was the tiger.

The tiger faced the water with her head resting on her front paws, her tail curled along her long body. She didn't stir, and Elliya considered tiptoeing past, but something about the tiger's posture stilled her movement. The tiger's eyes were open, but she wasn't lying in wait to pounce. She was merely lying there, watching the moonlight sparkle on the water's edge.

Elliya strained her Spark, trying to get a hint of the tiger's feelings. She couldn't detect anything, but something in the tiger's posture looked sad.

Could tigers be sad?

This tiger didn't look like the legendary cursed tiger that had killed the queen's power-hungry father. And even though the tiger had seemed terrifying on the day they met, Elliya now felt compassion toward the sad creature. She wished she could read the animal's thoughts to know what could make a tiger sad. She glided across the soft grass to the tiger's side, then sat beside her, joining the animal's contemplation of the sparkling water.

The tiger's eyes shifted, watching her approach, then returned to her silent vigil. Elliya thought it must be nice to be a tiger. Lounging in the sunshine ... stretching long, sinuous muscles ... the beauty of a cat with the strength of a bear. This tiger could defeat anyone who tried to hurt her. She was more than a match for any animal in the menagerie, and it would take multiple men to stop her. She was strong and beautiful and safe.

The answer felt like a punch in the gut, and her whisper came out as a quiet sob. "You're alone."

The tiger lifted her head and turned her startling green eyes on Elliya.

She swallowed her flash of fear and whispered, "You're the only one of your kind. You're alone."

The tiger studied her for several breath-held moments, then laid her head back on her paws.

Elliya looked at the water and took a deep breath. It was easier to speak without the tiger's piercing gaze. "I've been alone my whole life. My dream was only to escape the abuse, and continue on alone. I thought that would be enough ... Now I'm not so sure."

Elliya tried to imagine waking up in the monastery each morning, studying and cleaning, eating well, protected inside the thick walls—it was everything she'd ever dreamed. But the prince had wound his way into her daily life, and she could no longer think of the monastery without thinking about him. But after the ball he would leave for Verkeshe, and she might never see him again. Her breath hitched painfully in her chest.

"It's too late," she whispered. "I've already fallen in love with him."

This was exactly why she had made her vow. Her heart longed for something that would eventually lead to pain and loss. Why hadn't she stopped herself sooner?

But when should she have turned away from him? She replayed each moment all the way back to the day they met. From the first moment, it was already too late. His first smile had sent the boulder toppling down the mountain.

She had broken her vow by falling in love.

Elliya had been so lost in her thoughts she hadn't

noticed the tiger was now sitting up and staring at her. "I'm sorry. I sat down to comfort you, but I'm just talking about my own problems."

The tiger tilted her head.

Elliya bit her lip. She needed to confess, and perhaps a blessed/cursed tiger was the best option. "I vowed to the Goddesses I would never fall in love, but I broke that vow. I fell in love ... with Prince Hawthorne."

The tiger's brow whiskers twitched.

Elliya sighed. "I know. I'm a fool for falling in love, and a double fool for falling in love with the most charming prince in the queendom. Who knows how many women have fallen for him?" She wrapped her arms around herself. "Now he's leaving, and I'll get my wish to be alone, but I can't bear the thought of not seeing him again."

The tiger leaned closer, studying Elliya's face, then she focused back on the water, settling her face onto her paws. Without the tiger's penetrating gaze on her, Elliya let herself imagine Hawthorne boarding a ship and sailing away. Tears poured down her face, splashing gently on her dress.

The tiger stayed by her side as they held a silent vigil together.

20

Elliya woke to a loud knock on her door. She bolted upward in bed, trying to clear her groggy head. She'd stayed up too late grieving by the moonlit pool with the tiger, and now she'd overslept.

Lliadain's voice came from the other side of the door. "Elliya, are you in there?"

Elliya jumped out of bed and smoothed her unruly hair as she rushed to the door. "I'm sorry, Sister. Here I am."

The moment she opened the door, Lliadain pushed her way inside, a neat stack of clothing in her hands. "Scholars aren't lazy, Elliya. You'd do well to remember that if you want to succeed here."

She'd often been called lazy by her stepmother, so the admonishment stung. "Yes, Sister. I'm sorry."

Lliadain placed the clothing on Elliya's unmade bed. "It's time to be up and on to your special chore for the day. You've been assigned to assist at the ball."

Elliya's mouth dropped open. "The ball? Me?"

"Yes, you. I have no idea why—I'm sure there are more useful people. I was just told to bring you this uniform and send you to the palace. Find the other chambermaids wearing these uniforms and assist the royal family as they prepare for the ball."

"The royal family?" she squeaked.

Lliadain rolled her eyes. "Yes, that includes Prince Hawthorne. I thought you'd be pleased about that."

"Well, I—"

"Hurry and be on your way. There are a lot of preparations today, so they will want you there early. You won't continue with your laziness, will you?"

"No, of course not, Sister. I'll get dressed and go to the palace immediately."

Lliadain huffed, then strode from Elliya's room, and as the door opened, Luci ran in.

"Where have you been?" Elliya put her hands on her hips as the ginger kitten hopped onto the bed. "I haven't seen you for days."

The kitten ignored her and continued her task of sniffing the uniform Lliadain had deposited on the bed. Elliya rubbed her fingers across the soft fabric as the kitten looked up with her mouth open from serious sniffing.

"I'm sure it smells different from the clothes at the monastery. Much fancier. But I guess this is my job for the day. Assisting the royal family." The thought of seeing Hawthorne one more time both thrilled and terrified her.

I'm hungry.

Elliya sighed. "Of course you are."

After she finished dressing in the new uniform, she grabbed a quick breakfast for herself and Luci. She thought someone in the monastery might comment about her change of uniform, but as usual, no one paid her much attention.

Her walk to the palace was equally quiet until a carriage pulled up beside her and the door opened.

"Hello, little mouse!" said Geeni cheerfully. "Get in, and I'll take you the rest of the way."

Elliya hopped inside the well-furnished carriage and settled into the seat across from Geeni. "How did you know I would go to the palace?"

Geeni grinned, lowering the hood of her blue silk cape around her neck. "I pulled a few strings to get you invited onto the palace staff today. I thought you should have a chance to see a ball for yourself."

Elliya shook her head. "You're so kind to me, Godmother. I don't know what to say."

"I have one more surprise for you, dear." She lifted the box at her side and handed it to Elliya.

Elliya lifted the lid with careful fingers. Nestled inside, on a thick bed of fabric, was a pair of glass slippers.

Her mouth dropped open. "They're beautiful," Elliya whispered as she blinked back tears. "These are too beautiful for me."

Geeni leaned forward in the carriage, focusing deeply on Elliya's face. "Nothing but the best for my little mouse."

Elliya brushed her fingers against the cool glass. "But I'm just a servant tonight. I'm not actually going to the ball." The glass sparkled in the sunlight through the carriage window, lighting up the intricate designs carved into the bottom of the shoes.

Geeni gave her a warm smile. "I thought you deserved something pretty, even if you're just cleaning up after the royal family."

"Thank you, Godmother. I don't know how I can ever repay you." The tears she had been trying to contain finally spilled down her cheeks.

"Oh, little mouse. You repay me more than you know." Geeni wiped her fingers across Elliya's cheeks, sweeping away each tear.

Elliya ducked her head, ashamed at how often she cried in front of her godmother. "It's not just the shoes. You saved my life by getting me out of my stepmother's house." She swallowed a sob. "I don't think I would have lived much longer."

Geeni looked up from the bracelet she twisted on her wrist. "Well, then it's a good thing I found you when I did, isn't it? Qira the Trickster directed us to find each other that day."

Elliya's face lit with a smile. "You truly believe that? That the Goddesses used you to save me?"

Geeni grinned. "Perhaps you'll be the one to save me, little mouse."

"Why do you need saving? Are you in danger?" Anxiety flared in her chest as she considered not only saying goodbye to Hawthorne but also Geeni.

Her godmother's jade eyes glittered. "There is danger everywhere, little mouse. Even when you feel the most safe, danger might lurk right in front of you."

Elliya shivered at the woman's ominous words. "Aren't you afraid?"

Geeni's pink lips curved in a smirk. "There's too much to gain to waste time on fear. The only way to get what I want is to take the risk."

Risk was exactly what Elliya wanted to avoid. But maybe taking a risk wasn't as terrifying when you were as strong as her godmother.

Geeni tapped her fingers on the glass slippers. "Take the shoes with you, but don't put them on until you are inside the palace near the royal quarters. You don't want to scuff such pretty shoes on the rough cobblestones, do you?"

"Of course not, Godmother." She carefully lifted the shoes from the box and tucked one inside each pocket of her uniform. "You're exactly right."

"I usually am." Geeni winked. "Now be on your way. It should be an eventful night."

As the carriage pulled away, Elliya considered her godmother's words. *The only way to get what I want is to take the risk.*

What did Elliya want?

Her emotions were tied in knots ... She didn't know how to sort out her feelings for the prince without surrendering to the fear of falling in love. And was the prince correct? Was she afraid of love causing pain, or was she afraid of her own happiness?

But beyond that fear of love and happiness, a greater fear had risen to the surface. Greater than her fear of disappointing Geeni. Greater than her fear of the scholars discovering her Spark. And even greater than the fear of returning to her stepmother's home.

She was afraid she'd never see the prince again.

The idea stole her breath. She couldn't bear it. And the thought of him leaving without knowing how she felt was greater than the fear of admitting her feelings to herself. She had to take the risk, despite her fear.

And she only knew one way to convince him to stay— the only thing that had worked before.

She turned away from the palace and headed home.

21

———

Elliya quietly opened the kitchen door and repeated Geeni's words as a mantra. *The only way to get what I want is to take the risk.* Being discovered by her stepmother terrified her, but it paled in comparison to never seeing Hawthorne again.

She had to take the risk.

She crept through the quiet kitchen. The dishes were clean, and the pots and pans were neatly stacked. Had her stepmother's cleaning skills improved, or had she hired a full-time servant? Elliya peeked into the parlor, and though it was empty, she still tiptoed across the room and up the stairs. Her stepmother would be at her ladies' card game today, so Elliya didn't have long to grab one of her mother's books and get out.

She cracked open the door to the library and peeked inside. As her eyes landed on the bookshelves, her hand slid off the doorknob, sending the heavy door to smack against the wall. She didn't even flinch at the noise, because all her attention was on the shelves.

The shelves with gaps where her mother's books had been.

She ran to the bookshelves, her eyes scanning each gaping hole, hoping perhaps her stepmother hadn't found them all, but they were gone. All her mother's books, her ideas, her memory ... It was all gone.

Elliya had feared her stepmother would discover the origin of the books and use them as punishment, but now that her stepmother believed Elliya was dead, she'd thought the risk was over. How had her stepmother figured it out? Had she realized a book was missing? But no, her stepmother had no interest in books. Even if she'd realized a book was missing, she couldn't identify which one, much less connect that to the other books by the same author scattered among the shelves.

The loss shook through her. She had never truly possessed anything of her own to experience a loss like this before. She hadn't cried for her mother in years, but the familiar hole of grief expanded in her heart—the lost books opening that deep well of sadness. The last remnant of her mother was gone. Lost forever. She had nothing left.

Elliya wanted to sink to the floor and cry, but a quiet thought reminded her these were not her mother's only books. She rubbed her hands roughly against her eyes. Two of her mother's books were still at the monastery—the one Hawthorne had found in the labyrinth library and the one she had already stolen. And beyond that, one more remained.

She ran out of the office and threw open the small door at the end of the hall. She took the steps up to the attic two at a time, tripping up the last few steps, before sliding to a halt right before her bare mattress. The room didn't appear to have been touched since she left, but she had so few things in the room, there wasn't much to disturb. She pulled a loose nail out of the floor, then used it to pry up the floorboard.

Her mother's final journal was still inside.

She clutched the book to her chest, a sob breaking from her lips. All was not lost. She still had two textbooks and this journal. She would grieve the rest of the books later and use this journal to convince the prince to stay. Everything would be okay.

"I knew you'd come back."

Panic froze Elliya to the spot. She hated the feeling of her stepmother at her back, unable to see when the blow would fall, but her muscles had stiffened and she couldn't turn around.

Her stepmother stalked closer. "When that woman came to buy all the books by Yulia Zaleska, I realized you must still be alive."

Elliya spun, quickly tucking the small journal inside her pocket beside one of the glass slippers. "You sold them?"

Her stepmother's eyebrows shot up in surprise as she stared down at Elliya hunched on the floor. "You didn't send the woman? I assumed ..." She laughed wickedly. "If I had known they belonged to your mother, I would have destroyed them long ago and made you watch. But it's a good thing I didn't, because the woman paid me a fortune. I don't know what your mother wrote about, but apparently her ideas were worth a lot."

Who would have bought her mother's books? No one knew Yulia Zaleska was her mother, since she had changed her name when she arrived in Isandariyah. But a small shred of hope formed in her heart just knowing the books still existed.

Her stepmother studied Elliya's uniform, and understanding lit her eyes. "So that's where you've been! You've been working as a servant in the palace. It's the only job you're qualified for, but I'm surprised the queen would allow such lazy servants in her home." She clicked her tongue disapprovingly. "Now that you're back, I can fire the girl I hired, even though she was clever enough to come find me when she heard you poking around in the library."

Elliya swallowed, trying to remind herself how to speak. "I'm not staying here."

Her stepmother's eyes flashed. "I won't stand for your ungrateful nonsense, child. The queen has plenty of servants. You belong to me."

Her words summoned something from deep within Elliya. Even though her body was practically numb with panic, her heart rebelled against the words. Elliya didn't belong to her stepmother. She belonged to the Goddesses and to herself. And she wasn't just a servant. She was a scholar in training, and a prince called her ... friend.

She knew what she wanted. And she had to take the risk.

"I don't belong to you." She stood slowly. "I'm leaving, and I'm not coming back."

Fury radiated off her stepmother, along with a hint of surprise. "You will not speak to me that way, child."

Elliya bit back the habitual apology that sprang to her lips. If she wouldn't offer the woman an apology, she had no other words to say. "Goodbye, Stepmother."

Her stepmother's eyes widened in shock as Elliya breezed past her.

Before Elliya could duck through the small door, a sharp pain exploded against her back, knocking her against the doorframe. She gasped and spun. Her stepmother wielded the cane that had belonged to Elliya's father.

"You will not walk away from me. You'll remain in this house if I have to break your legs myself." She swung the cane at Elliya's leg.

A scream burst from her lips as the cane smacked into her. As she clutched her knee, she felt the outline of the glass slipper in her pocket. Her stepmother swung again, and Elliya turned *toward* the swing, the irrational part of her mind more worried about the delicate slippers than her own body. The woman swung the cane with such force, Elliya's knee nearly buckled. If she fell, her stepmother wouldn't stop until Elliya passed out.

She couldn't let this continue. She had to escape.

Elliya reached for the cane, startling her stepmother into stepping backward. Elliya had never fought back before. Her stepmother looked confused, but quickly recovered from her shock and swung the cane directly into Elliya's upper arm. She cried out, clutching her bicep, her lower arm going numb.

Glee sparkled in her stepmother's eyes. She grabbed hold of Elliya's wounded arm, her fingers digging painfully into her skin through the thin cloth. She dropped her voice to a slow and menacing whisper. "You belong to me, child, and I will never let you leave. I could have turned you out on the street when your father died, but I let you stay in this house, as the only scrap of a child the Goddesses let me keep. I might not be the best stepmother, but I am all you deserve, considering you killed your own mother."

The words chilled her to the core, and though she wanted to shake herself out of her stepmother's painful grasp, she couldn't move. Maybe it was true. She didn't deserve love. Maybe she deserved—

Her stepmother shrieked as a mouse ran across her foot. "Your room is infested, you filthy child!"

Elliya shook herself out of her frozen panic and focused on the mouse that had stopped in her line of sight.

We'll distract her. You run.

Her stepmother's grip tightened. "Your first task is to trap that mouse and kill it."

Elliya swallowed her fear and whispered, "No."

Her stepmother's eyes flashed, but before she could

strike, she shrieked as another mouse ran across the room, then under her long dress.

Elliya didn't hesitate and pulled her arm out of her step-mother's grip. Her stepmother's fingers clung so tightly to Elliya's dress, the seams ripped loose and the sleeve came off in her hand. She threw the fabric down and reached for Elliya, but another mouse scurried under her dress. She screamed and beat at her dress as the mouse climbed her leg.

Elliya whispered, "Thank you," to the mice, then ran away.

22

Elliya limped in the general direction of the monastery and the palace, still unsure where to go. Her mad dash from her stepmother's house had carried her far. Adrenaline and fear had helped her run faster than she had ever run in her life, but her escape had eventually slowed to a shuffling gait that hurt with each step.

She was expected to be serving at the palace now, but her trip home and back had taken so long, maybe they had already given up on her? The thought of going to the monastery, soaking her bruises in a hot tub, then falling asleep sounded so wonderful it brought tears to her eyes. Maybe she could sneak inside without the Sisters seeing her, and she wouldn't have to explain her bruises and ripped dress. She didn't have the energy to speak, much less to think of a reasonable explanation that didn't reveal she wasn't who she claimed to be.

But the whole reason she had gone home was to get one of her mother's books. She pushed down the unanswered questions about who had bought her mother's books and contented herself that they still existed somewhere. She gently patted the outline of the journal in her pocket and flinched as it brushed against her bruised leg. This journal would convince the prince to stay—she was sure of it. That meant she had to get to the palace tonight. If not, he would sail away the next morning, and she would never see him again.

But her uniform had a ripped sleeve, and her hair was a tangled mess. She couldn't just show up at the palace and demand to see the prince. They wouldn't believe her. She should go back to the monastery, change into her apprentice scholar uniform, then head to the palace. But that whole trip would take so long! How could she keep walking when she hurt so badly?

She finally reached the main thoroughfare of Isandine and had to make the choice: turn right toward the palace or turn left for the monastery. She stood there, unable to decide, her brain foggy and tears clouding her eyes.

A shiny carriage pulled up beside her, and the door opened.

A sob stuck in her throat. "Godmother?"

A white monkey hopped out of the carriage, followed by Alanna, dressed in a ball gown of red silk and rubies. "Blessed Twins! What's happened to you?" She told the driver to head to the monastery, then turned back to Elliya. "No, don't explain until you are inside. You look like you're about to pass out."

Elliya let Alanna help her inside the carriage. "I thought you were my godmother," she said groggily.

Alanna blew out a breath as she settled into her seat, the white monkey perched by her side. "You look in desperate need of a godmother right now. What happened to you?"

Elliya tried to pull the ripped sleeve of her dress to hide her bruise. "Um ..."

Alanna frowned. "And why are you dressed as a chambermaid?"

"I ... um ... I was assigned to assist at the palace during the ball. I'm late. I'm sorry—"

"It seems a little strange for an apprentice scholar to serve as a chambermaid, although I'm often confused about how the palace works. But what happened? Did someone mug you?" Her eyes flared. "What kind of pathetic thief targets a servant? If you're going to steal from someone, you should make sure they're rich and that they thoroughly enjoy the experience of having their wallet delicately lifted from their pocket." She looked at the white monkey at her side.

The monkey shook her head with disdain. *Amateurs.*

Elliya's eyes shot to the monkey, but then she looked back at Alanna, pretending she hadn't heard the monkey speak. "I have something for Prince Hawthorne—a book. He needs to see it so he won't leave. Will you take it to him?"

Alanna's eyes shifted from anger at the imaginary thieves to a careful consideration of Elliya. "You would convince him to stay?"

"Well, I hope the book will convince him. And it might be better if you give it to him instead of me. It would be ... less complicated."

Alanna tapped her lip. "Hmm ... I'm not sure I want to make Hawthorne's life less complicated. A handsome prince deserves a little complication, don't you think?"

The monkey flicked her tail. *It serves him right for being such a flirt.*

Elliya avoided looking at the monkey, but wasn't sure how to respond.

Alanna grinned. "I know exactly what to do." She tapped on the carriage roof, and when the driver peeked through the window, she said, "Take us to the theater instead."

"The theater?" Elliya gasped.

Alanna leaned back against her seat and looked Elliya up and down. "I have a few costumes that will fit you. Since they're just costumes, the jewels aren't real and the seams are a little loose from wear, but the dress should hold up for at least one night of dancing."

Elliya's eyes widened. "Dancing? Wait—"

"Of course! You can't go to a ball and not dance! Hmm ... I wonder if I have pretty shoes that will fit you."

"I actually have pretty shoes, but—"

Alanna clapped her hands. "Perfect! Then you're all set! I have to get going, since the ball is in my honor, you know, but the costume girls will help you."

"Thank you, Alanna, but I really shouldn't—"

The carriage pulled to a stop in front of the theater. "Don't be silly. Put on a fancy dress, then come to the ball and convince the prince to stay." Her eyes twinkled mischievously. "Using whatever means necessary."

Elliya choked. "What? No, I—"

Alanna folded her arms. "What would your godmother say? You thought she had come to rescue you ... I'm guessing a woman like that would want you to go to the ball."

Elliya blinked stupidly, unable to dispute her point. "Yes, she wants me to go to the ball."

"Of course she does. She can thank me later for stepping in as your temporary godmother." She opened the door, and the monkey hopped out. "Bibi will go with you to make sure everyone knows you have my blessing to take whatever you need."

Elliya stepped out of the carriage, biting her lip to keep from whimpering at how her muscles had stiffened during the carriage ride.

Alanna looked at her with compassion. "Ask the girls to give you the salve they use after stunt practice. It will help loosen your muscles enough that you can enjoy a few dances."

Elliya swallowed the lump in her throat. "I don't know how to thank you."

"You can thank me by stopping Hawthorne in his tracks." She chuckled fondly. "He's an even bigger flirt than I used to be, but I'm proof that even the biggest flirts can one day fall in love."

Elliya's mouth dropped open.

Alanna winked at her. "Enjoy the ball, dear."

The monkey proved an effective communicator, even without Elliya's Spark. Bibi hopped around the costume closet, her small hands plucking out ribbons and earrings while the costume girls pulled out a rack of dresses to sort through.

An older woman glanced at Elliya in the mirror while she styled her hair. "Maybe it's best if I leave it down ... to cover the bruises?"

Elliya ducked her head to hide her reddening cheeks. The woman had applied makeup over the salve, but the bruises were growing darker by the moment, and only so much could be done.

"There's no need to be embarrassed, child. It's not your fault." The woman rested a warm hand on Elliya's shoulder. "These bruises don't bring shame on you, but on the one who hurt you. You're going to a royal ball. You should spend the night dancing and only answer questions if you choose to reveal the bruises yourself."

Elliya blinked back her tears. "Thank you. I won't ever forget your kindness."

"Anything for one of Alanna's friends." She offered Elliya her hand. "Time to get dressed."

The costume girls had decided on a pale blue dress that brought out the blue in Elliya's eyes. They helped her into the full skirt with layers upon layers of shimmering blue tulle. The dress was sleeveless, but they had found long white gloves that hid the bruise on her upper arm, and her flowing hair hid the creeping bruise along her back.

"Let's find you a different necklace. That gold chain doesn't go with the dress." The older woman smiled. "This glorious dress has pockets, so you can just tuck the necklace inside."

Elliya's hand snapped closed over the charm from her godmother. She hadn't considered it much lately, though Geeni had been adamant that she wear the charm and keep it hidden at all times. Her godmother had never lied to her, so she had to believe that it truly was protecting her from the queen. She wrapped the chain around her wrist and hid it inside her glove.

When they started looking for shoes, Elliya showed them her glass slippers. The women oohed and ahhed over the delicate glass slippers with the intricate carvings along the soles. The monkey stopped sorting through the glittering earrings and hopped onto the table.

Bibi cocked her head. *There is something odd about those shoes.*

Two baby monkeys scampered into the room, stealing Bibi's attention. Elliya was curious about the monkey's interest in the shoes, but she couldn't reveal that she heard the monkey speak. Bibi and Alanna seemed very close, and Elliya wasn't sure what the monkey might reveal about her Spark.

Bibi groomed the twin monkeys, tidying the fur around

their faces. *No, you can't go to the ball. Remember what happened at the wedding?*

Elliya tucked the shoes into her pockets along with her mother's journal. "I don't want to risk ruining the shoes by walking in them outside. I'll wait to put them on until I arrive."

The older woman smiled as she led Elliya to the waiting carriage. "You really are such a sweet girl. I hope that for every measure of pain you've felt today, you receive a double measure of delight."

23

Elliya sat in the carriage, staring at the front entrance of the palace with her mouth open. The carriage had stopped in front of a grand staircase that led directly up to the ballroom on the second floor. Open balconies curved around the perimeter, and the ballroom's golden light spilled out of the fluttering curtains. She had been inside the palace many times but had always used the servants' entrances. Music and laughter filtered outside, and as she looked up, her mind told her to run.

The ceremonial guards lining the steps peered inside the carriage, probably wondering why she took so long to exit, but when they saw the white monkey hop out, they barely gave Elliya a second glance. Apparently Bibi was treated as an honored guest and allowed to do as she pleased. Elliya thought they should keep a closer eye on the monkey, considering how many jewels she had seen the monkey "collect" on the way from the theater to the palace.

This girl moves slower than my twins, thought the monkey. *Doesn't she realize how many sparkly things are inside? If she doesn't want to go to the ball, why is she even here?*

Elliya intentionally avoided eye contact with the

monkey, but she asked herself the same question—what was she doing here? She was an apprentice scholar, a servant of the Sisters and the Goddesses. What right did she have to walk into a ball wearing a gown as if she belonged? She should leave. Run back to the monastery and forget this whole day had happened.

But if she didn't find Hawthorne tonight, he would leave on a ship to Verkeshe, and she might never see him again.

She stepped out of the carriage.

When her foot touched the smooth cobblestone, she realized she still wore her simple work shoes. She mentally apologized to her godmother for being so forgetful and grabbed the glass slippers out of her pockets. A guard at the bottom of the stairs glanced her way, but when he saw her kicking off her work shoes and stepping inside the glass slippers, he looked away as if embarrassed for her. The cold glass soothed her sore feet, but their stiff shape felt strange. What a beautifully odd pair of shoes!

Bibi studied the slippers, then looked up, her posture impatient and a little suspicious. Elliya started up the stairs before the monkey could ask any more uncomfortable questions.

When Elliya arrived at the top step, she stared into the glowing ballroom and the swirling crowd. Bibi didn't hesitate—she hopped through the door and was quickly lost in the crowd. But Elliya stared at more people than she had seen in her life and broke out in a cold sweat.

As she took her first few hesitant steps inside the ballroom, her stomach suddenly roiled. So many people were talking and laughing and singing, and the twirling bodies swam in her vision out of time with the music. She couldn't catch her breath, and her perfectly fitted corset now felt suffocating.

Her eyes darted around the room, looking for a place to

hide. The closest place was one of the open balconies, and she walked there as fast as her stiff glass slippers would allow. Once she stepped onto the balcony, the noise of the crowd faded, and she could finally catch her breath. The thought of walking through that crowd to find the prince caused the nausea to rise in her stomach. But he was the only reason she was here. She had to find him.

She slowly peeked around the gauzy curtain into the ballroom. The dance floor was swirling chaos, but in the center danced Alanna and Jaemin. The prince watched her with fascination as she threw her head back and laughed. Alanna's ruby red dress sparkled with real jewels, and despite not being a princess, she looked like one.

Prince Finn danced nearby, and Elliya assumed Hawthorne was dancing as well—women would line up all night to dance with the charming prince. How would she ever find him in the middle of all these people?

Her eyes shifted to the dais at the front of the room. There sat a golden throne, empty. Elliya was very late to arrive, so why wasn't the queen here yet?

Her eyes drifted to the edge of the dais, where Prince Edric stood stiffly with his arms behind his back, wearing his red monk's uniform. Had no woman dared ask him to dance? Or had he refused based on his vows?

Hawthorne stepped up to the monk and offered him a glass of water. Elliya's breath caught in her throat at the sight of him. He usually wore loose linen shirts unbuttoned further than most men, but tonight he wore a long jacket with a raised collar. The stiff white fabric and his serious expression looked unusual on him. His playful smirk was gone, and the laughter had left his eyes. Even in the midst of a party, his expression was grim. His eyes focused briefly on the empty throne, and his frown deepened, before his attention shifted to the crowd.

While watching him, she had drifted out of her hiding spot, and as he scanned the ballroom, he caught sight of her in the balcony doorway. He stood so still that he appeared to stop breathing. His lips parted as if he might say her name, though the two of them were separated by a whole crowd of dancers. The glass in his hand had lowered unnoticed, and he flinched when the wine spilled.

He shook himself out of his stupor and handed his glass to his brother, who frowned at being forced to hold a glass of wine. The crowd parted as Hawthorne made a straight line for her.

Her heart fluttered like a trapped bird in her chest. She had so many things to say to him, and as he strode nearer, she had no idea what to say first.

He stepped onto the balcony, so close she would have taken a step backward if she could have moved at all. Instead, she stood frozen before him, her heaving chest all she could move as she tried to catch her breath.

"You came," he whispered, his eyes locked on hers. He stared at her like he had just discovered a great treasure.

How could she explain all that she had gone through to actually stand before him now? Wrestling with her decision to go home, the pain she still suffered from her stepmother's abuse, the tearful walk followed by a carriage ride with Alanna.

And that she would have gone through all that and more, just to see him one last time.

There was too much to explain, so she simply said, "Yes."

His eyes lit up with the sparkle that had been missing before. "I thought I might never see you again. I thought you'd hide in the monastery for the rest of your life, but you're here." He took her hands. "You're here, and you'll come with me to Verkeshe."

Words, so many words, crowded together in her mind.

He shouldn't go ... She didn't want him to go ... She wanted him to stay, but ... All her words were too much, and still not enough.

"No."

His face fell, and his hands gently released hers. "Oh ... I —" He shook his head roughly. "I shouldn't have presumed. I'm sorry."

She couldn't bear bringing the darkness back to his eyes. "No, I'm the one who's sorry. I—" She couldn't find the right words, so she pulled her mother's journal out of her pocket. "I brought you another book."

His eyes lit up briefly, then his lips turned down. "You brought me a book to get me to stay."

"Yes," she whispered. "Stay. Read it ... with me."

His lips hardened into a line. "Give this book to the Sisters. I'm going to Verkeshe tomorrow."

"No, please just stay and read—"

He drew in a ragged breath. "I need more than a book, Elliya!"

His voice had only risen a little, but still, she flinched.

He looked alarmed that he'd startled her, and he dropped his voice. "I need more than a book. I need to find Zaleska, I need answers for the queendom, I need ..." He trailed off as his eyes roamed across her face, landing on her lips. His voice was barely a whisper, yet it was the only thing she could hear. "Elliya, I need ..."

Her thoughts warred within her. Geeni had said, *The only way to get what I want is to take the risk,* but Elliya didn't know what she wanted. She had always dreamed of a safe, solitary life, but now that her dream was within reach, it had lost its appeal. However, the prince offered a future too terrifying to even consider. The only thing she knew for sure was she didn't want Hawthorne to leave.

But it was too many words, too many thoughts pressing

down on her. "Please, Hawthorne," she whispered. "Please don't leave."

Emotions flashed across his face—hope and desire, followed by a mixture of frustration and pride, melting into a sad uncertainty. "Elliya, you could ask anything of me, and I would give it to you, but please don't ask me to stay." He turned from her to look up at the empty throne. "I'm just a prince—basically useless to the queendom. But this is one thing I can actually do to help."

"Going to Verkeshe won't help, Hawthorne." She lifted the journal to his turned back. "This journal—"

Hawthorne's head tilted as he caught sight of his brother, Edric. The monk jerked his head to the side, summoning him. Hawthorne's shoulders sagged. "Edric needs me. I should go."

Her inability to explain anything properly suddenly caught up with her. She had failed in the one thing she had risked her safety to do: convince Hawthorne to stay. She couldn't explain anything, not about her mother, the science, her own feelings ... It was all too late.

He turned slowly and gave her one last look. "Goodbye, Elliya. I ..." Just as many unsaid words loomed behind his eyes. But he drew in a deep breath and said, "Goodbye."

She couldn't say the word in response, couldn't bear to admit it would be the last word she said to him.

He smiled sadly and walked away.

Her breath caught on a shaking sob as he walked away. She couldn't let that be the end. He needed to know he wouldn't find Zaleska in Verkeshe. But if Elliya saw him again, she would be just as unable to speak as before. She should have just handed him the journal and let him read it. He deserved at least that much.

The monk whispered in his ear, then led him into the hallway. It was too late for her to stop him, but she could give the journal to a servant to deliver to him. She took a deep breath and stepped out of the balcony into the ballroom.

The swarm of people and loud noises still made her nauseous, so she hurried through the swirling crowd into the hallway leading toward the royal quarters.

A guard blocked her way before looking closely at her face. "Ah ... sorry, Sister. You're dressed much differently tonight. That's a very fancy dress for sweeping ashes."

"Um ... yes, sorry." The apology sprang to her lips faster than the correction that she wasn't actually a full scholar yet.

The guard waved her ahead, and she walked further into

the royal quarters. Several chambermaids scurried down the quiet hall. Elliya herself would have been one of them if her stepmother hadn't ruined her uniform. She headed to the closest chambermaid, but the girl hurried away before Elliya could give her the journal.

"I'm going to Verkeshe," said Hawthorne.

Elliya froze outside the open door. She wasn't prepared to see him—just to hand the journal to a servant.

"You can't leave now." Jaemin's voice drifted through the open doorway. "Our other brothers haven't made it home yet, and the queen wants us all together."

Hawthorne's voice dropped to a ragged whisper. "The queen hasn't left her room for days! I'm no use to her here. I have to find an answer to our problem."

Alanna responded to his frantic tone with a calm voice. "Maybe she will come out tonight. She came to the last ball."

Edric answered dryly, "Yes, and that went really well, didn't it?"

There was a long pause before Hawthorne murmured, "She's not getting better. If we don't find an answer soon, Ginevere will make a play for the throne, and our mother won't have the strength to resist her."

Elliya vaguely recalled the name Ginevere from their discussion on blood testing other members of the royal family, and she shivered at the weight of his words. The princes were watching their mother slowly deteriorate from some mysterious illness, and none of them could inherit the throne. Their time was running short.

"I can practically feel Ginevere breathing down our necks," Jaemin growled. "We know she has spies among us. She probably has someone here watching us tonight."

Spies? In the palace? The thought made Elliya uneasy. Then she realized she was currently eavesdropping on their conversation. If someone saw her, it wouldn't look good. She lifted her skirts to tiptoe away.

Alanna sighed, "It's like Geeni is always one step ahead of us."

Elliya froze midstep.

"We can't let Ginevere get the upper hand," said Jaemin. "She's evil and will do whatever it takes to get the throne."

Elliya leaned against the wall, struggling to breathe. No, she must have misheard—

"Geeni already has the upper hand," muttered Alanna. "She almost killed you, Jaemin." Alanna grunted, as if suddenly confused. "My Spark is acting strangely again, just like when we were dancing. What's going on?" Her voice lowered. "What if Geeni's here tonight? Does she have a way to interfere with Sparks?"

"We have no idea what she can do," Jaemin growled. "She's manipulated so many people with magic that she has an arsenal of Sparks in the jewelry around her neck."

Elliya clasped the necklace she now wore hidden under her glove. Geeni had said it would protect her from the queen's magic, but never said how.

Alanna laughed darkly. "All she needs is a single tear to make one of her runes and use the person's Spark for herself. She's so cunning she could've stolen tears from half the city without their owners giving it a second thought."

Elliya thought of her kind godmother ... the woman who had found her crying in the marketplace and wiped away her tears ... the woman who had rescued her from her stepmother's house and held her while she cried ... the woman who comforted her like no one ever had ...

Geeni had stolen her tears while pretending to be her doting godmother. All those tears ... Geeni could turn them into runes to use Elliya's Spark for herself.

She had listened to Elliya's stories—stories that seemed

harmless, but in the hands of a manipulative woman after the throne ... What could Geeni do with the information Elliya had given her? By dropping Elliya off with the Sisters, Geeni had gained a source inside the monastery, and once they had assigned Elliya to clean the queen's shrine, her godmother also had a source inside the palace.

A spy.

Elliya was the spy.

She slapped a gloved hand over her mouth to hold back the sob that threatened to burst forth. How could her godmother betray her like this? Elliya had trusted her, but the woman had been using her since the day they met. Why couldn't Elliya see it before now?

"We will stop her," said Edric. "We will hunt Geeni down, along with all her spies, and we will end this."

Elliya trembled at the harshness of his voice. Her legs shook so badly that her bruises renewed their throbbing, and she wanted to fall down in a pile of tulle skirt and weep. But she couldn't. She needed to run and hide, but she didn't know where. There was no place she could go to receive mercy. Nowhere she would be safe.

"I will leave the hunting to you," said Hawthorne. "I'm leaving for Verkeshe tomorrow."

Hawthorne's voice sent a current of warmth racing through her. He was it. He was the one place of safety in the midst of betrayal. She didn't know if he could forgive her, but he was the only one she trusted to show her mercy.

The only one who loved her.

Before she lost her nerve, she stepped into the doorway, and all eyes shot her way. She cleared her throat, but her voice still only came out as a trickle of sound. "Hawthorne, may I speak to you?" Her voice dropped to barely a breath. "Privately?"

Alanna grinned and gave her a sly wink, and

Hawthorne's brothers rolled their eyes. They all obviously thought she was looking for a certain kind of "private" moment alone with the prince.

But Hawthorne's face proved he could read her better than they could. He quickly looked her up and down, as if searching for injuries. Her physical pain was hidden, but her emotional distress was clear enough to him.

"Of course, Elliya." He led her out of the room without a backward glance at Alanna and the princes.

25

The prince took Elliya's request for privacy seriously and led her to the labyrinth library. She followed him without a word as she tried to piece her confession together. He held her hand through the dark maze, starlight the only illumination shining through the glass roof.

When they arrived at the center of the labyrinth directly below the peak of the glass dome, he let go of her hand. He struck a match, lighting candles on the giant candelabra in the center of the stone floor. As the slowly lighting candles revealed his powerful silhouette, her breath came in gasps as she considered what she had to confess.

When he finished lighting the candles, he walked toward the curved leather sofa at the edge of the candlelight. "Sit down and tell me what's wrong."

Before he could sit, she fell at his feet. "Prince Hawthorne, I beg your mercy." She swallowed the lump in her throat. "I have betrayed you and the queendom. I'm so sorry. I've never been more sorry in my life."

She felt him hovering over her, though she didn't lift her eyes to look. She had never sensed violence in him, but perhaps her betrayal would be the act that caused him to snap. Her shoulders crept nearer to her ears as if to protect her head from an impending blow, and her knuckles were white from clenching the fabric of her dress. Her ears strained, waiting for the slightest sound, wondering if he'd yell or growl his accusations.

His clothing rustled as he lowered to meet her on the floor, and she flinched, sinking deeper into herself. His slight indrawn breath broke the silence before he came to a rest, kneeling before her and not moving a muscle.

"Elliya ... Tell me what's happened."

His soothing voice flowed over her bowed head and down her back, relaxing the muscles along her spine. She drew in a shuddering breath, but kept her head lowered. "She said she was my godmother. I thought she just liked gossip, but I didn't know who she was ... Exile me or throw me in the dungeon, but please—" She swallowed a sob and finally met his eyes. "Please, don't make me go home."

He drew in a sudden breath. "Don't make you go home?" He shook his head. "Elliya, whatever's happened, we will sort it out. Let's get you off the floor, and you can start from the beginning."

He placed a gentle hand around her arm to help her stand, but she flinched with a whimper. He immediately released her, his fingers springing apart as he studied her long white gloves.

Elliya bit her lip, ashamed she had cried out. His fingers trembled as he eased her long glove down her arm. His delicate touch raised goose bumps along her skin until he reached the hot bruise near her elbow. As his cool fingers brushed the swollen skin, tears sprang to her eyes.

She had cried many times in her life, but this was different. These tears weren't because of the pain. She cried because no one had ever touched her like this before.

With compassion.

Hawthorne swept her hair away from her face, baring her shoulder and revealing the bruise that peeked above the back of her strapless dress. He moved so slowly that she felt each individual hair as it caressed her back, his fingers whispering across her neck.

The prince's emerald eyes glimmered with unshed tears. His fingers fell away from her skin, and the sadness in his eyes hardened into something sharp.

His eyes flicked up to hers. "Who did this to you?"

The intensity of his words stole her breath. Prince Hawthorne spent most days with a playful smirk on his face, but his lips had tightened into a scowl, and his brows were pulled into a furious line. Even though she knew his anger wasn't directed at her, she still found his expression fearsome.

He must have detected a hint of her terror, because he smoothed his expression into a fake calm. "Let's get off the floor, shall we?" He didn't lift her again, but stood and offered his hand.

She allowed him to help her stand, then followed him to the curved sofa. Her legs ached as she lowered herself onto the seat, and she bit her lip to keep from making a sound. She pressed down the sparkling gown as she sat, the fluffy layers of tulle ridiculous in contrast to her betrayal. She wished she wore the rags her stepmother had given her.

He took her hand between both of his own. "Tell me, Elliya. What happened?"

She looked him directly in the eyes, owing him a proper confession. "Geeni ... Ginevere. I'm her spy."

He stared at her, barely breathing. "I don't understand."

Elliya drew in a shaking breath. "I told her about our experiments ... I told her I saw the queen ... Stories that seemed harmless, but I didn't know who she was, and I don't know what she can do with the information I've given her."

He shook his head as he tried to understand. "But who is she to you? How do you know her at all?"

Her lips trembled as she held back her tears. "She said to call her Godmother. She said she would protect me and never let me be hurt again, but she's been using me this whole time."

His eyes dropped to her arm with her lowered glove and exposed bruise. His gentle voice hardened slightly. "Ginevere did this to you?"

"No. She's never hurt me. She rescued me. That's why I thought I could trust her. She rescued me from my stepmother's house."

His eyes shot back to her face. "Your stepmother did this to you?"

All her secrets piled up around her, and she had no idea how to begin. "I'm so sorry, Hawthorne. I've kept so many secrets ... I thought hiding the truth would keep me safe, but I've ruined everything."

He scooted closer, her hand still in his. "You haven't ruined everything, Elliya. In fact, you are the one who will help us defeat Ginevere."

"Me? What can I do?"

"You are inside her circle and have access to her. She doesn't know you've realized who she is. You will give us information about her that will help us find and capture her."

"Wait ... so you want me to spy on *her*?"

His eyes lit up. "Yes, exactly! You can meet with her like nothing has changed and see what information you can gather from her."

She laughed, but the panic shone through. "She will know something is strange. I can't keep a secret from her."

He raised an eyebrow. "So you have no experience keeping secrets?"

"Um ... well, I guess I—"

"You have the skills, Elliya. You'll help us defeat her."

He spoke with such confidence, but not in himself—in her. How could he believe in her after she had betrayed him? Even though she hadn't known who Geeni was, she had willingly kept secrets from him. What made him so sure he could trust her?

The answer twinkled in his eyes, and the truth terrified her. But when she looked at him, she had to admit that if she was to take a stand against Geeni, he was the one person she would want at her side.

"Okay. I'll do it."

His eyes glittered with excitement and a warm current of desire running below the surface. "We need to figure out what her next move will be. She's preparing to strike against us, but we don't know how or when. That's what you will need to discover."

She nodded. "I'm sure she will want to meet with me soon. She'll want to find out what I thought of the ball." Her stomach knotted at what she might have revealed by acci-dent if she hadn't discovered Geeni's true identity.

He cocked his head. "She knew you were coming to the ball?"

"Yes, except she thought I was coming as a servant. Alanna is the one who gave me the dress after my uniform was ruined ... by my stepmother."

His mouth opened and closed as if he had too many questions, but he suddenly gasped. "Did she give you any gold jewelry with carved runes?"

She drew in a quick breath and pulled her glove fully off her arm to reveal the necklace with the rune. "She said it would protect me from the queen. That it would keep me from her notice."

He brushed his finger across the glistening rune. "This looks like a rune on the lamp Geeni gave Alanna. It kept her Spark hidden from Drazen and the queen."

Geeni had also given Alanna a rune? Had Geeni manipulated her, too? "That might be the one true thing Geeni ever said to me." She unwrapped the necklace from her wrist.

Hawthorne rested his hand on hers. "No. Keep it on. You don't want her to think you suspect anything."

She imagined meeting with Geeni and pretending nothing had happened, pretending she didn't know Geeni's true identity. What would she say about the ball? The dresses were pretty, and nothing unusual happened. Everything was normal—

A mouse cleaned its whiskers at the edge of the candlelight. Elliya cocked her head as she watched it.

"That's odd," she mumbled. "I can usually hear them."

Hawthorne turned to follow her line of sight. "The mouse? You mean your Spark isn't working?"

Her brows drew together. "That's never happened since I first discovered my Spark."

Thoughts raced behind Hawthorne's eyes. "Alanna said her Spark was acting strangely when she was dancing and then again when we were talking." His eyes flicked up to hers. "That's when you arrived. It was you."

Her eyes widened. "But I—"

"Did Geeni give you anything besides the necklace?"

"Yes," she breathed. "Glass slippers." She dug through the pile of tulle and removed one of her shoes. The moment she removed one slipper, she could hear the mouse chattering about not seeing Hawthorne in the library in a while.

The decorative pattern on the shoes clicked into place. "They're runes."

Hawthorne traced his finger across the carved glass. "I thought she could only engrave runes into gold ..."

"Gold would be easier to carve, but I guess gold shoes would be even more odd than glass ones." She pulled the other shoe off and shivered as both feet touched the stone floor. "So wearing both shoes disabled my Spark and interfered with Alanna's magic when I drew near her on the dance floor and again in the royal quarters. But what was Geeni's plan? If I had been cleaning the royal quarters as planned and Geeni managed to sneak inside, I assume her runes wouldn't work, either. What's the benefit?"

Hawthorne's golden brown skin paled. "It wasn't your Spark or Alanna's that she was trying to disable ... It was the queen's."

"The queen ..." she breathed. If the queen had no Sparks to defend herself, she'd be an easy target. Even though Geeni hadn't mentioned they were related, she had definitely revealed her feelings about the queen. If Geeni found the queen unexpectedly without her Sparks, there was no doubt what she would do.

"She's going to kill the queen," she whispered. Elliya jumped to her feet and tucked the glass slippers into her pockets. "We have to save her."

26

As they sprinted out of the labyrinth maze, Elliya wondered if she was crazy. If Geeni really was in the palace and wanted to kill the queen, Elliya didn't have the skills to stop her. But the thought of the sad queen, unable to fight back, made her sick to her stomach.

Her bare feet slapped against the stone floor as they left the library's long hallway and turned toward the queen's quarters. She had hoped to find guards or even chambermaids along the way and raise a warning, but the hallways were empty. Almost everyone was at the ball, and she didn't want to think about any stragglers Geeni might have found on her way to the queen.

As they approached the queen's door, Hawthorne slid to a halt and held up a hand to signal for silence as he peeked around the corner.

He turned back to her and whispered, "There are no guards outside, and the door is standing open." His eyes were haunted. "What if she's already …"

She took his hand. "I'll be with you."

He nodded gratefully, then his eyebrows pulled together.

"What if she brought her own soldiers? Maybe you should stay here."

"Will you fight them alone?" She recalled his sparring with his brothers—he would be no match for a trained fighter.

He snorted. "No, I'm a terrible fighter."

She had expected him to lie to protect his vanity, but he didn't appear embarrassed to admit it to her.

He squeezed her hand. "Neither of us will fight. We'll look inside the room and then decide what to do."

She nodded, returning the squeeze before letting go of his hand. They tiptoed to the door and peeked inside.

The sitting room looked like it had every time Elliya had been inside. No sign of a struggle, and a covered serving dish sat undisturbed on a rolling cart with a pressed linen tablecloth. No sounds came from deeper inside the queen's rooms, so they peeked into the next room, which contained the shrine.

The fire had burned down to ashes, which waited for Elliya to tidy up. The only unusual sight was the queen's door standing open.

"She's gone," whispered an unfamiliar woman's voice. "Where did she go?"

"I have no idea." A different woman, but not Geeni.

Hawthorne slowly peeked around the door into his mother's bedroom and sighed. "She's not here, Elliya." He spoke to the women inside. "Thank the Goddesses, it's you. I thought we'd find someone hurting the queen."

Elliya followed him inside the room. Two chambermaids waited with confused expressions, one with straight black hair and the other a blonde. The room appeared perfectly undisturbed, with no sign the queen had been there all night.

The black-haired woman stared at Hawthorne before falling into an awkward curtsy. "Prince Hawthorne."

The blond chambermaid's full lips rounded into a circle before she dropped into a curtsy.

The black-haired woman straightened. "We brought the queen's dinner, but she's not here. Do you know where she is?"

"No, I don't. But it looks like she took her guards with her, so I assume she'll be okay."

The blonde chewed her lip and looked to the other woman for direction. The black-haired chambermaid was the taller of the two, and thin compared to the blond woman's curves. Her brown eyes were sharp as she looked around the room, then studied the prince and Elliya. Her eyes dropped to Elliya's bare feet, visible since she had lifted her full skirt while tiptoeing in the room.

"Elliya ... You're not wearing shoes ..." She turned to the blond woman. "Trudy, she's not wearing shoes."

"What do you mean, Nix?" The blond woman—Trudy—still looked as confused as when they had first entered the room.

Nix sighed, fluttering her lashes. "That means we can go about our backup plan the easy way." She blinked a tear from her lashes, then lifted her uniform sleeve and wiped the tear on a golden bracer.

The black-haired woman moved faster than expected, shoving Elliya against the open door, a golden-handled blade held to her throat. The air whooshed out of Elliya's lungs as she hit the door, the bruises on her back screaming in pain. Elliya could only suck in tiny breaths because Nix pressed against her harder than her slight frame should allow. Elliya froze, just as paralyzed as she had always been when her stepmother had hit her. The only movement she allowed herself was moving her eyes to find the prince.

The blond woman had recovered from her confusion and held the prince against the opposite wall, a matching gold blade against his throat. Now that Elliya studied her more carefully, she saw Trudy had more than a curvy figure—thick muscles bulged beneath her chambermaid dress. Although, she also wore a gold bracer, so the muscles weren't the only source of her strength.

Fear shone in the prince's bright emerald eyes. With the cold dagger pressing against her throat, she knew her own expression was probably even more fearful. Then she realized the prince wasn't looking at Trudy or the dagger against his own throat—he stared at Elliya, his eyes shooting between her face and Nix's dagger at her throat.

His fear hardened into resolve. "You're Ginevere's henchmen."

Trudy huffed. "Henchwomen, if you please."

"What do you want with us?" he hissed.

Nix didn't turn but answered him with her eyes locked on Elliya. "We were supposed to grab the queen, but since she's wandered off, I guess we'll settle for a prince."

A hint of fear shone behind his resolve. "And what about Elliya?"

Trudy shrugged, but her grip on the prince didn't waver. "Geeni wants her alive, so we'll leave her here as long as she doesn't interfere."

Of course Geeni wanted her alive. Elliya was a source of tears containing a Spark. Geeni wouldn't throw that away unless absolutely necessary. And since Elliya was her spy, albeit unintentionally, Geeni would want her to stay where she could hear the most gossip.

"Elliya, you work for Ginevere? How dare you betray the royal family!"

Hawthorne's sharp voice snapped her out of her

thoughts. Why would he ask that? She had just confessed the whole story. Why ...

His lips were in a firm line, but a secret flitted behind his eyes. "You're training to be a scholar. How could you betray the queen like this?"

Trudy's full lips curled into a smirk. "You should know better than to trust pretty girls, Prince. We aren't always what we seem."

The black-haired woman shifted her knife, looking Elliya closer in the eyes. "You won't interfere with us, will you? You won't win any reward from Geeni if you try to steal him yourself, you know."

Her eyes flicked to Hawthorne in time to see his eyes light up before he again adopted his faked look of outrage. She swallowed and answered, "Um ... no, I won't interfere. I'm ... uh, very loyal to Geeni. I don't want to ruin her plans."

Elliya wasn't sure she was convincing, but the prince's eyes twinkled above the firm line of his mouth.

She must have done a sufficient job because Nix dropped her knife, then tucked it inside a hidden sheath. "Go get that tray of food and bring it here. Quickly."

Elliya nodded obediently and hurried into the sitting room. Though she wanted to run away or call for help, the thought of what would happen to Hawthorne made it impossible not to obey. She wheeled the cart into the bedroom, her heart relieved to find Hawthorne still unharmed. He watched her with an intensity that made her heart flutter.

Nix lifted the tablecloth to reveal wrapped coils of thick rope, then turned a sharp eye to Hawthorne. "We can do this the easy way or the hard way, Prince."

Hawthorne tore his eyes away from Elliya, then gave the henchwomen his most magnificent grin. "Have you ladies not heard about me? I have the reputation of being very easy."

Trudy snorted a laugh, but didn't relax her grip.

Nix rolled her eyes. "I've heard. So, you'll come with us like a tame little boy?" she taunted.

His grin grew wider. "Two strong women having their way with me? That's exactly how I thought this night would end."

Elliya's cheeks warmed at his provocative words, but he didn't glance her way at all.

The blond woman tilted her head to look up into his grinning face. "I like this one, Nix. I don't know what Geeni will do with him, but I have a few ideas."

The heat in Elliya's cheeks sank into her chest, where a wildfire of jealousy stirred to life.

"Try to control yourself, Trudy." Nix crossed her arms. "So, you'll go with us, nice and easy?"

The prince fluttered his lashes. "I'll be your sweet little lamb."

Trudy shifted her knife, then pressed herself closer to him. "Why are you so cavalier about this, Prince? Do you think you're strong enough to overpower me and escape?"

He laughed. "I'm no match for you, even without your runes, dear henchwoman. I'm a lover, not a fighter."

Nix rolled her eyes again and started piling the coils of rope on the floor. Elliya's focus shot around the room as she considered the rope. Would they break the window and scale the front of the palace? Someone would surely see them. She just needed to be calm and wait.

Trudy took a step away from him. "Time to prove how easy you are, handsome." She reached into her uniform pocket and tossed something toward the prince, who caught it by instinct.

He studied the small golden lamp in his hands. "This is like Alanna's lamp. The one Geeni gave her."

Trudy nodded. "Alanna used up all those runes, but this one is fresh. So feed it one of your tears and get into your disguise."

"Feed it a tear?" asked Elliya. "All the runes Geeni gave me worked the moment I put them on."

Nix looked at her like she had forgotten Elliya was there. Then she shrugged while dumping a load of rope at Trudy's feet. "Don't ask me. Some runes require a tear to activate and key it to yourself. Others, like the necklace she gave you, keep working no matter who wears it until the rune finally expires."

Trudy smiled proudly. "Geeni's smart. Very smart."

Elliya thought of a few other words to describe Geeni but kept them to herself.

Nix snapped her fingers impatiently. "Come on, Prince. Cry quickly so we can get out of here."

"If only the runes would take tears caused by pain," sighed Trudy. "I could find so many fun ways to make him cry."

The prince's eyes widened, then relaxed into their confident calm. "I told you I'd obey. Let me just think of something sad." His eyes locked on Elliya, trailing down her shoulder to land on her bruised arm. She self-consciously tugged on her glove, but tears had already sprung to his eyes.

Nix watched him with a raised brow. "You really are making this too easy. I can't figure out if you're so stupid you don't understand what's happening or you're so cocky you think you'll escape from us."

A tear fluttered at the end of his lash. "I'm not planning to escape. I have no doubt you will drag me back to the heart of Geeni's lair. I don't know what she will do with me, but I do know one thing ... I will be rescued."

Nix chuckled darkly. "You believe someone will sneak into Geeni's stronghold and set you free, little lamb?"

His eyes locked on Elliya. "Yes. Without a doubt."

Elliya's throat constricted. Why would he trust her like this? She'd already told him she didn't know if she could meet Geeni again and pretend nothing had happened. Now he was asking her to sneak into Geeni's lair and rescue him?

Nix shook her head. "If that delusion keeps you docile, then I'm for it. Rub your tear on that rune, then get dressed."

His eyes didn't leave Elliya's face as he wiped a tear from his eyes, then rubbed it on the lamp. Then he gasped, nearly dropping the lamp as his knees buckled, and he sank to the ground.

The shift happened so quickly Elliya couldn't explain what happened. Between one heartbeat and the next, strawberry blond hair had sprouted from his head, falling in soft waves down his back, and his body shrank. His jacket was too large as he drew in a deep breath, then raised his head.

A young woman stared back at Elliya. Hawthorne blinked his wide lavender eyes, then studied his small pale hands. The woman stood slowly, standing awkwardly in the prince's too large shoes. He turned to the queen's full-length mirror.

"I'm Princess Aliyabeth." He clapped a hand against his delicate throat. "I sound just like her."

Nix snorted. "This isn't the true form of Princess Aliyabeth, but it was close enough for anyone who never met her in person. This is the body of someone with a transformation Spark. Unfortunately, it's the same body Alanna used, so we need to keep anyone who met the fake princess from studying you too closely." She tossed him a chambermaid uniform. "Put this on. Trust me, people will look right past you."

Hawthorne glanced at Elliya before sucking in a deep breath. He set the uniform on the bed and removed his jacket. He had only removed a few shirt buttons when he saw himself in the mirror. The opened buttons revealed the princess's pale breastbone, with no undergarments.

A blush sprang to his cheeks, and he turned away from the mirror.

Trudy threw her head back and laughed. "Aww! The prince is blushing. Now that he's a girl, he's not so easy, I guess."

"Get on with it, Prince," snapped Nix. "It's time to go." She had gathered up her chambermaid dress, tying it at her waist and revealing pants and a harness underneath.

The prince looked helplessly between Elliya and the two henchwomen, but they were spaced such that he would have to face one of them while changing. Elliya was surprised he turned toward her. He stared at the ceiling as he removed his shirt, exposing his pale chest, and kept his head raised as he turned toward the bed to grab the dress. As he pulled the dress over his head, he finally lowered his gaze, and Elliya realized he hadn't been trying to hide his body from them—he'd been shielding the woman's body from his own eyes.

Protectiveness washed over her. Despite his flirty exterior, he respected this woman's body enough to shield his eyes and not look at her without her consent. He was willingly allowing himself to be led into Geeni's lair, believing Elliya would rescue him. He was the strongest, most gentle man she had ever met.

He bit his delicate pink lip as he reached behind himself, trying to fasten the dress. Elliya automatically moved to help him, but Nix stopped her with a glare.

"Don't touch him."

"I was just trying to help—"

Trudy laughed as she finished tying her own dress out of the way of her harness. "He's probably undone countless women's dresses, but the poor boy can't fasten his own."

Nix waved her hand as she attached a rope to her harness. "Help him with the dress, just don't touch his skin, or the magic bursts, and we have to do this the hard way. The hard way gets the job done, but it's extremely bloody." She sighed as if bloodiness would be a hardship for her.

Elliya stepped up behind him and slowly buttoned his dress with trembling fingers. She was terrified to touch his skin and leave the henchwomen to whatever bloodshed their "hard way" involved.

"Thank you," he whispered. A reasonable statement for her help with the dress, but she knew what he meant. He believed in her so much, he was thanking her in advance.

Nix tossed him a pair of gloves as she and Trudy both pulled on their own. "To make sure we don't accidentally burst the magic." She shoved her gold dagger into a sheath in her boot. "But don't worry, a blade won't pierce the magic, though your fake body will hurt just the same."

Hawthorne mumbled, "Good to know. I was worried about that."

Trudy summoned him with a curled finger. "Come here, sweetheart. Let's get you strapped in."

Trudy wrapped a harness around Hawthorne's pants, though they threatened to fall off his thin legs. She knotted a rope to connect his harness to hers, and she tugged, almost lifting Hawthorne off his feet.

Trudy grunted. "Ugh ... he still weighs the same."

Nix rolled her eyes. "You're strong enough to carry him down the wall even if the runes weren't activated, so stop complaining."

Seeing Hawthorne's slight form strapped to the strong blond woman's body sent a new spike of fear through Elliya. This was happening. They were taking him. And even though he believed she would come and rescue him, she still hoped the Queen's Guard would discover them as they descended the palace wall.

The women surprised her by moving away from the window and heading to the back corner of the queen's bedroom. Nix pulled a necklace from her chambermaid uniform, blinked a tear from her eye, and then rubbed it on the gold charm. She placed her hand on the smooth wall, and the marble rippled like a pebble thrown into a still pool. Nix slid her hand across the rippling stone, moving her hand in a searching pattern. Her eyes snapped open, and the stone settled back into place. She grabbed the gold knife out of her boot, then slammed the hilt into the wall in the exact place she had stopped.

The stone beneath her hilt slid into the wall in a perfect square, the wall expertly crafted to hide the secret brick. As the stone slid inward, a chunk of the wall swung outward on invisible hinges, opening to the night sky.

Hawthorne's pouty lower lip dropped as he stared open-mouthed at the secret door. Elliya tried to orient herself— the queen's quarters were at the corner of the palace, so while her window looked out over the front of the palace, this wall would be hidden behind decorative stonework facing the menagerie.

"How did you know about this?" whispered Hawthorne.

Trudy patted him on the rump. "It's magic, sweetheart."

Nix attached their ropes to the queen's massive bed, pulling the knots tight. Even with Hawthorne's weight unchanged from his true body, the giant bed weighed much more than all three of them.

Nix leaned out the hidden door and looked down. "It's a

clear shot down to the menagerie. Then three chambermaids will head out for the night. Trudy, I trust you can
distract the guards from noticing anything familiar about
this chambermaid by using your considerable 'charms'?"

Trudy sighed. "First, carry the prince down using my big
ol' muscles. Then distract the guards with my big ol'—"

"Yes, it's so difficult to be you, Trudy." Nix loosened her
rope, but before she jumped, her eyes fastened on Elliya, as
if just remembering her. "Hey, where are those glass slippers? We should take them with us."

Hawthorne's lavender eyes shot toward Elliya, but she
very carefully didn't look at him. "I'm sorry, but the shoes
broke. They were glass and ..." She shrugged, hoping that
was enough explanation.

Nix nodded, then swung away from the building, dropping out of view.

Trudy dragged Hawthorne to the door, pulling him close
to her chest. "Hold on tight, sweetheart. It would be a shame
to see you splatter on the ground, especially now that you're
just what the queendom has always wanted."

His pale brows pulled together. "What they wanted?"

She winked. "A princess."

Trudy swung out the window, pulling Hawthorne down
with her.

27

Elliya ran to the secret doorway and watched the henchwomen make their skilled descent. Hawthorne stared up at her through the lavender eyes of his disguise, his long strawberry blond locks billowing around him. Despite his harrowing descent down the palace wall, his pale face held complete confidence in her.

Why was he so confident in her? She didn't have the strength to follow them down the sheer palace wall using the ropes, and other than the door strategically cut into the wall, she could detect no other way down. If she took a running jump, she might land on the roof of the kitchen and climb down from there, but the roof was over twenty feet down, and she couldn't chase them if she broke her leg.

The prince's upturned face was growing smaller, and they would reach the ground at any moment. She took a deep breath, nodded to him in acceptance, and sprinted out of the queen's quarters.

It wasn't easy to run in a ball gown. She gathered as much of the tulle in her arms as she could and raced down the hall, her bare feet slapping loudly against the stone. Raucous music and laughter came from the direction of the ballroom, but she didn't head that way, not even to raise the alarm. She had to make it to the menagerie to catch them, and hopefully, the guards at the gate would stop them.

The prince wouldn't be happy with that rescue, though. He had the crazy notion that Elliya could trick Geeni into revealing her secrets, then Elliya would storm Geeni's lair and rescue him. She couldn't waste her time strategizing about such a ridiculous idea—all her thoughts were focused on stopping them before they passed through the palace gates.

She ran down two flights of stairs, then burst through the servants' door closest to the menagerie and headed down the path. She couldn't run as fast on the rough stone, but she ignored the pain in her feet and kept running.

From her first step inside the menagerie, she knew they had passed this direction. The animals were still, their voices barely a whisper in her mind. They were scared— more scared than if three women had only run down this path.

Something had happened.

Elliya stopped walking, her hope of catching up to them gone. She turned in a slow circle, straining her ears and her Spark for a hint of what had transpired. A faint rustling came from the direction of the moonlit pool of water to her right. She walked quietly through the grass, the dragging tulle dress louder than her bare feet.

She stopped near the water as the tiger limped out of the bushes. Her front leg was bleeding, and in her mouth, she carried a shoe.

The prince's shoe.

Elliya's indrawn breath caught in her throat. She tentatively approached the tiger and kneeled, the pale blue dress puffing around her. The tiger limped closer, then dropped the shoe on the grass before settling on her back legs and staring sightlessly at the moonlit pool.

Elliya moved slowly and picked up the prince's shoe. She wasn't surprised it had fallen off, considering how much smaller his feet were now, though the sight of the shoe in the tiger's mouth had felt ominous.

She scanned the tiger for other injuries. The big cat's fur revealed several minor scratches and a large cut on her front leg that dripped blood onto the grass by her paw.

"You tried to stop them."

The cat's green eyes shifted her way, then moved back to the water.

"It's not your fault you couldn't stop them. Geeni's runes gave them extra strength." She tried to imagine what a fight between a tiger and two magically strong women would be like. "I hope you took a bite out of them." She remembered the predatory gleam in Trudy's eyes as she'd looked at Hawthorne. "Especially the blond one."

The tiger's brow twitched, but she didn't turn Elliya's way.

Elliya scooted closer and looked at the wound on the tiger's leg. "Will you allow me to bandage you?"

The tiger tilted her head and studied Elliya with narrowed eyes, then shifted her front leg over, while returning her attention to the water.

Elliya took that as permission. She dug through the top layers of tulle on her dress until she reached an underlayer of delicate silk and ripped off a wide strip.

"He wasn't scared to go with them." She spoke in a comforting lilt as she gently wrapped the silk bandage around the tiger's muscular leg. "He has this crazy idea I'll come rescue him, though I have no idea how to do it."

The tiger held perfectly still, moonlight reflected in her eyes.

"I'm not the rescuing type. Goddesses know, I could never rescue myself." She tied the silk bandage neatly, then adjusted the knot so it wouldn't irritate the wound. She gave a quiet, dark laugh. "But at least I learned how to wrap bandages well."

She blew out a breath and rubbed the edge of her tulle skirt between nervous fingers. "You already know I love him. I confessed that to you the last time we met. But I have another confession ... I've been working as Geeni's spy, even though I didn't realize it."

Though the tiger didn't turn her head, her eyes narrowed and a low growl rumbled in her throat.

"Geeni used me to gather information from the monastery and palace. I just thought she was an eccentric benefactor who rescued me. But she's a truly brilliant actress who fooled me into believing she cared for me." She frowned. "Or maybe I'm the fool for not seeing through her deception sooner."

The tiger's growl stuttered, then continued even louder.

"Even the beautiful shoes she gave me ... they were just another trick. She hoped I'd get close enough to the queen to disable her Sparks and allow her to be captured. If Hawthorne and I hadn't run to save the queen, he wouldn't have been taken."

The tiger's growl reverberated in the still night air.

Elliya took a deep breath and continued her confession. "When I realized what I had done, he's the one I turned to. I always knew falling in love might put me in danger, but I never considered the danger to him. He went with them willingly because he thinks I will rescue him. He believes in me so strongly that he walked right into Geeni's hands." She swallowed before making the most painful confession of all. "He risked his life because he's in love with me."

The tiger opened her mouth and let out a roar that shook Elliya's bones. The sound echoed through the silent menagerie, and all the animals held their breath, including Elliya. The tiger turned her head slowly, and though Elliya couldn't read the animal's thoughts, fury and sadness warred in her wide green eyes.

Elliya tilted her head and bared her neck to the fearsome creature. A tiger ripping her throat out would be a fitting end for her betrayal. And a quick death would put an end to the terrified thoughts racing through her mind. The tiger's face hovered so close, Elliya shut her eyes to block out the sight.

But if she died, who would rescue the prince? What would happen when he realized she wasn't coming for him? The thought of causing him pain sent a sharp spike of courage through her soul.

Elliya whispered, "I know why I can't hear you."

The tiger huffed a warm breath against her neck.

She swallowed, and the tiger's whiskers tickled her bobbing throat. "I have a Spark. I can hear animals, but I can't hear you."

The tiger had already been unmoving, but now she fell into a predatory stillness. Her warm breath barely brushed Elliya's neck.

"You aren't an animal." Her voice dropped to a small trickle of air. "Your Majesty."

Elliya held her breath, waiting to see if she had misjudged the queen's level of rage. A soft sigh floated across her neck before the tiger withdrew.

She cracked open her eyes. The tiger sat back on her haunches, once again staring at the moonlit pool. Elliya's shoulders sagged in relief, and she blinked the tears out of her eyes.

Between one heartbeat and the next, the tiger became the queen.

She wore a thin silk shift, the delicate straps loose on her hunched shoulders. She sat with her legs tucked beneath her, the pose both catlike and oddly vulnerable. Her golden brown skin was scratched with multiple shallow cuts, and her long reddish-brown braid was as disheveled as if she had fought the henchwomen in human form. Elliya wouldn't have believed this woman could be the same creature as the tiger, except tied neatly around her upper arm was the silk bandage from Elliya's dress.

"She gave you a concealment rune," said the queen. "That's why I haven't collected your Spark."

Elliya had only seen the queen twice in human form, and she hadn't spoken either time. Her voice was as regal as Elliya had expected, though it sounded crackly from disuse.

Elliya answered the question that wasn't a question by removing her glove, revealing the necklace wrapped around her wrist and the charm with a shimmering rune.

The queen huffed, the sound more tiger- than queen-like. "I thought there was something unusual about you, but I couldn't decide what."

Now that the queen was in human form, Elliya's words were harder to find. The tiger had been terrifying, but surprisingly easy to talk to.

The queen picked up Hawthorne's shoe, rubbing her scratched finger across the teeth marks she'd caused by carrying it in her mouth. "How will you get him back?"

Elliya clutched the front of her dress. "Me? But you ... you can turn into a tiger! And your other Sparks. You have more magic than anyone since you steal—um ... since you collect—"

"I can't leave the palace. You must get him back your-self." Her voice was cold and resolute.

"But Geeni has so many runes, and she's given more to her henchwomen. It has to be you—"

The queen's head shot toward her with the stern glance of a teacher. "Have you considered what Ginevere wants? What she's trying to accomplish?"

"Um ... I guess she wants to overthrow you?" Elliya felt uncomfortable discussing the topic so candidly with the queen herself.

The queen waved her hand dismissively. "Yes, that, of course, but all she needs to do is outlive me since she is the only other woman with a valid claim to the throne. But she didn't try to kill me—she tried to kidnap me. Why?"

Her mouth opened as understanding dawned. "She wants your Spark."

"Ginevere can gather the Spark out of a tear and craft it into a rune. The only blessing is that her runes eventually run out of magic. But I collect the Spark of anyone I meet, essentially their magical ability becomes my own. So imagine if Geeni crafts a rune out of my tear, then uses it to steal someone else's Spark. Even if the rune with my Spark expires—"

Elliya gasps. "Would she still keep the Spark she had stolen?"

The queen looked at her with dark eyes. "I don't want to find out, do you?"

Elliya tried to imagine Geeni unbounded by the need to continually manipulate tears out of people. Once she stole someone's Spark, Geeni wouldn't need to keep them alive anymore.

Elliya shook the terrifying thought out of her mind. "You're hiding from her so she can't get one of your tears."

The queen laughed bitterly. "If she could just find me

alone in my room on a truly bad night, she could harvest a river of my tears."

Elliya's eyes opened wide, but she didn't speak.

"Being a tiger is the only thing that brings me a bit of relief on those dark nights." The queen's lips pinched. "Drazen and the scholars have been desperately searching for a cure for my illness, but until they do, I can't trust anyone with my tears."

Elliya studied the sad woman who possessed the hint of a sad tiger in her eyes. She whispered, "You believe you're alone."

The queen snapped her head and stared at her with narrowed eyes.

Elliya braved the woman's glare, which was more fearful than the tiger's. "When you were the tiger, I sensed you were sad because you were alone—the only one of your kind. But you aren't the tiger, and you aren't alone."

"Did you not hear me?" growled the woman. "I can't trust anyone with my tears."

Elliya crossed her arms. "You can trust your sons."

The queen blew out a breath, her anger dissipating on the wind. "I can't burden them with this. They already bear too much."

"They want to help you. Hawthorne was planning a fool's errand to Verkeshe, hoping he could discover an answer. They're desperate to help."

The queen looked at her, her bright green eyes weighed down by sadness and doubt. "And what if there is no way to help? What if there is no answer?"

Elliya rested a tentative hand atop the queen's. "Maybe there isn't an answer. But at least you won't be alone."

The queen raised a single brow, the movement reminiscent of the tiger's twitching brow. "And what about you? Aren't you joining the monastery to spend your life alone?

My son is now in Ginevere's clutches ... Do you plan to abandon him and enjoy your days in quiet contemplation, safe and alone?"

The queen's accusation stirred a ferocity she hadn't realized she possessed. "I will not abandon him," she growled. "I bared my throat to a tiger with the foolish hope you'd help me rescue him." After the heated words left her mouth, she bit her lip. It wasn't wise to speak to a queen or a tiger in anger.

The queen's mouth curved in the barest hint of a smile. "Good. It will take bravery to rescue him."

Elliya sighed, shoulders slumping. "I'm not brave. I lived with my stepmother's abuse my entire life, and I never tried to fight back. Eventually, I even stopped trying to run away. If I couldn't stand up to my stepmother, how will I fight Geeni and her magic?"

"There are ways to fight that don't involve violence. Though I wouldn't fault you if you turned to violence against a child abuser." Her eyes glinted darkly. "People like that should be stopped at all costs." She shook the dark look out of her eyes and studied Elliya. "I'm sure you found ways to rebel against your stepmother, though they felt small at the time."

She wanted to automatically deny any rebellious spirit, but a tiny rebellion popped into her mind. "I stole my mother's journal out of the library and hid it in my room."

The queen's eyes lit up. "She would have beaten you for that, wouldn't she?"

"Yes," Elliya whispered. "But it would have been worth it." More small rebellions popped up: spacing out her mother's books so her stepmother wouldn't detect them, reading late into the night, singing under her breath ... She had rebelled quietly, in the ways she could, in the places worth the risk.

"You're stronger than you think," said the queen. "And you're stronger than Ginevere or your stepmother can imagine." Her eyes took on a faraway expression. "They remind me of a man I knew when I was young. He believed I was a weak child and thought to control me. But eventually he learned the truth—that I was stronger than he ever expected."

Hawthorne's story about the queen's father ran through her mind, all the way to the man's violent death on the day of their wedding, courtesy of a cursed tiger.

The queen stood smoothly and looked down at an open-mouthed Elliya with a feral grin. "They never expect you to fight back. But sometimes, fighting back once is all it takes." The queen's grin widened, and suddenly she was the tiger with fangs bared. She dipped her head in farewell and began to limp away.

Elliya closed her gaping mouth, then choked out, "Your Majesty?"

The tiger turned with brow whiskers raised.

Elliya unwrapped the necklace from her wrist and dropped it into the grass. "Don't forget. You aren't alone."

The tiger tilted her head, and Elliya knew the queen could now hear the same conversation she did, from a pair of rabbits nearby.

Is that a tiger or a person? I'm confused.

Maybe both? That's why the tiger never ate any of us. Because she's a person.

People aren't scary—they give us snacks. But this one still seems kinda scary.

Elliya got the sense of tiny rabbit shoulders shrugging. *Maybe we'll invite her for dinner and see what happens.*

See what happens? What if she eats us for dinner?

Elliya chuckled quietly as the bunnies continued their conversation. The tiger queen stared at Elliya for several long moments, then opened her mouth and let out a roar that echoed throughout the menagerie. Instead of cowering in fear, the animals answered with chirps, squeaks, and grunts, welcoming her to the neighborhood.

A quiet growl of command rumbled in the tiger's chest, and though Elliya still couldn't read her mind, she knew what the queen had said.

"Yes, Your Majesty. I will get him back. I swear it."

PART III

28

Elliya woke to the prick of claws against her chest. She gasped, sitting up straight in bed, and the kitten tumbled onto the sheets beside her with an indignant glare.

I'm hungry.

Elliya sighed and rubbed her chest. In her dream, it had been a tiger's claws, but a tiny scratch marred her chest, not a gash caused by the tiger.

The tiger who was a queen.

She brushed her chaotic hair away from her sweaty face and tried to collect her thoughts. The tiger hadn't attacked her last night, but she'd done something more terrifying— she'd tasked Elliya with rescuing the prince. She had to track down her godmother, even though Geeni was always the one who came to her.

Elliya tugged the tight bodice of her ball gown, unsure how she'd slept in such an uncomfortable dress. Last night, she had stumbled barefoot through the menagerie and back to the monastery, then had fallen into her bed without changing. Her rest had been anything but restful, but it had produced at least one result.

She knew the first step.

Elliya dressed in her white dress and apron, then folded up the ball gown neatly, even though it was in rough shape. She found a new pair of shoes to replace the ones she had left in Alanna's carriage, then hid the glass slippers and her mother's journal in secret corners of the monastery. And after feeding the hungry kitten, she went to the lab.

Lliadain hadn't arrived yet, but Kensley was nibbling on a cookie as she took notes on a mouse's blood sample.

Elliya bowed politely. "Good morning, Sister. I need to beg a favor."

Kensley's golden brown eyes lit up. "I don't think you've ever asked for anything during your time here. What is it you need?"

Elliya took a deep breath and made her request. "May I please have the day off? I need to go ..." She swallowed her fear. "Home."

"Home?" asked Kensley. "I ... I thought you were an orphan?"

"I am. It's my stepmother's home." She averted her eyes. "It's complicated."

Kensley studied her a little too closely. "Yes, families can be complicated. That's why scholars vow to not have their own. Usually the families we are born into are more than enough complication."

Elliya bit her lip. "Yes, Sister. I just need to speak to my stepmother, then I'll come back. But it's a long walk. I made the walk there and back yesterday, but—"

"You saw your stepmother yesterday?" The scholar's eyes had fixed on Elliya's arm and the dark bruise that peeked out past her sleeve.

"Um ... yes, but it was in my free time—"

"I'm coming with you." Kensley began packing away the blood samples.

Elliya's mouth fell open. "Oh, um ... that's not—"

Kensley gave her a significant look. "Most families are complicated, but some are much, much more. You don't have to go alone, Elliya."

Elliya's heart warmed as she considered this sweet but fierce scholar taking on her stepmother.

For her.

She swallowed a lump in her throat. "Thank you, Sister. That means more than you know. But I must do this alone." She spoke quickly so Kensley couldn't interrupt. "I'll be okay. I promise. And ... after I speak to her today, this is the last time I will ever step foot in that house."

Kensley considered her with a thoughtful expression, then she sighed. "If this is something you need to do, I won't stop you." She dug inside her scholar's robes and handed Elliya a few coins. "But don't walk. Hire a carriage. It will be hard enough without the exhaustion of a long walk."

Tears sprang to Elliya's eyes at the scholar's kindness. She took the coins and headed out.

Elliya stood at the front door, trying to convince herself to knock. She had never entered through the front door and had only left through it once—the day Geeni had rescued her. Elliya always entered through the kitchen door, quiet and unseen. But she couldn't sneak in today. She needed an answer, and her stepmother was the only one with a clue.

She drew in a deep breath and knocked.

Her stepmother pulled open the door with a pleasant expression on her face. The moment she realized it was Elliya, her face shifted into her usual anger but mixed with a layer of confusion. Apparently, she was just as surprised by Elliya at the front door.

"What in the Twins' names—"

"Good morning, Stepmother. May I come in?"

This was not one of their usual scripts, and her stepmother seemed unsure what to do. She took a single step out of the way, and Elliya walked inside.

Once her stepmother closed the door, Elliya second-guessed her decision to come inside. Maybe she should have asked her question from the doorstep? The closed door felt like it sucked all the air out of the room. Was Elliya trapped? Would she ever leave again?

She closed her eyes and drew in a breath. Of course she would leave again. She had to save the prince. No one would stop her— not Geeni and not her stepmother.

Elliya's eyes snapped open. "You sold my mother's books."

Her stepmother still seemed a little off-kilter from the unusual conversation, but she recovered by falling into a common script. "Everything in this house belongs to me, you ungrateful child. I can do with it whatever I choose."

Elliya didn't let herself get distracted by falling into her usual response. "What did she say to you? How did she pay? Did she take the books immediately, or did she have them shipped somewhere?"

Her stepmother had said someone had offered her a lot of money for those books, which had only happened after Elliya retrieved one. And the only person who knew Elliya had come from this house was Geeni. This was the only clue she had to discovering Geeni's location.

Her stepmother looked confused at the barrage of questions. "Why do you want to know? Do you think you'll get them back?"

Elliya shook her head. "I don't care about the books—"

Her stepmother pounced. "Of course you care! You want

everything that weak woman once possessed. But I told you
—I own everything in this house—"

"You can have this house and everything in it!" Elliya
shook with a fury she had never felt before. "All I need to
know is where you sent those books, and I will leave and
never come back."

Her stepmother's eyes widened at Elliya's outburst, the
woman finding it as strange as Elliya did. Then her eyes
narrowed as an icy rage settled onto her face. She looked at
Elliya with pure disgust and whispered, "There is not a day
that goes by that I don't wish you had been the one to die
instead of them."

Though the rage was the same, her stepmother's words
weren't the usual script. The woman missed someone who'd
died? Not Elliya's parents—she obviously hated Elliya's
mother and resented her father for dying and leaving her
alone. Elliya shook her head. "Who died?"

The rage still simmered, but a deep sadness shifted
behind her stepmother's eyes. "Your stepsisters. My true
daughters. You lived, but it should have been them."

Elliya's mind raced as she considered this new revelation.
Her stepmother had never spoken of her daughters. She
must have lost them when Elliya was a young child, before
her father had died. Would Elliya's life have been any
different if those daughters had lived? Would her stepmother
have been kinder? Or would she have been just as evil?

A bird fluttered against the window. *Watch out!*

Elliya turned just as her stepmother raised the cane,
preparing to swing.

Elliya caught it between two hands, surprising both
herself and her stepmother. Her usual reflex was to duck
from the swing, so attempting to protect herself felt strange.
Though her hands stung and her arms hurt from catching

the weight of her stepmother's swing, triumph swelled through her.

Her low voice was fierce. "You will not hurt me again."

Her stepmother gaped at her, but didn't release her hold on the cane still held between them.

Elliya stared into the woman's eyes, though she rarely did. Even though tears threatened, she held them in. She didn't want her stepmother to mistake them for weakness.

She clung to the cane and spoke with a quiet intensity. "I would have been your true daughter, if you would have had me. There was no need to lay a hand on me—I would have cooked and cleaned to please you. I would have been the most loyal child, caring for you for your entire life. You could have had a true daughter and a legacy. But you rejected me. And now, your family line will end. You are the last, and you are all alone."

Elliya ripped the cane away, and the woman stumbled back a step, shocked.

Elliya rested the tip of her father's cane on the ground, showing her possession. "Goodbye, Stepmother." She strolled to the door, the cane clicking with each step.

Her stepmother hissed, "You'll never get those books back. That red-haired woman took them with her, and you'll never find them."

Elliya's hand stilled on the doorknob. "Red-haired woman?"

Her stepmother laughed. "Yes, she was quite determined to buy them for her mysterious employer. And now, you'll never see your mother's books again."

Elliya turned back, determination spreading across her face. "Thank you, Stepmother. That's exactly the clue I needed." She tilted her head politely. "Goodbye." As she pulled the door shut, her stepmother's look of outrage was the last thing she saw.

29

———

As the bouncing carriage bore Elliya away from her stepmother's house for the last time, her hands trembled so badly she could barely hold her father's cane on her lap. She still couldn't believe she had stood up to her stepmother. All the fear she had suppressed in that moment shook through her body now that she was alone. She couldn't stop the tears from falling, and a sob burst from her lips, mixed with wild laughter.

She had never felt so free. Not even when Geeni rescued her. Geeni had been the one to take the initiative, but today Elliya left of her own free will. She wasn't hiding from her stepmother anymore. She was alive and free.

She leaned her head back against the carriage seat and savored her freedom for exactly one exhaled breath before remembering Hawthorne. He wasn't free at all. She tried to imagine what was happening to him right at this moment ... Was he tied up? Shackled? Knocked unconscious? Was he still in the form of the young woman? If he had changed back into himself, had they given him new clothes to wear, or was he still dressed as a chambermaid?

She couldn't even smile at the adorable image because

of the question she was trying to avoid: what did Geeni want with him? And the even scarier question: what if she didn't need him alive?

When the carriage pulled up to the monastery, Elliya thanked the driver and put the questions out of her mind. She had to focus only on the next step, otherwise she would fall to pieces and never find him. So she deposited her father's cane in her room and walked calmly to find Lliadain.

Elliya had expected Geeni to retrieve the books herself, but her stepmother had met Geeni before, and she'd clearly said red-haired woman, not pink. Sure, there were a lot of red-haired women in Isandine, but there was a reason Geeni had only gone after her mother's books after Elliya had retrieved one and shown it to the scholars—because Geeni had another spy in the monastery.

And unlike Elliya before today, Lliadain *knew* she was a spy.

Elliya headed to the lab and once again only found Kensley. The scholar laid down her pen and hurried to the other side of the lab table.

"How did it go? Are you okay? You can take the rest of the day off if you need it."

Elliya's heart warmed at the woman's kindness. "Thank you, Sister. You've always been so kind to me." She took a breath and tried to speak as casually as she could. "I'm surprised to find you working alone."

Kensley gave her a pitying expression. "Ah, you expected to find the prince. I haven't seen him today. I think he's already left on his mission to Verkeshe."

"Oh ... um ... yes, that does appear to be what happened." She shook her head, unable to waste any time on explanations. "No, I meant Lliadain."

Kensley shrugged. "I haven't seen her today. She's been busy with a lot of her own projects lately."

Elliya muttered, "I bet she has."

Kensley didn't respond to the comment because she was still covertly checking Elliya for new bruises. A sudden thought struck Elliya, and she blurted out her confession before she could second-guess herself.

"I have a Spark."

Kensley's head pulled back in confusion. "What ... How do you know that word?"

"Um ... that's a long story. But I just wanted you to know I have a Spark. I can talk to animals. That's why the mice respond so well to me." She had heard their familiar chattering the moment she had walked in. "Oh, and the gray mouse in the far right cage says she has a thread wrapped around her foot. She could use help to get untangled."

Kensley's eyes opened wide, then her mouth split into a grin. "That's so wonderful, Elliya! What a blessing from the Goddesses!" She placed a gentle hand on Elliya's arm. "But we have to keep this a secret. You understand that, don't you?"

Dread curled in her gut. "I shouldn't tell the other scholars."

Kensley gave her an odd look. "Of course you can tell the scholars. It's the people outside the monastery who might be a danger to you. We're the only ones who can be trusted with this knowledge. No one else can know."

Elliya raised a brow. "Not even the princes?"

"Perhaps someday we can share this with them, but for everyone's safety, this information needs to stay only among Sisters." Kensley looked uncomfortable at this admission.

"What about Drazen, the queen's royal advisor? He knows."

Kensley bit her lip. "Yes, he knew before he arrived in

Isandariyah, because of his own Spark. As Sisters, we would have preferred to keep the knowledge completely to ourselves, but we have an agreement with Drazen based on the common goal of protecting the queen."

"Now that you know about my Spark, what does that mean? Am I trapped inside the monastery forever?"

"What? Of course not! This is not a prison. We offer sanctuary for those with Sparks to keep them safe, but many people choose to leave. We do our best to help them hide." Kensley dropped her voice to a whisper. "Outside these walls are people who would take advantage of your Spark for their own nefarious purposes."

Elliya spoke slowly. "Yes, I can imagine."

"If you don't believe me, ask Lliadain."

Elliya's brows shot up. "Ask Lliadain? About people with Sparks?" Lliadain had given Elliya a pretty strict warning about what would happen if she revealed her Spark. What did Kensley think Lliadain would say instead?

"Lliadain was good friends with a clever young man with an extraordinary Spark. He enjoyed his freedom and often ventured into the city, but one day, he never returned." She picked at the edge of her robes. "Maybe he went on a grand adventure, but I fear something terrible happened to him."

Lliadain had a good friend? Elliya couldn't imagine the prickly woman being friendly with anyone. And he suddenly disappeared? Maybe this man had been another of Geeni's spies? Although if he was, wouldn't it have made more sense for him to remain in the monastery to gather information?

"Thank you for sharing all that with me, Sister. I think I'll go find Lliadain to ask her all about it."

30

———

Elliya found Lliadain in the records room. Most of Elliya's work in the records room had been dusting files and organizing the scholars' experiment notes. Now that she knew who Lliadain worked for, everything the scholar did had a new meaning.

"Hello, Sister."

Lliadain jumped and snapped shut the file she had been reading. "Oh, Elliya, hello. You startled me. How did you know I was in here?"

Elliya stalked closer. "Luci told me."

Lliadain's brows shot up, and she whispered harshly, "I told you to keep your Spark—"

"Yes, but why? What will happen if I tell one of the Sisters?"

Lliadain crossed her arms, adopting her usual haughty glare. "You are accorded freedoms you wouldn't have if you were under the watchful eyes of the other scholars. No more working in the palace or going to balls—"

Elliya nodded as she finally understood. "Most people barely notice me, so I can slip into the palace basically unseen, but if the Sisters know I have a Spark, they'll suddenly pay more attention to me, and I'll lose my effectiveness as a spy."

Lliadain choked, her eyes shooting wildly around the empty records room. "What are you talking about? I—"

"I know we both work for Geeni."

The scholar's mouth opened and closed, but she didn't respond.

Elliya shrugged, as if the revelation were no big deal. "You don't have to hide anything from me, Lliadain. I know that Geeni—"

Lliadain grabbed her arm and hissed, "Stop saying her name!"

Elliya ground her teeth to keep from admitting that Lliadain had taken hold of her bruised arm. Instead, she used the pain to focus. "Fine. We both have the same benefactor."

Lliadain released her arm with a huff. "'Benefactor'? Is that what you call her?"

"I typically call her Godmother." Elliya had already used up most of her false bravado, so she resorted to the truth. "She saved me, Lliadain. Before she found me, I was sad and lonely and broken, but the day she pulled me out of that house, she changed my life forever."

A hint of pity shone through Lliadain's tough exterior. "Our 'benefactor' does tend to change lives." She tilted her head, studying Elliya closer. "Why did you seek me out? If you are truly as clever as you seem, you would realize we shouldn't have clandestine meetings like this."

"I need to contact her."

Lliadain's eyes narrowed in suspicion. "Why?"

Elliya's heart pounded. She didn't have any new information for Geeni, at least none she wanted to share. She only had one thing in her possession she could give. "I have something for her ... My mother's final journal."

Lliadain's eyes widened a fraction before falling back into their arrogant glare. "You can just give it to me, and I'll take it to her."

Even though she was prepared to sacrifice the journal if it meant saving the prince, she couldn't bring herself to just hand it over to the woman. "It's hidden at my stepmother's house. I want to tell my godmother where it's located."

Lliadain huffed and crossed her arms. "You can tell me since I'm the one she will send to get it."

This wasn't going the way Elliya had planned. Why did the prince think she could do this? She hadn't even known she was a spy, so how was she suddenly supposed to learn how to be a counterspy? Elliya couldn't let the conversation continue as it was, or Lliadain would convince her to return to her work, quiet and docile. She had to turn the conversation on its head.

"And how do I know I can trust you?"

Lliadain spluttered, "What? Of course you can trust—"

"I know nothing about you, Lliadain. Why do you work for her?"

Lliadain's pale face turned red, but it appeared to be a blush, not from anger. "It's none of your business why—"

"See? That's why I can't trust you. I don't know what you'll do with the information I give you. I need to speak to Geeni myself."

Lliadain flinched at the name, then she growled, "If you tell me where the journal is, I'll get it and take it straight to Gee—um ... to *her*. Just tell me and—"

"No, I don't think so. If you won't tell me how to contact her myself, I'll just wait until our next scheduled meeting. Although, that's several days from now, so hopefully she doesn't get angry about having to wait for new information." Elliya shrugged, as if it didn't affect her at all.

Lliadain bit her lip. "I can't tell you how to find her. Even if it sounds important, I can't risk the punishment if I'm wrong."

Elliya wondered how Geeni punished Lliadain. She had never noticed bruises on the scholar, and Elliya was skilled at noticing the signs.

Lliadain sighed. "Hold on to your information until your next meeting. If our benefactor decides this journal is important enough, she'll contact you."

Elliya wanted to continue to press her point, but she detected a promising restlessness in Lliadain. "Fine. But I will let Geeni know who to punish if she wanted this information sooner." She turned on her heel and strode out of the records room.

As she rounded the corner, she slipped inside a closet, holding the door open a crack. A few moments later, Lliadain hurried past, looking over her shoulder to see if she was being followed. She raised her hood over her coppery hair, then headed out of the monastery.

Elliya grinned and followed her out.

Even though Lliadain was dressed in white, Elliya had to keep a very sharp eye to not lose her in the crowd. But luckily, after only a few blocks, Elliya realized she had some co-conspirators.

She turned right at the next block, said a rat as it scurried behind a crate.

She slowed down, so be careful when you turn the next corner, said a squirrel.

She finished speaking to the guards at the city gate, said a soaring lark. *Then she headed down the main road and took the second narrow path to the left.*

The animals sensed her need to follow Lliadain and

kindly assisted her. Elliya thanked each animal as she passed, and at the gates, the guards saw her white dress and immediately disregarded her, allowing her to leave the city with no explanation. Geeni was smart to have spies dressed as Sisters. They could go anywhere without a second glance.

Elliya stepped outside the city walls and stopped dead in her tracks.

Tall trees rose on both sides of the road, the jungle only barely tamed even this close to the city. A wide road cut through the trees, and in the distance lay patches of farmland tucked inside the thick jungle. She had never ventured this far, had never imagined trees could grow so large or that the jungle was just a step outside the walls.

And she'd never imagined that inside the trees lived magnificent cities of animals. Their voices were so overwhelming that she stumbled and fell against a farmer's wagon.

The farmer asked, "Are you okay, miss?"

His horse asked the same thing.

She nodded to them both, but couldn't open her mouth to respond.

This was nothing like the menagerie. The animals at the palace were all neatly divided into their enclosures, and they chatted quietly, content and well fed. But out here, the voices were chaotic—calling out their location to one another, fighting for the best spot in the nest or fighting for their lives, songs of seduction and conquest, and a never-ending desire for food. The demands for food reminded her of Luci, but now it was magnified by an entire jungle's worth of creatures.

It was overwhelming and exhilarating. She suddenly felt larger than just herself. The animals were an extension of her body and thoughts, and she breathed in the heady power. Never in her life had she felt so strong. Had she always had this inside? What would her life have been like if she had recognized this power while living in her stepmother's house?

She's getting away! called a toucan.

Elliya jumped, pushing the animals' voices to the edges of her awareness, focusing only on the toucan. "Sorry, I'm coming."

She pushed her way past the wagons on the wide road and followed the toucan's flight onto a narrow dirt path. Though her dress was a lightweight cotton, she was still sweating fiercely. The trees curved overhead, blocking out the sun, but also stopping any breeze. She tiptoed down the path, out of Lliadain's sight, guided only by the voices of the animals.

I see something, said a soaring cockatoo. *A huge den built inside the trees.*

It belongs to that awful pink-haired lady, said an iguana chomping on leaves.

Elliya turned in the iguana's direction. "You've seen her here?" she whispered. "A woman with pink hair?"

She got the sense of shrugging shoulders. *I'm a local,* said the iguana.

"Is her den heavily guarded?" She wasn't sure how well an iguana could evaluate a stronghold's defenses, but then again, Elliya didn't know much herself.

She kicked us all out, said a jaguar. He sat calmly on the dirt path, watching Elliya closely. *Screamed at us, called us filthy pests, and threatened our lives if we didn't stay far away from the citadel.*

"She threatened you? In your own home?" A deep anger boiled in Elliya's gut at the thought of Geeni displacing these creatures and using Elliya's Spark to do it.

Not just threatened. The woman killed my mate to prove it.

A growl bubbled up in Elliya's throat. "I will stop her."

The jaguar blinked once, slowly.

Elliya straightened her dress and nodded at the jaguar. "Lliadain has taken us far enough."

The jaguar went from perfectly still to a blur of spots in a flash.

Elliya kept walking until she spotted them. Lliadain had frozen in the middle of the path, staring down the sleek jaguar. Elliya would have felt bad for the scholar if she didn't know the woman was a spy.

"Thank you, Lliadain. I can find my way from here."

The scholar jumped, half spinning to see Elliya, before turning her eyes back to the growling jaguar. "What are you doing, Elliya? You need to get out of here!"

Elliya crossed her arms. "I'm not afraid of the jaguar. I asked for his help."

Lliadain's brows pulled together, her eyes still locked on the big cat. "The jaguar isn't the most dangerous thing in this jungle."

"Are you trying to protect me? Or just protect yourself from Geeni finding out you led me here?"

The scholar took a step closer but shied back when the jaguar bared his teeth. "Please, Elliya." She raised her shaking hands and offered them in surrender. "Not everything is as it appears. I don't want to hurt you, but Geeni—"

"I don't want to hurt you either, which is why this jaguar will lead you to his den and watch you until I've finished what I need to do," said Elliya. "I can't have you running to Geeni to tell her I'm anything more than a scared little chambermaid." She stalked closer as if she were the jaguar. "Because I *am* a scared little chambermaid, but I'm also much, much more."

Lliadain's eyes widened. "You can't defeat her, Elliya. She has too many Sparks. She's—"

"I might not be strong enough to defeat her, but there's one thing I will do ... I will rescue the prince."

Lliadain huffed an incredulous laugh. "Rescue the prince?"

"Yes, I will rescue him. But I need to know what you told Geeni about my ... relationship ... with him."

Lliadain gave her an arch look. "What relationship? Neither scholars nor scholar apprentices should be distracted by relationships."

Elliya spoke slowly, "You didn't tell her anything about us? You definitely noticed how close we are. Geeni would want to know that information ... Why didn't you tell her?"

Lliadain acted as if Elliya hadn't spoken. "Geeni keeps her prisoners locked up using runes. You can't rescue him or the others. Believe me, I've tried."

Elliya's eyes snapped to her face. "You've already tried?"

Lliadain ignored her question. "She holds the only key to the prisoners' cages. Food and water are handed through the bars without opening the door." Her eyes took on a haunted look. "Some cages haven't been unlocked in years."

Elliya stalked closer, her eyes focused on Lliadain's face. The scholar ducked her head, trying to hide from Elliya's penetrating gaze, but with the jaguar so close, she couldn't move.

"Who else is trapped in her cages?" asked Elliya. "Is that the power she has over you?"

Lliadain bit her lip, still refusing to meet her eyes.

Elliya took the scholar's arm. "I will rescue the prince, along with anyone else I find in Geeni's cages."

Lliadain's usual haughty look returned. "Geeni has guards everywhere. You can't sneak past them."

"Oh, I'm not sneaking in," said Elliya as a mischievous grin spread across her lips. "I'm walking directly in the front door."

31

———

The guards discovered Elliya before she reached the front door. Two henchwomen escorted her inside, the same two who had captured Hawthorne—the curvaceous blond woman, Trudy, and the tall black-haired woman, Nix. They gave her a curious look, but didn't touch her. Apparently, they didn't believe her much of a threat. After all, how much threat could an apprentice scholar and occasional chambermaid be?

That was exactly what Elliya wanted them to believe.

She didn't need to fake her awe as they led her through Geeni's jungle lair. She had always known her godmother was wealthy—in addition to her expensive carriage and fine clothes, she had paid Elliya's stepmother enough money to allow her to leave. But Geeni's hideout was an actual fortress in the middle of the jungle.

The henchwomen led her down a curving path between massive banyan trees, and inside the wall of convoluted roots rose an ancient citadel. The moss-covered walls fit neatly beneath the giant banyans, and in some places, tree roots had cracked open the weathered stones.

Though the jungle had reclaimed the outer portion of

the citadel, Geeni had built a cozy hideout inside the ancient fortress. From the outside Elliya had expected dirt floors, but no sign of cracked stone marred the interior, only smooth marble floors and walls.

Her footsteps slowed. The citadel was so quiet. No mice scurried in the walls. No birds fluttered outside. Geeni had used Elliya's Spark to scare away every animal. After experiencing the heady feeling of power in the jungle, the silence inside was overwhelming.

The henchwomen didn't slow as they passed a laundry room, sleeping quarters, and a kitchen. Elliya scrambled to catch up to them, again noticing how unconcerned they were with her presence.

Nix knocked on the double doors at the end of the hall, and at a muffled word from within, she opened both doors and led Elliya inside.

Dark mahogany shelves filled with books and odd trinkets lined the walls of the study. Stone sconces highlighted the perimeter of the windowless room, and they glowed with a steady internal light, though Elliya couldn't determine how. A matching mahogany desk sat in the center of the room, piled with multiple stacks of books.

Elliya's mother's books.

Geeni sat with her boots propped on the desk, leaning back in her plush chair, and barely looked up from her book. "What is it?"

"We found her wandering around outside," said Nix.

Geeni's head jerked up, and she finally noticed Elliya. She blinked several times, confusion flickering in her jade eyes. Elliya had never seen the woman anything other than confidently calm. How many people had ever truly surprised Geeni?

Her godmother snapped the book shut, as if embarrassed to be caught reading Elliya's mother's book. In that moment, Elliya felt the power imbalance between them shift. She had found Geeni without her permission and had caught her in several lies, or at least several omissions of truth. She had surprised her godmother, and being surprised meant Geeni wasn't in control.

When that lack of control registered on Geeni's face, it was immediately followed by a flash of the expression Elliya was uniquely skilled to detect.

Anger.

Though Geeni's henchwomen didn't appear to notice, Elliya sensed the woman's fury boiling beneath her calm exterior. She couldn't afford to make her godmother angry enough to imprison her or worse. She had to return their relationship to the way it used to be. Geeni needed to believe Elliya wasn't a threat so she could free the prince.

So, despite her boosted confidence from shocking Geeni and the power she had discovered when she stepped into the jungle, Elliya reverted to the posture of her past.

She dropped to her knees, her head and shoulders bent, hands tightly clutching her dress. "I'm so sorry, Godmother. After these women took the prince away, the queen blamed me for not stopping them. She was so angry—I thought she would hurt me. Please, don't send me back."

Though she had debased herself with babbling apologies for her stepmother so many times, this time she felt no embarrassment. She wasn't afraid of the beating she might receive from Geeni—in fact, she would welcome the pain if it meant Geeni would view her again as a weak child. That would make her rescue of the prince even easier.

Geeni's bootsteps thumped around her desk and stopped before Elliya. "How did you find me?" Her voice was crisp, devoid of the sweetness from their past conversations.

"Lliadain told me." Elliya glanced up into the woman's cold jade eyes, then immediately ducked her head again.

"It's not her fault, Godmother. I begged her to tell me. She took pity on me because I was distraught."

"And how did you discover Lliadain knew me?"

Elliya bowed her head lower. "It was an accident. Please, don't be angry with her, Godmother. I'm so sorry."

"If someone followed you ..." The words were a cold threat.

Elliya lifted her head enough to see Geeni's boots standing on the rug before the desk.

The rug was the skinned hide of a jaguar.

Even though anger simmered in her veins, the ominous sight helped her to retrieve the only weapon she possessed.

Tears blurred her vision as she tilted her head up to Geeni. "I'm so sorry for showing up without your permission. After all you've done for me ... I'm just so grateful. Please, please don't send me away." She blinked, and fat tears rolled down her cheeks.

Geeni's gaze traced the path left by the tears. Elliya had a moment of panic that the woman might kill her, then gather the tears from her lifeless body. But her godmother reached out slowly and wiped away the tears with a gentle hand. "Oh, Elliya ... how can I stay angry at such a sweet girl? Your rough life has left you practically overflowing with tears. The Goddesses obviously sent you to me as a gift."

Her kind words set Elliya's teeth on edge. All the other nice things Geeni had ever said flashed through her mind, and she realized Geeni truly meant them. She saw Elliya as her treasure, as someone to protect.

Because her godmother planned to harvest tears from Elliya for her entire life.

Geeni calmly rubbed the gathered tears on the charm on her bracelet, then she looked up at Nix and Trudy. "Make sure no one followed her. If you see anyone, kill them first and ask questions later." The henchwomen nodded sharply and left.

Geeni softened her tone from the clipped command and spoke to Elliya as if to a child. "What am I going to do with you?"

Elliya continued to kneel, but she sat up as straight as a loyal dog. "I can cook and clean, Godmother. I promise I will do a good job."

Geeni leaned back against her desk and crossed her arms. "So you spoke to the queen? After the prince was taken?"

"Well, she did most of the speaking ... yelling, I guess." She lowered her head, feigning fear while trying to picture the imaginary scene.

"And what did you think of her? You told me before that she looked sad. Did she still seem like a pitiable creature?"

Her godmother was attempting to determine her allegiances. Elliya needed to prove her loyalty, while not giving Geeni any information she could use against the queen. "She was terrifying. But I held the necklace you gave me so she couldn't use her magic against me."

Geeni raised a brow. "She never saw the necklace? And you never removed it?"

"Of course not, Godmother," she said quickly. "You told me to keep it hidden and that it would keep me safe from her." No need to reveal the queen now had Elliya's Spark.

Geeni hummed thoughtfully. "Nix told me you were in a ball gown and that you broke the glass slippers I gave you."

Luckily, Elliya was prepared to give this explanation. "A drunk party guest attacked me." She lifted the sleeve of her white dress to fully reveal the purple bruise on her arm. "He ripped my chambermaid uniform, and I was too embarrassed to ask for a new one. I stole the gown, hoping I could escape into the crowd, but when I ran away, the glass slippers cracked. I'm sorry, Godmother. They were so beautiful." She trembled, and a shiny tear ran down her cheek.

Geeni smirked, her attention drawn to the tear and away from Elliya's flimsy story. She casually wiped the tear away. "Hmm ... I wonder why no one has announced the prince is missing. Why are they keeping it a secret?"

Sister Kensley believed Hawthorne had already left for Verkeshe, but Elliya gave Geeni the reasons she'd find more pleasing. "Maybe the queen is embarrassed that you kidnapped him out from under her nose? Or maybe she's waiting to see what you want for his return?" Elliya shrugged, as if the captured prince was not the entire reason for her appearance. "I bet the queen would give you anything you wanted if you'd return him."

Geeni grinned like a smug cat. "I bet you're right, little mouse. But I plan on keeping him a little longer. I'm prepared to let the queen sweat before I make my demands. Besides, he's a tame prisoner. He walked peacefully into his cage without even saying a word."

Elliya's heart clenched as she imagined Hawthorne walking silently into a cage, cooperating solely because of his belief in her. She couldn't let him down. She tried not to reveal her true feelings, but at Geeni's raised eyebrow, she wondered if she'd failed.

"Tell me, little mouse, are you not concerned that I have kidnapped a prince? That I hold him prisoner in an underground cage with plans to use him against the queen? Does that not concern you?"

"I trust you, Godmother." Elliya swallowed her disgust and turned it into a pleading sincerity. "You changed my life the day you rescued me, and I will never be the same. I promise I will serve you even more faithfully than I served my stepmother. I'll be so quiet you won't even notice I'm here."

Geeni grinned. "I believe you, little mouse. Someday I might give you a new palace to clean, but for now, you can stay here with me. Just keep the citadel tidy and come find me if you feel sad. Can you remember to do that?"

She gave Geeni a beatific grin that was only partially fake. "I promise I'll remember everything you've ever said."

She would remember everything, like how Geeni had revealed Hawthorne was in an underground cage. Elliya now knew where to look first. She would learn her godmother's secrets, then sneak away and give the information to the people who could defeat her.

Geeni's little mouse was finally ready to be a spy.

32

───────

The moment Geeni dismissed her, Elliya wanted to look for stairs leading down, but instead she calmly walked to the kitchen. The room was lit with the same steady light as Geeni's office, and smelled of strong curry. A tired-looking man stirred a large pot and barely glanced in her direction when she entered. Did he follow Geeni of his own free will, or did her godmother have some leverage over him?

Elliya walked quietly to the counter, picked up a knife, and started chopping carrots. The man studied her, his eyes roaming from her apron to the neatly sliced carrots. He slid an onion next to her cutting board, then turned back to the curry without a word.

As she chopped, Elliya contemplated the knife she held. She had been inside the citadel for less than an hour and already had a weapon in her hand. How easy would it be for her to lure Geeni close with a few onion-induced tears, then slide the knife between her ribs?

Her hands shook when she truly considered it. Elliya was not a fighter, much less a killer. She couldn't stop Geeni with violence ... She had to find her own way.

The man had stopped stirring and had arranged fine porcelain dishes on a wooden tray. He neatly plated the curry with rice and a warm piece of flatbread, then poured mint tea with a heaping scoop of sugar. A stack of sturdy clay dishes waited on the countertop for the rest of the citadel inhabitants, so there was only one place this tray was headed.

"I'll take this to Geeni," she said.

The cook barely shrugged before scooping rice evenly onto the clay dishes.

Elliya lifted the tray, careful not to spill a drop. She had helped cook at the monastery, but hadn't served anyone a meal on a tray since her stepmother. Instead of filling her with dread, the similarity of serving Geeni brought a sly smile to her lips. She was no longer trapped in her stepmother's house, and she wasn't trapped here. She was here by her own choice. Perhaps a reckless choice, but it was hers.

She knocked on Geeni's study door, smoothing her face into placid subservience. Geeni was sitting at her desk again, but this time, she appeared smugly at ease, the power shifted back in her favor. Elliya tiptoed to the desk and lowered the tray without a word. Geeni watched Elliya's movements with twinkling delight in her jade eyes, like a child with a new toy.

Elliya bowed, then backed out of the room without saying a word. She itched to explore the citadel now and find Hawthorne, but she walked back to the kitchen where the cook sat at the counter with his own plate of food. He glanced at the other plate, and Elliya obediently took a seat and ate.

The food was good and still hot. Her stepmother had demanded Elliya wait nearby during her entire meal, which meant Elliya didn't eat until the food was long cold. What would her life have been like if Geeni hadn't dropped her off at the monastery but had brought her to the citadel instead? Elliya imagined that past version of herself—sad and broken, then suddenly safe with plenty to eat ... She would have worshipped Geeni as a benevolent patron and gratefully served her, tucked safely inside the citadel. She would have never stood up to her stepmother, never worked with the scholars, never met the prince ...

Even when she thought herself weak, he believed in her. He didn't baby her by offering protection like Geeni did—he challenged her by walking into Geeni's lair and expecting her to follow. He didn't manipulate her like Geeni did—he asked permission to kiss her, then respected her wishes when she said no. He called out the best in her because of his faith in her.

She would rescue him. Then she'd worry about the dangerous emotions raging in her chest later.

The cook finished his meal, and Elliya accompanied him into the dining room to gather the other dishes. Elliya counted eight women around the table, which didn't seem enough to guard the entire citadel, although judging by the golden bracers they wore, they were each likely much more than they seemed.

She gathered the plates of leftover scraps alongside the quiet man. Nix eyed Elliya thoughtfully as the cook picked up her plate. When they passed Trudy, the blond woman patted the cook on the backside while winking at one of her fellow henchwomen. They laughed loudly, and the man gathered the last plate and shuffled out of the room. Elliya bit her lip and trailed him back to the kitchen.

He moved as if by rote, pulling four wooden bowls off a shelf without looking at Elliya. She deposited the plates on the counter near his stack and watched him work. He dumped the scraps off the plates into the bowls with the leftover bits of burned flatbread he hadn't served. He arranged the bowls on a tray in one hand and hefted a bucket of water in the other hand.

Elliya's breath hitched as she realized where he must be headed. She hurried to his side, taking the tray from his hand. "I'll help."

His eyes said she was strange, then he shrugged and lifted the bucket with both hands.

She walked behind him out of the kitchen, her footsteps silent and her gut tied in knots. She expected one of Geeni's soldiers to call out at any moment and stop her, but no one gave her a second glance. The man stepped into a dark staircase headed down. Elliya tried to still her racing heart and followed him.

At the bottom of the stone staircase waited a barred wooden door. The man lowered the bucket onto the dirt floor and lifted the heavy bar with both hands. The door creaked open, revealing an underground forest of roots.

The banyan trees above had slowly overtaken the ancient storeroom, with thick roots shooting through the ceiling down to the cracked stone floor below. The roots and their creeping tendrils were so thick, she couldn't even see to the edge of the room, other than a faint glow.

This was Geeni's prison.

Even though Elliya's entire goal had been to find where Geeni was holding Hawthorne, now that she was here, terror ran down her spine. What if Geeni had hurt him? What if her godmother's soldiers had beaten him and left him bleeding in a cell all alone? The thought of what Elliya might find terrified her, but she couldn't race ahead of the man with the heavy bucket of water, so she followed him quietly through the twisting path of roots, until they arrived at the source of the glow.

Thick golden bars shone with the light of shimmering

runes carved into their surface, and it took a minute for her eyes to adjust. Between the thick roots stood four cages, and she quickly scanned the prisoners ... Two prisoners lay on the ground, curled in on themselves. One prisoner sat hunched against the bars. And there, in the last cage, stood Hawthorne.

Her breath caught on a sob of relief. She couldn't detect any wounds, and since he was shirtless, it would have been obvious. Shocking images raced through her mind as she considered what Trudy might have done that would leave him shirtless until she remembered he had removed his shirt to put on the chambermaid uniform when he transformed into the princess.

He only wore one shoe—his other shoe was in her pocket. The sight of his bare foot on the dirt floor upset her even more than the lack of a shirt. She would have immediately returned his shoe, except she worried it would give away her true intentions.

She stepped closer, and as Hawthorne's eyes locked with hers, she froze in her tracks. While the other prisoners' postures showed defeat, he stood with his shoulders thrown back and head raised. He looked triumphant. Not because he had conquered anyone, but because he was right.

He'd known she would come for him.

He had been watching the door, waiting for her. And in the light of the glowing gold bars, his eyes plainly revealed his emotion.

Desire.

Not a desire to escape or to defeat Geeni or even to save the queendom, but a desire for *her*. The strength of his desire filled her with a delight as thrilling as it was terrifying. He was so still he barely appeared to breathe, but his lips parted, and he breathed out with no sound, "Elliya ..."

She trembled under the weight of his stare, and the

wooden bowls rattled against the tray. The clatter provided a reminder of her supposed chore, and she spun back to the cook, who stared at her with pinched brows. She hurried to his side as he approached the imprisoned woman, who had slowly raised herself to a seated position. The woman was filthy—the only clean part of her body was her cheeks. Elliya considered the oddity as she handed a bowl of food to the woman while the cook filled her cup with water from his bucket.

Elliya placed a bowl on the ground before the young man in the next cage. He had barely stirred from his place on the ground, and his long black hair hid most of his face.

The cook finished handing out the water, then stood there, watching the prisoners drink. It didn't appear to bring him joy or distress. He just numbly waited.

Elliya guessed his intentions. "I'll wait for them to finish, then gather the dishes and clean them myself."

He stared at her, as if confused by her long string of words. Then he shrugged and shuffled out the door.

Elliya carried a bowl to the next prisoner. His beard was long and his hair tangled, but his cheeks above his beard were clean. He numbly took the bowl from her hands.

She left the tray on the ground and carried the remaining bowl to the last cage.

Hawthorne stood in the same place, his eyes tracking her every move. As she approached his cage, he watched her with an intensity that sent sparks racing across her skin. Her legs trembled so badly she almost tripped. Had she forgotten how to walk?

She stepped in front of his cage, directly before him. She tried to swallow, but couldn't remember how. As she opened her mouth to see if any words would come out, his eyes dropped to her lips, and suddenly, her lungs forgot how to breathe. So, when she spoke, it was with no air. "I've come to rescue you, Prince."

A reasonable person would have laughed at the ridiculous statement, but Hawthorne's eyes sparkled with delight, a whirlwind of desire still raging below the surface.

"I don't have a way to get you out right now, but I promise I'll discover Geeni's weakness and bring the Queen's Guard back to rescue you." She handed him the wooden bowl with trembling hands. "You should eat. Keep up your strength."

His lips curved in a grin. "In this moment, I feel even stronger than Trudy wearing a bracer full of runes."

Elliya's eyes narrowed as she considered the blond henchwoman. "Did she hurt you? You were disguised as the princess ... Did Trudy turn you back by ... touching you?" Fear and fury warred in her heart. If that woman—

"I'm okay, Elliya. And now that you're here, I'm more than okay." He held his wooden bowl with one hand and gripped a shining bar with the other. "With you here, I feel like I could tear these cages apart myself."

She looked closer at the glowing runes lining the bars. "What do these runes do?"

"The other prisoners told me the cage blocks the Spark of anyone inside. Kind of like those glass slippers, except since these bars are gold-plated steel, they unfortunately aren't as breakable."

Elliya tilted her head as she reached out with her Spark. "Geeni used my stolen Spark to keep every animal out of the citadel, so I can't tell if it's working."

Hawthorne glanced at the other prisoners, a frown spreading across his face. "I don't think it affects the Spark of anyone outside the cage. They told me Geeni comes down at least once a week and her Spark appears to work just fine."

The prisoners' clean cheeks suddenly made sense. She hissed, "She's harvesting their tears?"

Hawthorne nodded sadly. "From what I can gather, some of these prisoners have been here for years. She doesn't torture them—apparently pain ruins the tears—but she finds other ways to convince them to cry. They have been here so long, they've all but given up hope for escape."

Elliya saw something of herself in the hopeless expressions of the prisoners. Though she hadn't been behind gold bars, she had felt just as trapped. Even now, Geeni believed Elliya was just like these prisoners, except so harmless she didn't need a cage.

She growled, the sound reminiscent of the tiger. "Geeni won't keep them any longer. I'm rescuing them, too."

When she turned back, Hawthorne pulled himself closer to the gold bars, his eyes hungry. "I've always said you are truly stunning when you're angry."

The wildfire brewing in her chest commingled with the blush that heated her neck and chest. She cleared her throat. "I can't stay down here much longer. It will raise suspicions, and I need them to forget I'm here to have any chance of smuggling you out."

He straightened from the bars with a resigned sigh. "The runes stop the others from using their Sparks to escape, but the bars themselves are still the true cage. Geeni wears the golden key around her neck. She locked me in herself." He scooped curry onto a burned piece of flatbread and ate while he watched Elliya think.

She bit her lip. "How will I get the key from Geeni? She let me close enough to serve her dinner, but I think she would notice if I tried to lift jewelry from her neck. Maybe someone in the Queen's Guard will know how..."

He leaned casually against the side of his cage as he scraped the bottom of the bowl with his finger. Was this the first meal he had eaten since they captured him? He seemed relatively unbothered to be trapped in a cage, shirtless, slowly licking curry off his finger, black stubble forming on his cheeks. But the sight made her breathless with anger ... and more.

She gripped the gold bars with both hands, pressing her body against the cold metal. "I'm so sorry, Hawthorne. For everything. I don't know how, but I will get you out of here. I swear it."

He dropped the wooden bowl and stormed toward her. He had moved so quickly that she had no time to step away, and now his face was before her, his hands gripping the gold bars just above hers.

He was so close, he could merely dip his head, and his lips would brush hers. He gripped the bars tightly, the muscles in his arms and chest straining under the weight of his restraint. The bars were no barrier to a kiss, but still, he didn't move. He merely stared down at her, waiting.

Her heart pounded a fierce rhythm, forcing her to acknowledge the question burning in her chest.

Why doesn't he just kiss me already?

She thought the guilt of her broken vow would follow the admission, but she only felt a rush of relief at admitting the truth. Yes, she had broken her vow and had fallen in love. And yes, she wanted to kiss him more fiercely than she had ever wanted anything in her life. And she knew the desire in his eyes was reflected in her own. He knew she wanted him to kiss her, but he still resisted. Why?

Because he had asked her for a kiss before, and she had told him no.

He'd said he wouldn't take a kiss without her permission. He had respected her answer then and was still respecting it now.

He didn't kiss her, even though she clearly wanted him

to. Even though she'd faced her stepmother again to find him. Even though she loved him so fiercely, she had walked straight into Geeni's lair to save him. Despite all that, he wouldn't violate her consent.

She would have to ask for the kiss herself.

Asking for what she wanted was foreign to her. Acknowledging her wants had been a sure way to guarantee her stepmother would take them. Better to give up all wants, all desire, and live a safe, bland existence.

But there was no room for someone like Hawthorne in a safe, bland existence. If she wanted him in her life, she had to take the risk. A risk scarier than walking alone into Geeni's lair.

She wet her lips, her mouth suddenly dry.

His eyes shot to her lips, and he drew in a slow breath through his nose while his teeth bit his bottom lip.

"Hawthorne ..." she whispered.

A wooden bowl clattered to the ground.

Elliya sprang away from the bars, her eyes focused on the wooden bowl rolling near her feet.

The bearded man in the next cage stared at them with wide eyes, but when she turned to him, he glanced away. "Um ... sorry, it slipped out of my fingers." He rubbed a hand through his disheveled hair. "I'll face the other direction ... Please continue with whatever ..." He let his words fade away as he took a seat on the ground, occasionally stealing a glance over his shoulder.

Hawthorne hadn't removed his hands from the bars, and he pressed his forehead against the cage with a soft chuckle. "I guess I'll just have to wait until you get me out of here to find out what you were going to ask me."

She bent to gather the wooden bowl, and when she straightened, a new determination filled her. "You won't have to wait long. I'm not waiting for the Queen's Guard. I intend to get that key tonight."

Hawthorne's eyes never left hers as he picked up his own dropped bowl and held it out to her through the bars. "I know you will, Elliya." His hand brushed hers as he gave her the bowl. "And I look forward to speaking to you without bars between us."

It took all her strength to leave him there, trapped inside a golden cage, a captured prince with desire burning in his eyes.

33

Elliya scrubbed the prisoners' wooden bowls more thoroughly than they had ever been scrubbed. Then she wiped down the countertops and swept the kitchen floor. Cleaning helped her organize her thoughts, and her thoughts were currently a raging mess. When she started reorganizing the pantry, the cook merely shrugged and left for the night.

Her thoughts about the prince caused her heart to race, but surprisingly, those thoughts were the most organized. Even though she had no idea what her feelings for him meant about her future as a scholar, she knew what she wanted: to get him out of that cage.

Her hand had floated unconsciously to her lips as she leaned against the pantry shelves. She shook herself out of those thoughts and considered the problem she had to solve first: how to get him out of Geeni's clutches.

First, she had to get the key from around Geeni's neck. The woman didn't seem like the hugging type, so Elliya didn't know how to get close enough to take it without the woman noticing.

Maybe she could convince her godmother to let Elliya

brush her hair? Geeni often wore her pink hair in elaborate styles—if Elliya styled it, maybe she could unclasp the necklace. Elliya had said she'd get the key tonight, but this plan required her waiting until morning, or maybe waiting for days while she convinced Geeni to trust Elliya with her hair.

She pushed that problem aside and considered her next problem: she needed to get the prisoners out of the citadel. Some of them appeared so weak that she wasn't sure if they could walk all the way back to the city, much less run through the jungle with henchwomen on their trail. Elliya had to sneak them out, so no one noticed they were missing until they were long gone.

As she mopped, she considered ways to break them out of prison. The dirt walls were promising for tunneling out, but even if she could gather an army of tunneling creatures willing to sneak inside Geeni's border, it would take them too long to dig a long enough tunnel to make it outside the guards' perimeter.

Sneak onto the roof and see if she could lower the prisoners? No, other than Hawthorne, they were too weak for that.

Disguise them as servants and sneak out? No, there were too few inhabitants of the citadel—it wasn't like the palace, with dozens of servants moving around at all times.

Create a diversion and sneak the prisoners out the front door? No, when the guards realized the distraction, they'd come running and easily find them.

She had scrubbed the kitchen until it sparkled, yet still didn't have an answer. She rubbed her eyes, her exhaustion sinking in. Even though she desperately wanted to rescue Hawthorne and the prisoners tonight, she was forced to admit she had no plan. She needed to rest and see if an answer presented herself.

As she put the mop away, she paused. Where would she

sleep? Everyone had forgotten about her so thoroughly, no one had told her where to find a bed. She imagined curling up beside Hawthorne's cage, falling asleep while holding his hand through the bars ...

Elliya shook off the foolish thought. She couldn't reveal her feelings about Hawthorne or let anyone suspect she considered the prisoners at all. So she headed in the complete opposite direction. When the cook had led her down the old stone staircase, she had noticed another staircase leading up. In her stepmother's house, her room was in the attic, so walking upstairs for bed felt natural.

Geeni had reinforced this staircase with new materials, so it looked like the rest of the renovated citadel, unlike the ancient staircase headed down. When she opened the door at the top of the stairs, her breath caught on a gasp.

Stars lit up the sky, brighter than she had ever seen inside Isandine. Not that she had stargazed much before—her room in the attic only had a small vent leading outside. She had noticed the stars during her walk home from the palace each night, but the interesting sights of the city often distracted her.

But out here, there were only stars.

She stepped closer to the edge of the tower and looked down. Even though the tower was shorter than the massive trees, the ground was still so far away. She was forced to discard any remaining hope that this might be a means to escape.

As she looked out, eyes shone in a banyan tree. She sighed with relief—she hadn't realized how much she enjoyed the voices of the animals until they were gone.

Elliya could speak to the animals without saying a word, but she found it more natural to speak aloud. "Hello, Sir Owl," she whispered. "It's lovely to see you on such a beautiful night."

The owl launched himself off the branch. His wingspan was so wide, Elliya had expected his flight to be a dramatic fluttering of wings, but the owl was perfectly silent as he swooped and landed on the worn stone ledge.

Are you the new boss of this castle?

Elliya whispered, "New boss? No, definitely not. I'm just here trying to help the people she captured."

The owl gave her a considering look. *What a shame. You'd be a much better neighbor than the pink-haired woman. She never greeted us as kindly as you have. She sent out a loud warning, like a mental scream, threatening to kill the children of any animal she found inside her walls.*

"That's awful!" Elliya gasped. "I'm sorry I'm not strong enough to capture her or force her to leave. I can't even figure out a way to complete my much smaller mission of rescuing the prisoners."

The owl fluffed his feathers, settling into a more comfortable position. *What do you need?*

She leaned against the stone parapet, grateful to have someone to talk through the problem with. "I need a secret way out of the citadel."

There are many exits the pink-haired one doesn't know about.

She gasped. "Really?"

The owl's wide eyes looked smug. *If she would have simply asked us about the entrances or watched us long enough to track our movements, she could have discovered them herself and sealed them up. But she just yelled at us to leave, so many of our pathways still remain, especially near the roots.*

"The roots! Yes, that's exactly what I need. Is there a pathway big enough for an animal of my size?"

He shrugged. *I've never been inside, but I can find you one who has.*

She got the sense of a mouse running into a hole near

the trunk of a great banyan tree. The owl's eyes glittered in the dark night.

Elliya gave him a stern look. "I know mice are your dinner, but I'd appreciate you not eating them around me."

He tilted his head to consider her. *If you promise to overthrow the pink-haired one, I swear to eat no animals from your household.*

She frowned. "I can't oust her myself, but once I help the prisoners escape, I will lead the Queen's Guard here to capture her."

The owl nodded, as if that was enough. *So, an exit is all you need?*

She sighed. "No, I also need to get a gold key from around Geeni—the pink-haired lady's neck while she's sleeping. I'm quiet, but not that quiet."

You need a thief. I know exactly the one.

Her mouth dropped open. "But—"

I'll go find the ones you need. The pink-haired one keeps owl hours, so it will be a while until we can steal the key. You should sleep. I'll wake you when it's time. The owl flicked his wings and took off in a silent flurry of feathers.

She wasn't sure whether the owl could deliver what she needed or if he was just an overly confident creature, but since she had no other plan, she curled up beneath the stars and fell asleep.

34

Elliya woke to the tickle of tiny fingers touching her face. Her eyes snapped open. A small monkey patted her cheek, similar in size to Alanna's monkey, except with brown fur and a white face. When her eyes opened, he raised his other hand, which held a key that shimmered faintly in the moonlight.

Is this what you need, boss?

Elliya took the key in shaking fingers. "Yes," she breathed. "How did—"

He shrugged. *I've stolen from her before.* He looked up at the moon. *I stopped after she had one of my brothers killed. Didn't seem worth the risk anymore.* His small eyes shot back to her. *But if you're going to overthrow her and become the new boss—*

"Um ... I didn't say—"

—I decided it was worth the risk. Sometimes you have to take the risk, you know?

She bit her lip, holding back any further explanation, and simply said, "Yes, sometimes you have to take the risk."

The owl silently soared over her head and deposited a

furry creature in her lap. Elliya picked up the trembling mouse as the owl landed on the stone parapet.

The mouse took a deep breath and spoke to the owl. *I can't believe you told the truth about not eating me.*

The owl looked smug.

The mouse sat on her haunches and gazed up at Elliya. *You need a secret exit out of the roots?*

"Yes. Do you know one big enough for animals my size?"

You might have to dig a little at the doorway, but the path was originally for your kind, so you should fit.

Elliya's eyes filled with tears as she looked at the three creatures. "How can I ever repay you?"

Defeat her, boss, said the monkey. *For the sake of our lost kin.*

Elliya tucked the key inside her apron pocket and stood, holding the mouse carefully. "We shouldn't talk to each other once we go back inside. I don't know if Geeni could hear us or not."

The mouse nodded, then allowed Elliya to tuck her inside the apron pocket alongside the key.

Elliya didn't speak to the monkey or the owl, but bowed to them as she reentered the citadel.

As she came to the bottom of the stairs, she looked down the hallway, where a soldier paced back and forth. Elliya prayed she would be just as unnoticeable as she always had been. She walked calmly down the hall, stopping briefly in the laundry room, before heading to the ancient stairs. Her pulse roared in her ears as she descended the old staircase, but she made it all the way to the bottom without the guard calling out to her.

She took a deep breath and lifted the heavy wooden bar on the door. As she pulled the door shut behind her, she realized the missing bar would reveal someone had been inside, but she couldn't fix that. She headed for the glow through the maze of roots.

The other prisoners slept, but Hawthorne stood in his cage exactly as he had when she left. She would have thought he hadn't moved, except his dark hair was mussed like he had just woken. He watched her approach, his eyes as hungry as before. Her instincts wavered between freezing in panic and running to him, but she marched calmly to not jostle the mouse in her pocket.

She stopped directly in front of his cage, and he waited in breathless anticipation. His eyes never left her face as she pulled the golden key out of her pocket, slid it into the lock, and turned it with a soft click.

The door swung open on oiled hinges, and Hawthorne stepped out before her. His presence was overwhelming. The golden skin of his bare chest, the fire in his emerald eyes, his full lips, slightly parted ... She wanted to drown in the intensity of him.

But she had to keep her head, or she could lose it all.

She swallowed her desire and whispered, "Once we are out of here, there is something I would like to ask you, Prince."

His eyes twinkled, the fire undimmed. "I dreamed of your question, Elliya," he whispered.

She shook her head, trying to focus on her prison break, and remembered what she had wanted to give him before. "You dropped this." She pulled his shoe out of her apron pocket.

His fingers brushed hers as he took the shoe. "You are a very considerate savior, Elliya." He bent to slide on his shoe, and Elliya bit her lip as the muscles in his back flexed with the movement.

She cleared her throat and dug in her apron for what

she'd picked up in the laundry room. "And I brought you something else."

He took the shirt from her hand with a playful grin. "You're tired of seeing me shirtless already?"

She ducked her head as a blush rose to her cheeks. "You're too distracting."

He buttoned the shirt with a smug smile.

Elliya unlocked the cage of Hawthorne's neighbor, and the bearded man came awake with a start. "What are you doing?"

"I'm rescuing you," she said. "All of you. Most of the citadel is sleeping, so we need to move as quietly as we can."

The man stared numbly but didn't move. Hawthorne walked slowly inside the cage and lifted the man under his arm to lead him out. The moment the man stepped outside the bars, he straightened with a jerk and clapped his hand over his mouth to cover a laughing sob.

"My Spark," he whispered. "I forgot what it felt like … Oh, Goddesses, my Spark!" He reached for the golden door of his cage and ripped it off its hinges.

Elliya's mouth dropped open. She prayed the thick roots dampened the sound enough the guards couldn't hear.

Hawthorne stared at the man as the glowing runes faded. "It was your Spark the henchwomen used when they captured me. They were so strong and had no problem descending the side of the castle with me."

Even though the runes had faded, the cage continued to glow. The man lowered the glowing door to the ground quietly —funny, considering how much noise he'd already made.

However, as the man wept for joy, Elliya wondered if Geeni could sense tears from a distance …

"We have to hurry," she whispered.

The man's face split in a wide grin. "My name's Renaud,

and I'm ready to go whenever you are. But I'm not sure about the others."

Elliya unlocked the young man's cage next, and while Hawthorne checked on him, she unlocked the last cage. The woman still lay on the floor. Her curled body looked barely more than a pile of rags, and her wide eyes were the only sign that she realized anything unusual was happening.

Elliya whispered, "Will you let me help you walk out of here?"

The woman raised a shaking hand, and Elliya helped her stand. When the woman stepped over the threshold, she removed her hand from Elliya's and stood without moving. The woman didn't shed tears like Renaud. She seemed numb, despite her freedom and the return of her Spark, although she didn't show any signs of what her ability might be.

"Are you okay?" asked Elliya.

Renaud came to stand beside them and whispered, "Marielle has been here longer than the rest of us. I think she's been held prisoner for many years—long before Geeni even came to this citadel. It might take some time for her to begin to speak again."

As Renaud murmured comforting words to Marielle, Elliya went to check on Hawthorne.

He had ripped a strip off the bottom of his shirt and was tying it around a wound on the young man's leg. "Elliya, this is Daelin."

The man's black hair hung limply around his face, and he appeared thinner and sicker than the other two prisoners. And while he seemed more aware than Marielle, his face was contorted in pain.

"This wound is infected. We need to get you to a doctor." Hawthorne helped the man stand and growled, "You'd think

Geeni would take better care of her prisoners, considering she needs them to have any power at all."

Elliya backed out of the cage as Hawthorne helped the limping man out. When the man stepped out, his face lit up, delight twinkling in his dark eyes, before they suddenly turned lavender.

The princess raised a delicate hand to her mouth, hiding her trembling lips.

Elliya had to remind herself this wasn't truly a princess, that this man had the transformation Spark Geeni had used on her lamps. But Elliya had recently seen Hawthorne wearing this form, and it was strange to see it on someone else.

Hawthorne appeared just as surprised by the transformation. He let go of the woman and tilted his head, as if he recognized her, but not quite. The woman wore the same rags the man had worn, and considering how thin the man had appeared, they hung equally loosely on this form.

Daelin flickered back into his male body before transforming back into his female form with tears streaming down his face. "So many years ... Geeni stole this from me for so many years."

Elliya wanted to give Daelin a moment, but the prisoners' tears caused her fear to spike again. "We have to go."

The princess—Elliya couldn't help but think of her as a princess—smiled through her tears and took a step, then immediately crumpled to the ground. Though the rest of Daelin's skin appeared a healthy pink, her leg was just as injured as it had been on her male body.

Hawthorne reached for the woman, then stopped himself. Daelin reached out her hand, and Hawthorne took it hesitantly, his eyes on the woman's face, exhaling when his touch didn't change Daelin's form.

Elliya looked at the glowing runes on the remaining

cages. "Renaud, do you mind taking care of those? I'd rather not leave those in Geeni's possession. If she wants to capture someone else, she'll have to remake her runes." She didn't mention aloud that Geeni would need to steal more tears from whoever had the Spark to dampen the magic of others.

Renaud lifted his hand in salute. "It would be my pleasure." He ripped the door off Marielle's cage. When the runes faded, the storeroom grew darker, though the gold bars continued to faintly glow. Elliya looked at the shadows around them and groaned. "I forgot to bring a candle or lantern with me. Some prison break."

Renaud easily hefted a glowing door. "I can bring this with us so we can see."

Marielle was staring blindly at her empty cage, the runes dead but the bars still a faint gold. She bent and picked up a chipped stone the size of her palm, and as she stood, it blazed to life, shining brighter than the cages.

"Geeni used your Spark to light the cages ... and the lights in her office ... Thank you, Marielle." She turned to Renaud. "I guess you can continue."

The man gave Marielle a fierce salute, then ripped the doors off the other two cages, and bent the bars with runes for good measure. The metallic screech set her teeth on edge, but the guards hadn't heard it the first time, and hopefully they still wouldn't.

Hawthorne helped Daelin limp closer to Marielle and her light, while Elliya reached inside her apron and lifted out the mouse. She turned to the former prisoners. "We need to get as far away from the citadel as we can before Geeni discovers we are gone. This mouse knows of a secret exit, so we will follow her." The polite part of her wanted to talk to the mouse, but she didn't know if Geeni could "hear" their communication if she was using Elliya's Spark. So, instead, she lifted the mouse to look her in the eyes in greeting, then set her on the ground.

Hawthorne's eyes twinkled as he watched her, fascinated by her Spark. And if any of the others thought it odd to follow a mouse, none of them said it aloud.

35

———

The five humans and one mouse wove their way through the maze of roots and tumbled-down walls. Elliya followed the mouse's path, with Renaud leading Marielle right behind. The mouse occasionally ran too far ahead of Marielle's light and had to double back. Elliya thought it would be more efficient if she carried the light herself, but Marielle stared at the glowing rock like a precious artifact, and Elliya couldn't bear to take it from her.

In a few spots, they had to climb through small openings between the roots, so it was no wonder Geeni or her henchwomen hadn't explored this far. Even with Marielle's bright light, the roots cast flickering shadows as they moved, and Elliya couldn't wait to make it aboveground again.

Elliya followed the mouse through one more narrow space between thick roots. On the other side lay an ancient brick hallway. "This must have been a secret escape in case the citadel was ever attacked. I'm surprised it hasn't collapsed after all this time."

Hawthorne helped Daelin through the opening, then looked down the dark tunnel. "We've passed through the ring of banyan trees surrounding the citadel. Let's hope this gets us outside the range of Geeni's guards as well."

They followed the mouse down the brick corridor, moving faster now that the path was straight. The further they walked, the more Elliya noticed the animals sleeping in dens above her. For a moment she sensed the jaguar she had left to watch Lliadain, but was careful not to reach out with her Spark yet.

The mouse raced ahead of them into the shadows before coming back into Marielle's light, then scampering off again. Elliya hadn't seen the mouse for a while when the light revealed cracked steps leading up to a door. The mouse scrambled up the steps, then darted through a hole left by a fallen brick, then raced back in and turned in circles.

"This is it," Elliya whispered. "This is the way out." She walked up the steps to the iron door set at an angle and tried pushing it open, but it didn't budge.

"It probably hasn't been opened in centuries," said Hawthorne.

Renaud let go of Marielle, carefully putting the unresponsive woman's hand in Daelin's. "I think I can help."

Elliya surrendered her place on the stairs, stepping to Hawthorne's side. Renaud pressed his shoulder against the heavy door and pushed.

Iron hinges squealed as dirt trickled in around the edges. Outside the tunnel, centuries' worth of roots snapped as the opening door disturbed their path. Elliya held her breath, hoping the sound wasn't loud enough to warn the guards of their escape.

Renaud gave one final push, which loosened the last of the debris, and the door fell open to the side. He tilted his face to the night sky, moonlight reflecting off the tears on his cheeks.

Elliya whispered to Hawthorne, "Geeni trapped them

underground for so long ... How will we get them safely through the jungle and back to Isandine?"

"They've survived so much, and they will survive this, too." He watched Marielle, who clutched her light to her chest as she stared wide-eyed at the open door. "Sometimes strength is just surviving at all."

Elliya took his hand, clasping it tightly before releasing it with a sigh. "We have to keep moving."

He nodded and turned to Daelin with a question in his eyes. The woman answered by putting her arm around his neck, and he scooped her up and carried her up the stairs.

Marielle still stood at the bottom of the stairs, looking up.

"Geeni's guards might see your light from a distance." Elliya spoke quietly, but didn't underestimate the woman by speaking slowly. "Can you hide the stone until we get away?"

Marielle didn't respond, but she took a deep breath, and the light was suddenly snuffed out. The dark shadows of the quiet tunnel crept closer. Elliya wanted to sprint up the stairs, but waited patiently as Marielle began the slow ascent on her own.

When Elliya stepped out, Hawthorne was hunched over Daelin's leg, while the woman bit her lip.

"We have to get her to a doctor soon," he whispered. "She's in a lot of pain."

Renaud turned his attention from the sky to focus on Daelin's leg. "We should take her to the monastery. Two of the Sisters have healing Sparks."

Elliya's attention shot to Renaud. "How do you know that?"

"I lived there for a while." He frowned. "I never should have left ... It's how Geeni captured me and extorted tears from me for so long—by only allowing me to see Lliadain if I freely offered her my tears."

Elliya's brain tried to piece together the bits she had heard from Kensley and Lliadain, but couldn't figure out how everything fit. "Why did you need to see Lliadain?"

Renaud looked at her as if it was a silly question. "Because she's my wife."

"Your wife?" choked Elliya.

Hawthorne's snort of laughter proved he was just as disbelieving as Elliya.

Renaud studied Elliya's white dress as if for the first time. "Are you a scholar? Do you know Lliadain?" He bit his lip. "I shouldn't have said anything ... She has to keep our marriage a secret. We had plans to run off together, but once Geeni captured me, she forced Lliadain to stay inside the monastery."

Elliya couldn't imagine the cold red-haired woman married to this thoughtful man ... couldn't imagine her in a relationship with anyone. Elliya shook her head in disbelief and sent her Spark reaching out for the jaguar she had sensed earlier.

Daelin tried to stand on her own, which finally knocked Hawthorne out of his dumbfounded stare. "Lliadain ... wow ..." he said while he helped Daelin stand.

Elliya murmured to him, "We don't have time to figure that one out." She reached out with her Spark, asking the animals nearby for the closest path to the road back to Isandine. A bright green frog with yellow feet hopped onto a fallen log. "Thank you, sir," she whispered to the frog. To the others, she said, "That's our escort."

Elliya followed the frog on his winding path through the forest, while Hawthorne brought up the rear. He walked slowly, supporting Daelin while she limped and also keeping his eye on Renaud, who kept staring at the stars, and Marielle, who occasionally stopped walking to pick up an unusual rock.

Elliya had to keep her eyes firmly on the frog. Without Marielle's light, she depended on moonlight, and she lost track of him anytime he passed through a shadow.

She glanced at the sky, anxiously anticipating the first hint of dawn. She stopped to give them a chance to rest and murmured to Hawthorne, "The sun will rise soon, and we aren't far enough away yet. It's only a matter of time before someone notices I'm missing and thinks to check downstairs."

Hawthorne frowned. "They can't go much faster, especially with Daelin's injury and Marielle so unused to walking. Maybe Marielle would permit Renaud to carry her, and I could carry Daelin ... Then we could move faster."

Elliya gazed up at his serious face, his emerald eyes shimmering in the moonlight. He was stunning—more beautiful than a man had a right to be. She was grateful she'd taken the extra few moments to grab him a shirt, because his presence was overpowering enough as it was. She wanted nothing more than to walk by his side for the rest of her life.

"I have to go back," she whispered.

He shook his head. "Elliya, we can move faster—"

"No, we can't," she said firmly. "The moment they discover I am gone, they will come for me. I can't allow you to be captured again. Get the others safely to Isandine, then call the Queen's Guard to come raid the citadel."

He opened his mouth to object when a growl ripped out behind her.

She thought it was the jaguar, but the animal's thoughts were calmly amused, not angry. When Elliya turned, she found the source of the furious growl.

Lliadain's usually neat red hair was tangled with sticks and leaves, and her face was smeared with dirt. She was even more filthy than the prisoners who'd been held captive for years. Her back was smeared with mud, and two paw prints stained the front of her formerly white scholar's robes.

Elliya glanced at the jaguar, who sat calmly licking one paw.

She tried to escape. I convinced her otherwise.

Lliadain hissed, "How dare you use your Spark to keep me captive? This filthy animal chased me into a cave last night, then woke me up by chewing on my robes and—"

"Lliadain?"

The scholar's head shot around at the soft whisper, and her eyes opened wide. "Renaud?" His name came out as a choked sob.

He ran to her and picked her up in a twirling hug, showering kisses all over the scholar's face. Lliadain laughed through her tears, her fingers tangling in his matted hair.

Elliya and Hawthorne exchanged shocked glances, then stared at the couple. A laughing Lliadain was so astonishing that Elliya couldn't turn away, even though the couple's passionate kiss brought a blush to her cheeks.

The sky brightened infinitesimally, but enough to remind Elliya of the danger. She stepped closer to the couple and cleared her throat. "I'm sorry to interrupt, but you have to get out of here."

Renaud set Lliadain back on the ground, and the scholar's face settled into her familiar grimace. "I know that, Elliya, even better than you."

Elliya didn't rise to her challenge, instead asking Renaud, "Can you carry Daelin? It will help you move faster." She very carefully kept her attention on Renaud. "Even though I'm sure you'd rather be holding your *wife*."

Lliadain gave her a glare equal parts anger and embarrassment.

Renaud scooped up Daelin and grinned at his wife.

"Don't be jealous, dear. Once we are out of the jungle, these arms are all yours. I'll carry you wherever you want to go."

A blush of embarrassment rose to Lliadain's cheeks, along with the faint hint of desire. Elliya found it so startling she turned to address the jaguar.

The big cat batted at a tiny glowing pebble. Marielle watched his big paws swat the shining rock, and a hint of a smile curved her lips.

The sight warmed Elliya's heart, but she cleared her throat again, trying to get the cat's attention this time. "Can you lead the way back to the road?"

Of course. I'm not a cub. He gave her a dismissive look before hopping playfully, jumping onto the pebble with both front paws.

Elliya rolled her eyes, then said to the others, "Follow the jaguar. He will lead you out."

Marielle picked up the glowing stone, and the jaguar sighed dramatically. When he moved through the trees, Marielle stayed at his side. Renaud carried Daelin, now delirious with pain, and Lliadain clung to his arm.

The scholar turned at the last moment. "Aren't you both coming?"

Hawthorne opened his mouth, but Elliya cut him off. "Hawthorne will catch up in just a moment. Keep walking and don't worry about us, Sister."

The scholar gave her one last glare before turning and walking beside her husband, resting her filthy hair against his powerful arm.

36

———

As the footsteps of the former prisoners faded, Elliya realized how long it had been since she was alone with Hawthorne. He watched her with a calm intensity, his eyes sparkling with desire. How could he be so confident about what he wanted, when admitting her own desire felt fraught with risk?

His lips parted. "I'm coming with you."

The ridiculous claim startled her thoughts away from his lips. "No, you aren't. You're going with the others."

"No, Elliya." He shook his head slowly, his eyes still locked on her face. "I'm coming with you."

She huffed a breath between her lips. "I can do this on my own, Hawthorne. I don't need you to protect me."

"To protect you?" His brows rose. "Of course you don't need my protection." He stepped closer, his wide shoulders filling her vision. "You survived your childhood without my protection. You faced your stepmother again without my protection. You walked alone into Geeni's citadel without my protection." He dipped his head, his eyes unwavering. "There are many things I want to offer you, Elliya, but protection isn't one of them. Because frankly, you don't need it. You're the strongest person I know."

Elliya's breathing slowed, and the jungle animals quieted, until it was only Hawthorne in her mind. Hawthorne, who believed in her so strongly he'd allowed himself to be taken prisoner. He had already proven he didn't feel the need to protect her, but the logic of his decision failed her.

"If you aren't trying to protect me, why won't you leave with the others?"

He whispered his confession. "Because I love you, Elliya. And I don't want to be parted from you ever again."

Hawthorne had confessed his feelings for her many times and shared his emotions plainly for her to see, even though she had shared nothing. The fear of opening herself up to love still shook her to her core, and her heart thudded so loudly in her chest, she was sure he could hear it. How could he reveal his love for her, over and over again, without his heartbeat racing as wildly as hers?

Elliya placed her hand on his chest. She felt his indrawn breath of surprise at her touch, and under her palm, his pounding heartbeat. His heart pulsed as rapidly as hers, the rhythm heavy with fear and desire. He wasn't so confident that he shared his emotions without fear.

But he took the risk.

She looked Hawthorne deep in his emerald eyes and took a risk of her own. "May I kiss you, Prince?"

His reply was a quick and breathless, "Yes."

Hawthorne held perfectly still as she lifted her trembling hand from his chest and placed both hands on his cheeks. Stubble prickled under her fingertips, and her little fingers grazed his throat above his wildly thudding pulse. He raised his hands as if he might embrace her, but his fingers merely hovered near her arms, the heat of his closeness tingling against her skin.

She pulled his face to hers, slowly, savoring each moment. Hawthorne had stopped breathing, and his heavy lashes finally fluttered closed. Elliya leaned in and lightly pressed her lips against his.

If she had found his closeness overwhelming before, it was nothing compared to kissing him. His soft lips and rough stubble … his earthy spiced scent … the heat radiating off him …

Hawthorne accepted her delicate kiss, his only movement the quickening of his pulse beneath her fingertips. She finished the tender kiss but didn't release him. Her lips lingered before his, the memory of the kiss still tickling her skin. She didn't pull away when she spoke, letting her words brush across his lips.

"Hold me."

He obeyed her hushed command with wholehearted commitment. His arms closed around her, avoiding her bruises yet pulling her body against his. Her hands slid from his cheeks to loop around his neck and shoulders, dragging him into a deeper kiss.

He kissed her with the ferocity of a man uncaged—confident and strong, yet still remarkably gentle. She melted against him, surrendering to the emotions bursting in her chest.

Hawthorne loved her, and she loved him. She had believed falling in love was dangerous, but with Hawthorne's arms around her, she felt safer than she ever had in her life. Not with the safety of his protection, but safe because he made her feel strong. With Hawthorne by her side, she could take on anything. She would face Geeni, her stepmother, the possibility of loss and grief … She would face it all because she was strong enough to handle it. He believed in her, and she loved him enough to trust in that belief.

She would no longer run from love.

She didn't want to stop kissing him. She wanted to kiss him until the sun rose so she could discover what it was like to kiss him in the sunlight, but instead, she pressed her lips firmly against his for one more moment, then lifted her head.

Hawthorne's grip loosened at the first hint of resistance until his hands rested loosely at her lower back. Elliya untangled her fingers from his hair and rested her palms on his chest, his heartbeat still pulsing with desire, but with no hint of lingering fear.

She cleared her throat, trying to remember how to speak after being kissed so soundly. "I need to go."

He opened his mouth to object, but Elliya placed her finger gently on his lips. The argument brewing in his eyes faded with an inhaled breath of longing.

She gave her reasoning while he was distracted. "I trust Lliadain will do anything it takes to get Renaud out of here, but I don't trust her with the other two. She'd leave them behind in a moment if it meant keeping her husband safe. Geeni will be desperate to get them back. They need your protection."

Her finger slipped from his lips as she sensed his reluctant acceptance. "You're right," he sighed. "Though I'm not much good in a fight."

"Hopefully, there won't be any need to fight. Just keep them moving toward Isandine until you can send the Queen's Guard to do the fighting."

He drew her closer, his hands against her lower back lighting a fire up her spine. "I'll try to focus on leading everyone to Isandine, but I'll be very distracted thinking about that kiss."

Her cheeks warmed, and her lips twitched into a smile. "If you bring the Queen's Guard beating down Geeni's door, I'll kiss you again. It will be your reward for rescuing me."

"That's kind of you to say, but we both know you won't need any rescuing. However, I appreciate you letting me pretend." His voice dropped to a husky whisper. "I'll be back soon to claim that kiss from you, but until then, one last kiss, this one from me to you."

He kissed her so thoroughly that her thoughts grew fuzzy around the edges. She could no longer remember why she had felt urgency, other than the need to continue kissing him. Though her lids were closed, her eyes rolled back and her lashes fluttered as she sighed against his lips. The moment she realized her hands hung loosely, she reached out to grab him, but he took a smooth step away.

Hawthorne looked smug as she tried to catch her breath. He bent in a sweeping bow. "I'll be back to rescue you." He winked as if it were a grand joke, then walked into the trees to catch up to the others. After two steps, he stopped and turned with a grin on his lips. "I love kissing you, dear, but perhaps you should tell the animals to mind their own business next time."

Elliya finally took note of her surroundings. The animals in their vicinity were all cooing and purring and chirping. The sounds were embarrassing enough, but some of the animals' suggestions were quite explicit. She hissed a reprimand and tried to will the blush off her cheeks.

He gave her a knowing grin, then started walking again. "Hawthorne?"

He spun back around at her quiet call.

"I love you, too."

A contented smile curved his lips before he headed into the shadowed trees.

Leaving him in the jungle wasn't as hard as leaving him

inside his cage, but her heart still rebelled at the thought. However, her plan was the best option, so she began her trudging walk back to the secret entrance.

She would go back through the dark tunnel, and into the prison with the now destroyed cages. She kicked herself for not asking Marielle for a glowing stone to take with her, but she would just have to find an animal with excellent night vision who could lead her inside.

The sky was streaking with the first bright hints of dawn. Elliya assumed the cook would make breakfast soon. After she made it back through the prison, she would bar the door and sneak into the kitchen as if nothing had happened. Even though it would take the prisoners some time to make it back to Isandine, she hoped trained soldiers could make it through the jungle quickly—

A bird cried out, then was suddenly silenced.

Elliya spun in a circle, looking for danger, but couldn't see anything.

The animals still chirped and cawed and snorted, but their voices were unrecognizable to her. Dread curled in her gut as she scanned the trees, trying to decide which way to go, but in the end, her decision was obvious.

She headed back toward Hawthorne.

She knew she was close when the animal sounds grew louder and more panicked. Though she couldn't understand them in words, she knew what they said.

Be careful!

Watch out!

Danger!

Elliya stepped into a clearing and discovered her instinct about the animals' meaning was correct. There was a predator close.

And the predator had found the prince.

37

———

Hawthorne was bound to the thick trunk of a teak tree, his wrists bound at his waist, his mouth gagged. The fresh shirt she had given him was ripped from his fight to avoid capture. It could have been a henchwoman who'd captured him, but Elliya had a sick feeling it had been Geeni herself.

Elliya couldn't see anyone else nearby, so she guessed Geeni must have left him to continue her search for the other prisoners. Hawthorne was shaking his head, trying to pull off the gag, and Elliya ran to him and began untying the knot.

"I'm so sorry, Hawthorne. We should—"

The moment his mouth was free, he said, "Geeni is still—"

"Is this any way to repay your godmother?" Geeni spoke with a slow drawl, her hands casually resting on the two daggers strapped to her sides. "I rescued you, gained you entrance to the monastery, where you could live the rest of your life in peace ... I even gave you beautiful, priceless gifts, yet this is how you repay me?"

Those "priceless gifts" were currently on Geeni's feet,

which explained why Elliya could no longer hear the animals' voices. The glass slippers looked completely out of place in the jungle with Geeni's tight pants and cropped vest, but the woman stood as if the shoes were normal hiking attire.

"You found the slippers," said Elliya.

"I sent Nix to retrieve Lliadain, and when she couldn't find her, she searched the monastery. Under a pile of laundry, dear?" Geeni clicked her tongue. "Very amateurish spy work, but since you didn't even know you were my spy, I guess that's to be expected."

"But why are you wearing them? Don't they affect your runes, too?"

Geeni's hands tightened on her daggers. "I don't need a Spark to be dangerous, little mouse." She stalked closer. "How did she convince you to betray me?"

Elliya's mind flooded with questions: How long before the others sent back the Queen's Guard? Was Elliya safer with those shoes on or off Geeni's feet? Could she untie Hawthorne quicker than Geeni could run in heels?

But the most immediate question came to her lips. "She who?" Did Geeni know Elliya had spoken to the queen?

Geeni gave her a flat look. "Lliadain. I know she put you up to this. What could she possibly say that would convince you to betray me after all I've done for you?"

Elliya's mouth fell open. She truly had no response to the number of wrong assumptions Geeni had made. Her mind raced to figure out how to use that to her advantage, but lying wasn't natural for her. So she fell back on her instinct when confronted by an angry woman bent on violence.

She dropped to her knees. "I'm sorry, Godmother. You've been so good to me. I shouldn't have listened to Lliadain. Please forgive—"

"Enough groveling," said Geeni. "It's extremely tedious, little mouse. Tell me where the others are, and I'll allow you back into my household, and all will be forgiven."

"The others?" asked Elliya, stalling to find a reasonable lie.

"Don't play stupid," snapped Geeni. "Where has Lliadain taken the other prisoners?"

"Oh, yes, of course, Godmother! Lliadain sent the prince and I ahead to watch for guards. The others were further behind us because they had to walk slowly."

Geeni tapped her lips. "I expected if Lliadain attempted a rescue, she would only take her husband and leave the others. She must have greater plans than I thought."

Elliya had been purposefully avoiding looking at Hawthorne, but while Geeni was lost in thought, she stole a glance. He was attempting to work loose the rope around his wrists. But even if he worked the knot loose, what would they do? The two of them couldn't beat Geeni in a fight, with or without her runes. They needed Geeni looking in the wrong direction so the prisoners could escape. And if Elliya led Geeni away, Hawthorne might escape his bonds and join them.

Elliya scrambled to her feet. "I'll help you find them."

"Elliya, no!" said Hawthorne, straining against his bonds.

She frowned as Geeni's attention shot his way. Elliya faced him directly and tried to communicate her actual message, despite her words. "I'm sorry, Prince, but I know where my true loyalty lies."

"Please, don't—"

She growled, "Don't make me gag you again."

Hawthorne pinched his lips shut, but continued to strain against the ropes. It appeared to be anger—the way he leaned against his bonds ... the ropes pressing against his muscular chest. But Elliya was close enough to see it wasn't anger pulling him toward her.

It was desire.

Desire that she would stay. Desire that she would find another way. Desire to simply be close to her.

Elliya's body pulled closer in response, but she stopped herself, turning toward Geeni with a jerk. "Let's go. I'll show you where we split off from them."

Geeni studied her with a raised eyebrow. Elliya wasn't sure if it was because she had just given her godmother a direct order or if the woman had detected some hint of the desire between them.

Elliya stepped swiftly away from Hawthorne. "They're this way, Godmother. I'll show you—"

Geeni moved faster in glass heels than Elliya had expected. Her godmother strode through the jungle debris and raised her dagger to Hawthorne's throat in one smooth motion.

Elliya froze, panic squeezing her chest until she couldn't breathe.

Geeni's eyes locked on Elliya, while the tip of her dagger brushed gently against Hawthorne's neck. "Before we go, I think I'll get rid of the prince. I had planned to keep him prisoner for a while, but I've found princes are much more trouble than they are worth."

Hawthorne had stopped straining against his bonds and held perfectly still, his eyes flitting between the dagger, Elliya, and his bound hands. She sensed him trying to escape, and with every glance in her direction, a silent command for her to run.

Elliya's muscles quaked from two competing instincts: one, to drop back onto her knees and beg Geeni to spare his life; the other, a fierce and overpowering need to rip the woman's throat out.

She had never felt such a strong desire to commit violence, not even when her stepmother had abused her. Elliya had thought only evil people like her stepmother had the capacity for violence, but in that moment, she realized she not only had the capacity, she would savor the experience. The thought both sickened and fascinated her.

Geeni shook her head sadly, the knife still poised at Hawthorne's throat. "Oh, little mouse ... You poor thing. You let yourself fall in love with the too-charming prince."

Elliya bit her lip—anything she said would reveal the truth of her godmother's accusation.

"What is it with scholars?" Geeni placed one hand on her hip, the other still holding the dagger. "Are any scholars truly committed to their vows? A woman like Lliadain betraying her vows was surprising, but you, little mouse ... I'm honestly shocked."

Elliya wanted to point out she wasn't a scholar yet and hadn't taken her official vows, but Geeni was right—Elliya had betrayed her vow to not fall in love. And Elliya still found it shocking herself.

Geeni sighed dramatically. "It seems like you all have secret husbands, secret families, secret lovers. You, Lliadain, Alanna's mother, your mother." She ticked the names off on her fingers. "All of you forsaking scholarship for—"

Elliya tilted her head. "My mother?"

Geeni waved a dismissive hand. "True, Yulia Zaleska didn't take vows like the Sisters, but being a woman scholar in Verkeshe takes even more commitment than here in Isandariyah. Together we could have used her research to gain unimaginable power, but she gave it all up and ran away. What a waste."

Understanding dawned on Hawthorne's face as he finally realized the identity of Elliya's mother, but Elliya didn't have time to explain it to him. She was still too surprised by what Geeni had revealed.

Elliya whispered, "You knew her in Verkeshe?"

"She was younger than you are now." Geeni smiled fondly, despite her dagger still at Hawthorne's throat. "We attended a girls' school together. The school attempted to turn Verkeshian girls into proper wives, but your mother was always studying topics that were decidedly unladylike. When I found out one of those topics might be beneficial to me, I used my family's resources to get her a suitable lab to conduct her research."

Elliya's eyes widened. "You were her patron. The one who used her. The reason she fled Verkeshe."

Geeni's jade eyes sharpened. "And just how do you know that, little mouse? I now have her complete collection of work, and it says nothing about why she left Verkeshe. Unless she wrote something else?"

Elliya's heart fluttered, and she pinched her lips to keep from smiling. Nix hadn't found her mother's journal mixed in with the other books in the monastery library. She had managed to keep the last of her mother's secrets out of Geeni's hands.

Geeni pricked Hawthorne's neck, and he flinched. "Are you holding out on me, little mouse? For who? This prince? What exactly do you think he will offer you?" She traced the blade down his jawline. "This one has had dalliances with countless women. You're just one of his many playthings. Whatever he's promised you, he's promised the same and more to all the women before you. Once he's done with you, he will leave you with nothing but pain and a broken heart."

Geeni's words nipped at her old fear, bringing it back to the surface. What did she truly think the prince offered her? Marriage? A lifetime as his mistress? A brief dalliance, then nothing more? They had never discussed it, probably because she had only confessed her love for him moments earlier, but the doubt lingered.

The corner of Geeni's lips rose in a small smirk. "He's a beautiful young man, so I don't blame you for losing your head. But you're a smart girl, Elliya. Think about your future." Geeni lowered the dagger, but didn't sheathe it as she stepped closer to Elliya. "Stay with me and continue your mother's research. I'll build you a lab and buy you books—whatever you need to pursue her study of bloodlines."

"But why do you want to continue her research? What if it can prove one of the prince's children is truly of the First Queen's bloodline?"

Geeni laughed. "Don't think so narrowly, little mouse! I possess written proof that my bloodline is true, and my claim to the throne is stronger than the princes' nonexistent children. No, this research is more valuable for what it means for the rest of the world. Isandariyah is the only queendom civilized enough to hold to matrilineal succession while every kingdom struggles with questions of paternity. What if we could provide proof that not every royal family was as pure as it seemed? What if there were farm boys with purer blood than princes? Imagine what would happen."

Elliya breathed, "War. War is what would happen, Geeni."

Her godmother winked. "Exactly, little mouse."

Elliya spared a brief glance at Hawthorne, who appeared as shocked as she was. She kept her voice as neutral as she could. "You told my mother this, and she ran away."

Geeni's lips tightened. "I didn't tell her, but she must have guessed. I know she discovered something about the Verkeshian princes. Something everyone suspected, but no one could prove. Except somehow Yulia could."

The brothers from her mother's journal. They were the Verkeshian princes. And her mother had discovered that only one might belong to the king, while the other surely did not. Elliya held perfectly still, hoping her shock didn't register on her face.

Geeni appeared lost in a memory of the past. "For such a brilliant woman, she was extremely shortsighted. Imagine the rest of the world in chaos, with a queen in Isandariyah using her stability to gain power. Imagine the world she could create."

Elliya could barely breathe, but she whispered, "You will be that queen?"

Geeni's jade eyes glittered. "I won't just take this country, I will take them all."

Elliya stared at her, trying to understand the magnitude of the woman's plans. "You started this scheme when you were still in school?"

"I was always a precocious child." Geeni's face showed a hint of pride, then she waved a dismissive hand. "Besides, I have more plans than just this one. Don't you see, Elliya? I am not only the future of this queendom, I will lead the world into a new age. And you can be there with me."

Elliya froze as Geeni stalked closer, dropping her voice. "Falling in love with the prince only leads to pain and grief. He will betray you and break your heart. What happens when I take over and he is no longer a prince? He will need to seek wealth and power somewhere else, and he will leave you alone with no one to protect you." Geeni lovingly brushed Elliya's cheek, though it was tear-free. "But I won't abandon you, little mouse. You are my treasure. And I can offer you the protection he can't."

Geeni's jade eyes demanded her full attention, but Elliya glanced over the woman's shoulder at Hawthorne. She thought she would find fear in his eyes, fear she might accept Geeni's offer, but his emerald eyes held no hint of doubt in her.

"She's right, Elliya." He had stopped straining against his bonds and appeared at ease, as if he was patiently waiting for rescue. "There's only one thing I refuse to offer you. Protection."

Elliya barely noticed Geeni's triumphant grin, because she couldn't take her eyes off him. He wouldn't offer her protection because he didn't believe she needed it. He believed she was strong. Stronger than she had ever realized. And he believed she would rescue him once again.

Geeni didn't believe she was strong—she believed Elliya was so weak she would exchange her freedom and her intellect and her tears in exchange for a false sense of safety. But Geeni had miscalculated Elliya's strength while forgetting her own weakness.

Tears pooled in Elliya's eyes. "I'm so sorry, Godmother. You're right. You're the only one who can protect me." Elliya glanced at the prince through blurry eyes to find him biting his lip on a smug grin. "Please don't be angry with me. I'll do whatever you ask."

Through her tears, Elliya noticed their audience had grown. Birds and monkeys perched quietly on branches overhead while the brush stirred with the gentle movement of mice and iguanas. She couldn't understand them since the glass slippers on Geeni's feet still smothered her Spark, but she could read their body language clear enough.

They were waiting just as patiently as Hawthorne.

Elliya pulled up every happy moment with the prince, every bittersweet thought about her mother, the tragedy of the prisoners' lost years ... She collected her happy tears and sad tears and angry tears and offered them up to Geeni.

As bait.

Fat tears shimmered on Elliya's lashes but hadn't

dropped down her cheeks yet, and Geeni's eyes glittered with greed. "Of course I forgive you, little mouse," she cooed. Her fingers twitched, and she absently touched the charm on her wrist, then glanced at the glass slippers with annoyance.

Elliya kept her eyes on Geeni, but dotted fur flashed beyond her godmother's shoulder. The jaguar wouldn't have left the prisoners alone. Not until they found their way out of the jungle.

Elliya tensed her lips, trying to hold her frown. Then she blinked, and the tears rolled down her cheeks.

Geeni wet her lips. "Let's dry your tears and get you safely inside the citadel."

Elliya nodded obediently, fluttering her wet lashes.

Geeni lifted her hand to Elliya's cheek and stepped out of the glass slippers.

Elliya mentally shouted a string of commands, and the waiting animals sprang into action.

A flock of birds took flight, and when Geeni glanced up, two monkeys shot from the trees, grabbed the glass slippers, then scampered away. The jaguar leaped from the shadows and landed lightly beside Hawthorne—the cat's attention locked on Geeni with his muscles poised to spring again.

Geeni raised her dagger to Elliya's throat and growled, "What have you done?"

A strange confidence rolled over Elliya as she wiped away her remaining tears. "I sent the prisoners to find help. The Queen's Guard will be here soon."

Rage flickered in Geeni's eyes, and she pressed the blade closer to Elliya's throat. "I can kill you and Hawthorne before they arrive."

The fury she had felt seeing Geeni's blade at Hawthorne's throat returned, and Elliya answered her with a deadly calm. "If you even look at the prince, that jaguar will rip your throat out. You will never touch Hawthorne again."

Geeni's eyes widened in surprise, and Elliya stopped scowling at her godmother long enough to glance at Hawthorne. He watched her in rapture, his muscles coiled just as tightly as the jaguar, except he wasn't poised for attack, but to take Elliya in his arms and kiss her with reckless abandon.

Geeni leaned in closer. "But I can kill you right now, before the jaguar can pounce."

Elliya spared one last look at Hawthorne and the mouse chewing through the ropes binding him to the tree, then her eyes flicked back to Geeni. "You could kill me right now, but the moment you do, every animal within a hundred-foot radius will come for you."

Geeni snorted dismissively. "You forget, little mouse. I have your Spark. I can command these animals just as well as you."

Elliya's mouth fell open, then she laughed. "You haven't used my Spark much yet, have you? Otherwise, you'd know I can't control animals."

Geeni's mouth twisted in anger, but a hint of doubt showed in her eyes. "I commanded all the pests to leave the citadel, and you just ordered those monkeys to steal my slippers. Of course that's your Spark."

Elliya grinned, pleased her godmother wasn't all-knowing. "My Spark isn't to command animals—it's communicating with them. I understand them, and they understand me. If they follow a command from me, it's only because it aligns with their own wishes or because they want to do me a favor. For example, I wouldn't have to command the jaguar to rip your throat out. He's wanted to do that from the moment you killed his mate. However, I asked him to please only kill you if you approach Hawthorne." Elliya shrugged. "It's just a request. He's free to change his mind."

Geeni drew the blade closer as the doubt flooded her eyes. "But once you are dead, they will only have me to listen to. They'll obey me."

Elliya met her godmother's gaze and held it. "Use my Spark right now. Listen to them before you make any rash decisions."

Geeni didn't lower her dagger, but her eyes unfocused slightly as she paid attention to the animals around her.

Focusing on a single animal in a crowd was difficult, but Elliya had been practicing since she entered the jungle. Her godmother didn't have as much practice, so the experience must be overwhelming. The animals were practically screaming with their desire to attack Geeni, but one conversation between a pair of condors soaring overhead rose to the surface.

When can we eat her?

Do not eat her!

Why not? Everyone agrees she needs to go.

Kill her, yes, but look at that pink hair ... Remember the last time you ate a frog that brightly colored? You were sick for days!

I won't eat the hair. Just the good bits.

Elliya could pick out dozens of conversations debating the merits of eating Geeni or if she was rotten meat. From Geeni's look of outrage, Elliya guessed Geeni understood plenty.

"A bunch of filthy rodents," hissed Geeni. She didn't need to yell for the animals to hear her. "I have Sparks of strength and speed ... I can kill any animal that tries to touch me."

Elliya raised a brow. "But can you kill *all* of them, Geeni? You killed the jaguar because she was alone, but can you defeat every snake and monkey and bird and rat if they swarm at once?"

Geeni glanced at her bangles marked with runes. Strategies formed and reformed behind her godmother's eyes, but the woman didn't move.

Elliya looked up at the woman who had betrayed her and whispered, "Surrender, Geeni. Turn yourself in, and I'll beg them to let you live."

Geeni's attention shifted from her runes to Elliya's face. "You would see me surrender rather than die?"

"I know you've used me from the day we met, but you saved my life when you pulled me out of my stepmother's house. And for that gift, I would spare your life. Surrender yourself to the Queen's Guard, and I'll testify on your behalf to the animals in the jungle and to the queen herself."

Geeni studied Elliya as if she had never seen her before. "You're so peculiar, little mouse. Sparing my life proves you don't understand what kind of game I'm playing at all."

Animals at the perimeter of Elliya's awareness stirred, but she couldn't tell if they reacted to the Queen's Guards or one of Geeni's henchwomen drawing close. Geeni scanned the clearing, probably wondering the same thing.

Geeni turned back to Elliya with a shake of her head. "My plans stretch over decades, child. There is no surrender for me." She slowly lowered her blade and took a step back. "I will win it all, or I will take the queendom down with me." Then she sprinted barefoot into the trees.

She moved so quickly Elliya could hardly see where she went, but several animals decided against obeying Elliya and ran after her. Elliya called out to them, asking for one more favor. "Please be careful! She's dangerous, and I wouldn't see you hurt."

She sensed a slight lessening of the recklessness from most animals. The jaguar fought his desire to run after

Geeni, determined to honor Elliya's request to stay and protect Hawthorne.

Elliya turned slowly and met Hawthorne's eyes. The mouse had almost finished chewing the ropes looped across his chest and binding him to the tree, but his wrists were still tightly bound. Instead of asking her to untie him, his eyes asked her a different question.

Running to him was her answer. As she drew closer, he pressed hard against his restraints, and the ropes dropped, the mouse scampering away. She slammed into him, fingers tightly clutching his shirt, and pressed herself against him. The fear she had felt when Geeni held the dagger to his throat clenched her heart again, and she let out a sob against his chest.

"I thought she would kill you," she whispered.

His deep voice rumbled against her cheek. "I knew you'd rescue me again, Elliya. It's just who you are." He lifted his bound hands and tenderly cupped Elliya's cheeks. "You've saved my life twice. I'll grant you any favor you ask."

Gold or riches didn't even cross her mind. She raised her head and whispered, "Kiss me."

His emerald eyes glittered as he lifted his bound wrists over her head and pulled her into a kiss. Elliya whimpered a plea, and he responded by spinning her toward the tree and pressing against her. She wrapped her arms around his waist, pulling him close, deepening the kiss, while his bound hands tangled in her hair.

The animals' internal voices and external noises exploded in a cacophony of sound. Their cheers and indecent suggestions were so loud, Elliya almost missed the gentle cough.

"Um ... Your Highness." The sound of a politely cleared throat repeated. "Are you okay?"

Hawthorne lifted his head and gave the Queen's Guard a lazy smile. "Oh, I'm more than okay, Captain."

Elliya blinked several times, trying to bring herself back to some level of consciousness. She was grateful for the sturdy trunk at her back and Hawthorne holding her so tight, because her knees felt so weak, she might have collapsed.

The uniformed man looked at both of them, his eyes unsure where to land. "We heard Ginevere has a stronghold nearby ..." He looked over his shoulder at a dozen Queen's Guards standing in a neat formation. "We should hurry if we're going to catch her."

Unable to give the prince a direct command, he didn't speak his true meaning: Stop kissing that girl and help us capture Ginevere.

When Elliya saw how fast Geeni had run, surely due to a rune, she had given up hope of catching the woman by natural means. And no matter how many animals Elliya had on her side, it would take more than just her Spark. They would need a careful plan and a lot of magic to stop Geeni. And that wouldn't happen today.

Elliya licked her lips, which still tingled from their kiss, and spoke to the soldier with an authority she hadn't formerly possessed. "The prince is currently occupied. This jaguar will show you the way to the citadel."

The captain's eyes widened—whether from receiving a command from a maid or the sight of the previously unnoticed jaguar, Elliya wasn't sure.

"You heard the lady," said Hawthorne with a wide grin. "I'm busy." He didn't wait for the guards to leave before he resumed their passionate kiss.

38

Elliya arranged her mother's books in neat stacks on Geeni's desk. She hadn't truly believed she would see them again, so finding them all safely inside Geeni's office was an unexpected blessing.

There were signs Geeni had come back to the citadel briefly before she fled. The bookshelves hadn't been touched, but the desk drawers had been emptied and two cabinets were cleared out. Geeni had left no runes behind, other than on the glass slippers Elliya had retrieved from the monkeys.

The Queen's Guard didn't find Geeni or any of her henchwomen. Even the cook was gone by the time the soldiers arrived at the citadel. Elliya had assumed Geeni would give her people runes, letting them quickly flee the scene, but it still disappointed her that there was no sign of them.

No sign except the booby traps.

The monkeys had warned the soldiers by hopping near the hidden trap at the front entrance. The soldiers had disabled the trap, and the monkeys had already found one more by the time Elliya and Hawthorne had caught up.

The soldiers were professional enough to not mention the couple's tardiness.

The first thing Elliya had done when she arrived at the citadel was to gather the remains of the jaguar's mate from Geeni's office and take her outside for a proper burial. The jaguar had watched with solemn eyes while Hawthorne helped Elliya dig a grave beneath the shade of the banyan trees. After a prayer to the Goddesses, Elliya had dropped a tear into the fresh soil as an offering.

Now seated back at Geeni's desk, she looked at her white dress and wondered if it would ever truly be white again. White dresses were fine for scholars working in a monastery, but they weren't practical for escaping an underground prison, trekking through the jungle, or grave digging.

Hawthorne looked just as rough as she did.

He stood at the office door, speaking quietly to the captain. He hadn't left her side since they walked together back to the citadel. After the jaguar's burial, he had helped her gather her mother's books onto Geeni's desk, then had started exploring the other bookshelves, giving her space to read without hovering over her.

Although Hawthorne was not a member of the Queen's Guard like his older brother, the captain nodded at him, his rough face bearing hints of a fond smile. Elliya's lips twitched into a fond smile of her own. Hawthorne could charm even the roughest of soldiers.

The captain saluted and walked off, and when Hawthorne turned to find Elliya watching him, he gave her a smug grin. "Have you finished reading? Considering other ... activities already?"

She didn't touch her lips at the memory of those "activities," though she instinctively wanted to. "I doubt the captain wants us lingering here."

Hawthorne carefully scooted the glass slippers away from the corner of the desk before hitching up his leg to take a seat. "The captain isn't concerned about us. You can stay as long as you want."

She looked at the stacks of her mother's books. "Do you think someone can help me carry these to the monastery?"

Hawthorne watched her with keen eyes. "Is that what you want, Elliya? To go back to the monastery?"

She opened her mouth, but couldn't answer. Her vow to the Goddesses was irrevocably broken. She had fallen in love—fallen so hard that even if she managed to push Hawthorne away, her heart would never be as it had before. She couldn't take the scholars' vows, devoting her life to scholarship, when her heart was no longer just her own.

He watched her with his breath held but didn't interrupt her thoughts. What did she want? There was too much—an entire lifetime of suppressed wants. She had no experience believing those wants could come true, much less the ability to express those wants out loud.

She decided to start with an easy want. "I want a bath and clean clothes."

Hawthorne sat perfectly still, his eyes intense. "The monastery isn't the only place with clean clothes."

How could she explain what the monastery meant to her? Even if her dream of being a scholar had shifted, the monastery still held a special place in her heart. The monastery was safety and peace and books and food and her kitten.

She swallowed the lump in her throat and declared her next want. "I want a home."

Hawthorne exhaled, as if that was the answer he had been waiting for. "That's been arranged. I told the captain this citadel now belongs to you."

Elliya's mouth dropped open. "You did what?"

Doubt crept into his eyes. "It's your choice, of course. If there's somewhere else you want to live, you obviously can. I just thought you'd want—"

"You're giving me an ancient citadel?" she asked in disbelief. "In the middle of the jungle?"

"Um ... I guess it's not exactly the most practical home. It's so large that you'll need help managing it." He chewed his lip. "I can hire you a housekeeper and cook so you don't have to worry about that ... There are so many books and artifacts here, scholars will probably drop by for research, so it might feel like an extension of the monastery." A hint of embarrassment colored his cheeks. "I shouldn't have assumed you'd want this place. But I thought you'd like a home in the middle of the jungle, surrounded by animals. You seem so powerful and confident here. I just thought—"

Elliya reached across the desk, grabbed the front of his shirt in her fist, and pulled him into a kiss. After his initial surprise faded, Hawthorne melted into the kiss, sprawling lazily across the books between them.

She didn't release him, but she lifted her head and whispered, "I love you, Hawthorne."

"And I love you, Elliya."

She let go of his shirt, allowing him to straighten. "Thank you for my new home. It's exactly what I want."

Though she had released him, he held still, staring into her eyes. "It's just the first of your wants that I intend to fulfill."

His sultry tone sent a tingle racing across her skin, and Hawthorne grinned as if he knew his effect on her. He stood from his perch on the desk. "As for your other two wants, I'll ask the captain to send someone to fetch us clean clothes, then I'll discover the citadel's bathing options. Geeni strikes me as the type of person who'd install a modern bathroom in an ancient citadel." He winked and turned to go.

"Hawthorne?"

He turned back at her soft call.

She walked to the front of the desk. "I want to ask you something."

He moved toward her and whispered breathlessly, "Ask me."

In his eyes, she could see the answers to all the questions she would ask him someday, from "Will you kiss me again?" to "Will you marry me?" His answers were clearly written, unashamed and unafraid.

She smiled tenderly, loving him now more than ever. "I have a lot of questions for you, Hawthorne. But I can't ask them all today."

"I'll wait." His words were patient but confident.

She asked one of many. "Will you help me study my mother's books? I read them before, seeing only the science, but I need to read them again to understand what Geeni was looking for. There's something about the Verkeshian princes, but I'm not sure why it matters to her, other than for sowing chaos. I think studying my mother's work is the only way to figure out what Geeni has been planning for so many years. Will you help me?"

His eyes lit up, sparkling with intelligence and desire. "I'd love to."

She pictured the two of them seated at this desk, reading her mother's books, debating the ideas and making discoveries ... The citadel truly would be her home as long as Hawthorne was in it.

"Good," she said with a grin. "Now that we've settled that, will you kiss me quickly, then find out about that bath?"

His emerald eyes twinkled in the affirmative, but it was the only time he didn't do what she asked.

The kiss was *not* quick.

39

EPILOGUE

Geeni stood on the dock, watching the great sailing ships load. A pink curl fluttered across her cheek, and she tucked it under her wide-brimmed purple hat. The sun was particularly oppressive today, but it was probably just because she was unused to wearing long sleeves. The lavender cuffs were loose enough to give her access to her jewelry, but she felt smothered in so much fabric.

Boots clicked against the wooden planks, and Geeni turned as Nix headed her way. The black-haired woman's eyes roved the crowded dock, and her hand twitched anxiously above her sheathed gold blades.

"Report," said Geeni.

Nix's eyes never stopped their examination of the crowd as she said, "The ship is almost loaded. We can leave shortly."

"And our remaining safe houses? Are they secure?"

Nix nodded once, sharply. "Bribes paid and threats made."

Geeni would have preferred to pay bribes and make

threats herself, but since the Queen's Guard was on high alert, she had begrudgingly left the task to her soldiers.

"Good," said Geeni. "I don't want to lose another safe house." Losing the citadel stung. She had finally finished her renovations, only to lose it because of a mousy little maid.

"Where are we going?" asked Nix.

Geeni looked at the open sea. "I need to spring the trap I left floating out there."

The soldier's eyebrow rose. "Intriguing. What kind of trap?"

"A red-haired captain who sails faster than anyone on the Dharijian Sea." Geeni pulled out her pipe and began packing it.

Nix just stared at her.

Geeni lit the pipe and took a few quick puffs. "Rhielle is more comfortable on water than dry land, so that's where we'll find her."

Geeni breathed out a slow trickle of smoke as she stared at the bright sea. The girl was a spitfire, but the young captain's ambition would further Geeni's own plans. The mousy little scholar had proven to be more trouble than she was worth. What Geeni needed now was a shark. "Rhielle will steal exactly what I need her to, all while believing it's her own idea."

"You want her to steal something?"

Geeni lowered the brim of her purple hat across her eyes. "Theft on the open sea is her specialty." She drew in one last pull from the pipe, then blew the smoke out to sea. "Time to track down a red-haired pirate."

To be continued in
A Spark of Seas: A Little Mermaid Retelling

AFTERWORD

I initially started this book with a different prince. He was a gruff scholar type, and I thought they'd be a grumpy/sunshine couple. But as I wrote the first few chapters, I realized though Elliya was sweet, she wasn't truly "sunshine." She would have been, had she grown up in a loving household, but a lifetime with an abusive stepmother left her understandably traumatized. I wrote two separate "meet-cutes" with this grumpy prince, but I couldn't find an instance where Elliya wouldn't react to his brashness with anything other than self-protective withdrawal. She needed someone who could sneak past her rightfully built defenses and allow her to feel immediately safe.

By feeling empowered.

Thankfully, I had a Prince Charming waiting in the wings. The moment I wrote Hawthorne into the scene, sweet Elliya came alive.

I dedicated this book to women like Elliya—women who are stronger than they know. If you or someone you know is living in a violent home, there is help available.

National Domestic Violence Hotline
https://www.thehotline.org/
1-800-799-7233
SMS: Text START to 88788

ABOUT THE AUTHOR

Susannah Welch lives in sunny South Florida with her brilliant husband and a magically hypoallergenic cat. She enjoys singing and dancing and showing off. She likes her stories with a little bit of drama, and a whole lot of sparkle.

facebook.com/susannah.welch.author
instagram.com/susannahwelchauthor